ONE LAST

ALASKA AIR ONE RESCUE | BOOK THREE

PROMISE

ONE LAST

ALASKA AIR ONE RESCUE | BOOK THREE

PROMISE

SUSAN MAY WARREN

Revell

a division of Baker Publishing Group
Grand Rapids, Michigan

© 2024 by Susan May Warren

Published by Revell
a division of Baker Publishing Group
Grand Rapids, Michigan
RevellBooks.com

Printed in the United States of America

Library of Congress Cataloging-in-Publication Data
Names: Warren, Susan May, 1966– author.
Title: One last promise / Susan May Warren.
Description: Grand Rapids, Michigan : Revell, a division of Baker
  Publishing Group, 2024. | Series: Alaska Air One Rescue ; book 3 |
  Summary: "Waitress Tillie Young never thought her ex would track her to
  Alaska. When he kidnaps her daughter, she'll do anything to get her
  back-even enlist help from her favorite grumpy customer, pilot Arlo
  "Moose" Mulligan. It will take all of Moose's Alaskan savvy to keep them
  alive-but who is going to protect him from the love he never saw
  coming?"—Provided by publisher.
Identifiers: LCCN 2024001842 | ISBN 9780800745493 (paperback) | ISBN
  9780800745967
Subjects: LCSH: Alaska--Fiction. | LCGFT: Romance fiction. | Novels.
Classification: LCC PS3623.A865 O545 2024 | DDC 813/.6—dc23/
  eng/20240117
LC record available at https://lccn.loc.gov/2024001842

Scripture quotations are also taken from the Holy Bible, New International Version®, NIV®. Copyright© 1973, 1978, 1984, 2011 by Biblica, Inc®. Used by permission of Zondervan. All rights reserved worldwide.

For more information about Susan May Warren, please access the author's website at the following address: www.susanmaywarren.com.

Published in the United States of America.
Cover design by Emilie Haney, www.eahcreative.com

24 25 26 27 28 29 30   7 6 5 4 3 2 1

For Your glory, Lord

PROLOGUE

Let's start with this . . .

IT WAS TIME TO TELL LONDON THE TRUTH.
Shep sat with the Air One Rescue team around a fire table on the deck of Moose's amazing log home overlooking the Knik River, listening to Oaken Fox strum his guitar as the Air One Rescue team razzed Axel about his big appearance on *Good Morning, Alaska!*

But Shep's gaze couldn't move off London. She sat, cross-legged on a chair, her blonde hair down, the firelight in her eyes, and all he could think was—

Tell her.

Because frankly, any day, any rescue could go south. And it might not take an accident on the job either—look at Tillie, Moose's waitress friend. Gone, into thin air, and despite Moose's efforts to find her, he'd turned up nothing.

But the look on the man's face betrayed worry, even if tonight he'd tried to put on a smile. Now, the man stood next to the smoking grill. He wore an apron and held a grilling fork, now putting

7

ribeyes on a platter. "Steaks are off the grill and setting up," he shouted. "Grab plates."

The team got up, Oaken putting away his guitar, and Shep didn't miss Axel pulling Flynn into the shadows of the deck, kissing her.

Yeah, see—even Axel had found the one.

Although, Shep had known exactly who the one was for years. Now, London helped carry the plate of steaks to the table.

"C'mon, you two! Dinner is getting cold!" Moose's voice.

Axel broke away from his kiss with Flynn and shook his head.

The team sat down at Moose's long wooden outside table. Boo had lit candles, and the steaks glistened on a plate next to grilled garlic bread, a salad, and some fried potatoes.

Moose prayed, then the team "amened."

They nearly missed the ring of the doorbell. But someone sat on it, so Moose got up.

"Expecting someone?" Axel said.

He wiped his mouth, then dropped his napkin. "Nope."

Then he headed into the house.

"So, Oaken, how's that movie you're working on?" Shep asked.

"I'm not in it, but I did a little video promo in a town called Ember a few weeks ago."

"Ember, Montana?" asked Shep.

"Yeah."

"I have a cousin who used to work for a smoke-jumper team out of Ember." Shep dug into his steak.

"There's a big forest fire raging right now, so hope he's not in danger."

"Naw, he's married and lives in DC with his wife. Directs a Red Cross SAR team—"

"Boo! Flynn!"

Shep looked up at Moose's voice. He'd come out of the house, and his stricken expression put a fist through Shep.

Especially since his voice had thinned. "Can you guys . . . come here?"

The entire team got up and followed him into the house.

And then Shep, too, felt a blow, right to his lungs.

Tillie.

She sat on a bench in the kitchen. Long, dark hair pulled back, a black jacket, grimy jeans, and tennis shoes, brown eyes that widened when the crew came in. She held an ice pack to her cheek, her lip broken, her eye swollen.

Boo walked up to her. "Tillie? What happened?"

Poor Moose. He stood near the end of the counter, holding on like he needed balance. Or maybe just tucking in emotion behind the fierce, dangerous expression.

Everything stilled, waiting.

Then Tillie said, her voice quiet, even a little shaken, "I'm sorry, but I had no other choice." She looked at Moose. "My daughter has been kidnapped. And I need your help to get her back."

ONE

Twenty-four hours earlier...

A S IF MOOSE MULLIGAN DIDN'T HAVE ENOUGH problems, the mountain tried to bury him.

The cracking sound spiked the clear blue air as the ice cones hanging off the eastern cliffs detached and careened toward the Byron Glacier, a frozen river spilling out through a valley of granite.

Moose looked up from where he was dipping his thermos into the crystalline meltwater stream of the massive blue-veined plane of ice—

"Run!" This from his copilot, London, who'd been capping her water bottle. She wore a red rescue suit and mirrored aviator sunglasses, her long blonde hair pulled back in a braid, and had already leaped to her feet.

He'd heard the dog barking some fifteen seconds before, so perhaps Moose should have seen it coming. In his defense, he had a lot cluttering up his brain—like the lawsuit that could take down Air One Rescue, and the unrelenting worry about the disappearance of

Tillie Young, a woman he really shouldn't be obsessed about, and the gnawing problem of the inheritance that didn't really belong to him—the one that funded everything he owned. Just little things that could blow apart the life he'd built.

Whatever.

Still, when they'd first landed on the ice with his chopper, he'd spotted—and hadn't liked—the way the serac of old snow and blue-gray ice clung to an upper lip of granite.

Now, his body went cold as the entire wall cascaded into the valley, thirty tons of icy boulders and snow and silt thundering toward them.

They were dead where they stood.

"Move!" He hit his feet and tried to locate the three tourists who'd purchased his day charter to the glacier, a clearly not-so-brilliant idea to keep his rescue flight service in the black. Two sisters and their brother wanted a close-up view of the glacier. One of the sisters was a photographer, intent on capturing the sunset just as it winked off the icy plane. Another worked with a dog, a beautiful Malador that looked a little like Balto and possessed the energy of an entire dog-sled team, the way it explored the area.

He spotted his people already sprinting.

"There!" He pointed to a cavern nearby, carved out of the rock, a cleft born from earlier ice flows. The dog bolted for the entrance—the one littered with boulders and silt, like teeth.

Behind them, the ice flow gathered speed, chunks of lethal ice roaring toward them, a cloud of debris like a volcano rising above it.

London hit the cave first and pulled in one of the sisters to crouch with her against the wall.

The brother came in beside her, and next to him, his other sister.

Moose practically dove into the space, some twenty feet deep, grabbed the dog into his arms, and hid behind a Volkswagen-sized barrier. Then he ducked his head and prayed.

Sort of prayed. More like a repeated, *help, help, help.*

Moose and the Almighty had been in a sort of ongoing conversation for the past month, mostly about Tillie, but also his depleted bank account and the lawsuit, and yes, really about Tillie and—

And then the avalanche swept across the mouth of the cave like a freight train, loud and consuming. One of the women put her hands over her ears and screamed, and all Moose could think was . . .

This was how it would end.

Him, trapped in an ice cave, freezing to death.

Talk about being buried in his job.

Okay, that wasn't funny, but Moose had nothing else as the roar subsided and silence filled in between the gasps. He lifted his head and looked around.

"Everybody alive?"

He heard crying, so hopefully. As it was, blue ice chunks and dirty silt and grimy, crusty snow had all tumbled together to form a wall, sealing them in. A hard, musty odor raked up from the debris, a chill shivered through him, and an echoing drumbeat of silence filled his soul as their predicament settled into his bones.

And it occurred to him then, weirdly, that this might have been how Jonah had felt, running from a God he loved, swept into the belly of a whale.

Except Moose wasn't running. Just . . .

Certainly, there were things he didn't want to face, but *really*?

And that's when he got giddy. Or morose. But either way, he wasn't quite himself when he turned to the huddled, terrified tourists, along with a wide-eyed London, and said, "Hope nobody is claustrophobic."

One of the women just looked at him. Midtwenties, brown hair that trailed out under a felt cap, her eyes a hazel blue, and now she blinked at him as if he'd lost his mind. "Seriously?"

"He's just in shock," said London and got up.

The dog barked as if agreeing with her, and the woman held out her arms. "C'mere, Rome."

The dog obeyed, crouched, and started whining.

Yep, exactly how Moose felt.

Cool-headed London pulled out her walkie.

The other woman started to cry, and the brother put his arms around her. Moose thought his name might be . . . *Ridge?* See, this was why he wasn't good at the tourist game. But desperation had clouded his vision after taking a look at his cash flow.

Or lack thereof.

He stood up to examine the ice wall.

The woman with the dog—Rome—stood up and came over to Moose. "How could you let this happen?"

"Sorry. My epic powers of avalanche control are clearly on the fritz."

She closed her eyes, pinched the bridge of her nose with her thumb and forefinger. "Sorry—no, I mean . . . isn't there a weather forecast or something you should have checked before we flew up here?"

"I did. Clear skies. No sign of lethal glacier avalanches." Although, if he were honest, he might have paid better attention to the heatwave that had descended upon Alaska this summer, and especially the past few weeks. He'd lived in a small town under the shadow of Denali long enough to know heat caused ice to groan and shift.

Again, too much clutter in his head. Him trying to do it all. But if he didn't, who would?

He turned to survey the group. "Anyone hurt?"

The man shook his head. "Aspen, you okay?" He addressed his sister, tucked into his embrace, and she lifted her head, nodded.

"How about you, Stormi?"

The woman standing in front of him also nodded, then sighed, her voice softer now as she addressed Moose. "Please tell me that you have a plan."

He drew in a breath, looked around the cave. "Not yet. But I'm working on it."

Sort of what he'd said every morning since Tillie had disappeared from the Skyport Diner. He shouldn't be so undone by the absence of his favorite waitress, but she was more, oh so much more, than that.

So far, he'd unearthed a big fat nothing about her disappearance. Which only dragged up the earlier conversation with London as they'd been wandering around the glacier. *"Have you heard from Tillie?"*

Certainly, she hadn't meant for it to hit him like a blow to his chest, nearly whuffing the breath from him. As if she could read his mind.

"Nope."

But the question was always there, wasn't it? A month of searching—he'd even asked his cousin Dawson, a cop, to look into it. Nothing.

"Maybe she wants to stay gone." He hadn't meant to let that tidbit out, and clearly his tone had carried an edge to it, because London had raised an eyebrow. *"Just saying—I left a note at the diner weeks ago. If she wanted to get in contact with me, she would."*

"Mm-hmm."

"Maybe I'm just poking my head in where it doesn't belong."

"It's the rescuer in you," she'd said. *"You and Axel are cut from the same cloth."*

Hardly. His brother shone in the limelight. But Moose didn't care for any of it. He wasn't the guy to live on the edge, make the papers. Just wanted to keep his head above water.

That could mean letting Tillie go. She had walked away, no foul play suspected. He was simply overreacting to being ghosted.

"Everyone just stay calm," London said now, her voice confirming exactly that. She was a bit of a mystery to him. When Shep had suggested he bring her aboard the private SAR team, he hadn't quite expounded on her skills. She could fly planes and choppers, was an expert climber and skier, and spoke at least three languages. What she was doing flying for his tiny SAR outfit, he didn't know. He just knew he didn't deserve her.

Didn't deserve a lot, really. Like this entire gig, the Air One team, his house, even his very life.

So he got it, and didn't ask questions—of London, or even of God, because he didn't want to question the goodness of the Lord. He just embraced the grace, frankly, and thanked God every day for it.

Which meant even now, in their snow tomb. *God, please save us.*

"I'll see if I can raise the team on the radio," London said and turned away to speak into the walkie. Static filled the airway.

He wanted to tell her that they were out of range anyway, some thirty miles from Air One HQ.

When she turned back and shook her head, all eyes burned into him.

And that's when he realized . . . *light.* By rights, they should be in darkness. He looked up, and indeed, light spilled through from the top of the cavern, possibly where the flow had washed by.

This time of year, end of August, twilight started at nine, so he had a good four hours before it turned pitch dark.

Four hours to freedom. Four hours before the sun set and the ice turned them hypothermic.

Four hours before they all died.

But they weren't dead yet. He turned back to the wall. He couldn't believe he'd left his gloves in the chopper. One more thing that had simply dropped out of his brain. "Okay, I'm going to try to dig us out. I need your hat, um—"

"Stormi," said the woman and pulled it off her head. Aspen also handed him hers.

London walked over. "I'm a better climber."

He ignored her. Because the last thing he wanted was one of his teammates getting hurt on his watch.

His ride, his responsibility.

He had issued crampons for the glacial trek, and Ridge carried a walking stick, which he handed over. London stood back, her arms crossed over herself. "There are a few handholds at the top, but it's going to be slick."

Moose surveyed the wall. It rose some fifteen feet, mostly massive boulders, some smaller jagged pieces of ice. Not a terrible climb, but precarious.

"Ridge, give me a push." He chipped out footholds, then a handhold, and Ridge got behind Moose and helped balance him as he wedged his foot into a slot between two ice boulders.

"To your right, Moose," London said, stepping up to catch him.

What was the phrase—pride goeth before the fall?

He found another foothold, but his hands, inside the hats, lacked purchase.

His grip slipped—"Falling!"

Ridge helped break his fall, but Moose landed on his back with a *whoof*, his breath hitching out. Rome backed away from him, barking.

"Yeah, I know, I know."

London made a face.

Moose rolled to his feet, glanced at the light. He couldn't afford to waste any more precious time. "Okay, let's do this again—"

"Let me," said London. "This isn't my first ice climb. And I'm about half your weight." More, she wore thin gloves. She stepped up to the wall. "Plus, you're a foot taller than all of us—you can get me up higher."

"I don't like this."

"What? Don't be crazy. We're all having a blast." She shook her head, but he caught a smile.

17

Rome backed up, barking as London went to the wall. She dug one foot in, and Moose braced her as she climbed up and put her other foot in the next hold.

"Don't get handsy," she said as he moved to push her up.

"That's what you're worried about?" Moose shook his head but watched his hands anyway and managed to help her to the next foothold.

"I can see the top." She shoved her hand into the hold—the ice closing around it—and then pushed up. "I'm almost there!"

She lunged for another hold, one he couldn't see—

Her shout echoed off the granite as she slipped. He caught her coming down—not pretty, but enough to break her fall. They stumbled back and he thunked against the cavern wall.

Okay, so this wasn't funny anymore.

And now it really felt like a metaphor, thank you, for the fact that no, he wasn't getting out of this one this time. Even if they managed to escape, he still had the lawsuit, and the slide had probably damaged his chopper parked on the ice, and sometimes it just felt so . . . well, like his life had avalanched in around him.

Swallowed him whole. Again, sort of like Jonah.

London disentangled herself and stood up. Glanced at him. "Good catch."

He managed a wry smile.

She walked back to the wall.

Stormi crouched next to her dog, who was barking.

"Did you go through Navy boot camp at Great Lakes?"

London's question made him glance at her. "Yep."

"I hear they have an obstacle course, not unlike the one in San Diego."

"You mean the one for BUD/S? It's not even a little like that one. But yeah . . ."

"When I was in training, we had a wall. The only way over it was to work together." She looked at the group. "Make a human ladder."

He wanted to ask, *What training?* but with the sun setting . . . "What do you have in mind?"

"Moose, you think you can hold Ridge?"

He glanced at the guy. About five-ten, lean and solid, about one-eighty. "Yep."

"Okay. With your six-feet huge and his five-something, that's about eleven feet."

"The wall is at least fifteen feet, and then you have to climb out. You have nothing to grip onto—"

"You'll need another person," said Stormi. She got up, came over to stand by London. "I'll go up. I used to water-ski. We did pyramid tricks like this." She glanced at her brother. "Remember Brainerd?"

He nodded. "Yep."

Okay, now they were getting somewhere. "So, you climb up on London's shoulders and get free. Then what?"

"Then I'll help London up," Stormi said.

"And I'll go for help," London said.

He drew in a breath.

"Stop being so heroic." London met his eyes, hers sharp. "If we want to get out of here, you need to let some of us do the work."

Fine. "Everyone take off your crampons."

Except him. He went over to the snowpack and leaned against the icy wall. Bent his knee. "Let's do this."

Ridge braced his foot on Moose's thigh, then got a knee on Moose's shoulder. He used the ice pack to brace himself as he put his other foot on Moose's shoulder and pushed up.

Maybe one-eighty had been a little underestimated. The man's feet dug into Moose's shoulders, burning through Moose's body. Wow, he was out of shape.

Ridge leaned against the ice pack.

London followed, climbing up Moose, then behind Ridge. He bent his knees, and she used his thigh to leverage herself onto his shoulders.

Please, don't fall.

"I can see the opening."

"Can you get through?" Moose grunted, his hips and shoulders burning.

"I think so. Or Stormi can, if I push her."

"Can you hold us, Moose?" Ridge said, looking down.

It might be the only thing he could do. An old Bible verse filtered up to him. *"Therefore put on the full armor of God, so that when the day of evil comes, you may be able to stand your ground, and after you have done everything, to stand."*

He blew out a breath. "Do it, Stormi." He braced himself as she put her foot on his leg, then a knee next to Ridge's foot, and used Ridge to climb up. Then, by the sounds of the grunting, she climbed Ridge and stood up behind London.

"Stormi, be careful!" Aspen, now holding onto Rome, who was losing his mind.

London had found a handhold on the ice. So much for the cold, too, because sweat pooled and now dripped down Moose's back. His legs shook as he fought against the weight.

London bent her knees and looked at Stormi. "Don't pull on me or we'll both go down."

He didn't want to think about that crash. There was grunting from above, and London made a sound but then—

"I can see daylight," Stormi said. "Just a sec—"

And then she pushed off from London. He got a glimpse of it, craning his neck for a second as Stormi's boot clipped London's mouth. She jerked, rearing back—

"Don't fall!" Aspen shouted.

But London didn't come crashing down, and a moment later,

Moose spotted London leaning into the ice, trying to find footing in a wedge as Stormi pulled her up.

"I'm up!"

Just like that, the weight lifted from his shoulders.

Moose stepped back, and Ridge jumped from his perch. Moose steadied himself on the wall and spotted London, looking down at them. Her lip bled, red dripping down her chin. But she grinned, her teeth reddened, and gave him a thumbs-up.

"Hang tight! We'll be back."

He found himself braced against the wall, then sliding down to his knees.

Ridge sat beside him, pulling Rome into his lap. Aspen joined them.

"Think they'll get here before we all freeze to death?"

Moose looked at him. "Could be worse."

"You're right." Ridge ran his fingers through Rome's fur. "We could be claustrophobic." He smiled at Moose.

Moose found a smile. Held up his fist. Ridge bumped it.

"You do this a lot?" Ridge ran his hand down the dog's back. The animal put his head on Moose's knee.

Moose rubbed the dog's ear. "No. I run an SAR outfit. I just needed the extra cash. Probably the last time I do this."

Ridge looked at him. "So it's just fate that I happen to be trapped with an SAR professional?"

"I don't believe in fate."

"Then what is this?"

Moose leaned his head back against the rock. "Ever hear the story of Jonah?"

"From the Bible? The guy in the fish?"

"Mm-hmm." He closed his eyes. "This, my friend, is a warning. Welcome to the whale."

Silence, then laughter next to him. "It can't possibly be that bad."

Moose looked away. "It's not. I know God is in control. It just feels—"

"If I remember my Bible stories right, Jonah was running from God. You running, Moose?"

"No. I learned long ago that running wasn't the answer." He looked at Ridge. "I made a promise, a long time ago, to a dying man. And I didn't keep it."

"And now you think God is punishing you?"

"No. Not punishing. But maybe reminding."

"Thanks a lot. Now I feel like one of those poor fishermen on the boat with Jonah."

He liked this guy. "Sorry."

The sunlight had started to dim, the cave turning clammy.

"What was the promise?"

Moose closed his eyes. "It's a long story. Let's focus on getting out of here."

"We're not going anywhere, so—" Ridge glanced at him. "Rome is a good dog to tell your problems to. We won't listen."

Moose gave a wry smile. *Yeah, no.* The last thing he needed was to start unpacking his regrets.

"Why'd you need the extra cash?" Aspen asked. She sat next to Ridge, cross-legged, dressed in a pair of insulated pants, her hair short and tucked into her hat. Her camera had survived the avalanche, and she held it in her lap.

He shoved his hands into his pockets, fisting them against the cold. "This year was a particularly busy year on Denali, and in the area. With the warm weather, we had a lot of tourists—hikers and climbers—who got in over their heads. Which meant we went through our cash reserves. We're funded by donations, and we were a little short going into this year, so I had this stupid bright idea to let a reality show film us."

"*The Sizeup*?" Aspen said. "That was you?"

"Yep. I suppose you saw the episode where the woman died in a blizzard?"

"Yeah. Rough."

"Not only are we broke, but her family is suing us for not continuing the rescue efforts and discontinuing the search while she was still alive."

"There was a blizzard!" Aspen said.

"Yes. But we did shut down the search for a while. And it's possible she could have been rescued if we'd kept looking." He couldn't get that nightmare out of his brain, either. The vision of a woman shot and left for dead. So yeah, even he'd find himself guilty.

And in truth, he'd been trying hard to hold on to his faith, because where he sat, Moose didn't have a clue how the Almighty might get him out of a lawsuit. Legal fees alone would wipe him out.

"What about the Good Samaritan law?" Aspen said.

"It only protects people who accidentally encounter someone in need, not people involved in an official rescue effort. And it doesn't cover SAR teams." This from Ridge, and Moose stared at him.

Ridge smiled. "As fate—or providence—would have it, you're trapped with a civil lawyer."

What? He shook his head.

"I'm local. My sisters came out to visit, and this day tour was my bright idea," Ridge said. "You get us out of here, and I'll give you my card and see what I can do to help."

Hello, that was fast.

Rome leaped to his feet, barking, and Moose looked up just as a light broke through the shadows. A headlamp, and on the other end—

"Bro, you down there?" Axel pushed up his light, his smile showing in the dim light. "Guess you never thought you'd be the one getting rescued, huh?"

"Zip it and get me out of here."

23

But see, clearly God was about solving all his problems while he was trapped in a cave. *O ye of little faith.*

And if he was in here, with Moose, solving his crazy problems, rescuing him, Moose should remember that the Almighty was also out there with Tillie.

Even if Moose wasn't.

Please. Keep her safe. Bring her help if she needs it.

TWO

SHE'D KNOWN THAT SOMEDAY HER MISTAKES would catch up to her.

Unfortunately, Tillie had stopped looking in the rear-view mirror for a while now, believing that she'd outsmarted the bogeyman.

So, her fault for not paying attention. Her fault, and Hazel would pay the price.

"Mommy, will you come back?"

Hazel stood in her coral-and-green Moana nightgown, the ruffle on the hem torn from where she'd put her toe into it in the night, wearing her favorite pink cowboy boots, holding her ratty stuffed dog. Good new was, they didn't have to sleep in their car any longer. And they'd both taken long-awaited baths, so at least she was leaving her daughter clean and fed and hopefully, please, safe.

And most important, hidden.

Tillie crouched in the entryway of Rosalind Turner's small two-bedroom tract home in a cozy, fenced safe lot in an old family neighborhood near Earthquake Park. The place smelled of pumpkin soup and Roz's incense candles, and if anyone could keep Hazel safe, it was a former cop.

A former vice cop from Miami, one who knew Rigger and what he could do.

"Of course, honey. Mommy just needs to take care of . . . something. I'll be back as soon as I can." Tillie pulled Hazel close, held her seven-year-old lanky body to hers, savoring her skinny arms around Tillie's neck and the smell of shampoo and bubble bath. She was everything Tillie lived for.

Tillie met eyes with Roz, who stood behind her, arms folded over her barrel body. Their conversation an hour ago returned to her—

"If I'd known Rigger was back and after you, I would have come home sooner."

Tillie knew what it meant to Roz to visit her grandchildren, and frankly, she'd thought it was fine.

Thought she could handle Rigger, if it really was him that'd appeared at the Skyport Diner a month ago, looking for her.

She'd slipped out the back and returned home to scoop up Hazel, pay the sitter, and move them to a hotel.

But her money had run out while she was trying to figure out her next play, and that's when they'd landed in the car and—

"What are you going to do?"

Tillie couldn't tell her. Couldn't face the barrage of reasons why this might be a terrible idea. In her head, she saw no other way to bargain for her freedom. Hazel's freedom.

So here she was, saying goodbye to her only treasure, the one reason she had for living. She pushed Hazel away and held her by the arms, meeting those green eyes. "Obey Grandma Roz. I'll be back by morning, okay?"

Hazel nodded, but fear swept her expression, so Tillie held out her pinky.

Hazel hooked it and smiled.

"Okay, then." She got up and lifted a hand to Roz, walking to the door.

"I got this. You be safe."

Tillie swiped the moisture from her cheek and headed out into the twilight, something inside her jerking when she heard the lock click.

Rigger wasn't going to take anything else from her, so help her. . . .

She got into her car, closed her eyes, and offered a foxhole prayer, although she doubted that anyone might be listening, and turned the engine over.

Someone might be listening, though, because the old Ford Focus started, and she let out her breath.

Then she pulled out and headed east, toward Eagle River.

It wasn't a fancy house, and perhaps she should have sold it, but after her sister Pearl died . . . well, it was all they had of her. Memories, laughter, and stories embedded the painted panel walls, hard work in the remodeled kitchen, the bathroom, Hazel's ocean-scape bedroom.

As Tillie drove up Highway 1 to Eagle River, the absurdity of her thinking wound around her chest, squeezed.

Of course Rigger would know to look for a house in the name of his former girlfriend. Deceased girlfriend, but Tillie had never changed the deed.

Stupid! She slammed her palm into the steering wheel.

Even more stupid was sticking around Anchorage for a month, hiding. She should have pointed her car south, headed toward the lower forty-eight. But she just as easily might have ended up on the side of the road, steam coming out of the radiator.

And then there was the whole driving through Canada part, and the necessity of a passport. And while hers might work, Hazel's had expired two years ago, which meant that driving over the border was out of the question.

So, yeah, she'd fled, bunked in the Bird Creek Hotel, then over at the Puffin Inn, then the Ramada, and finally the one-star Mush Inn.

Cash only. But who knew what Rigger would do to track them down? After all . . . she had his treasure too.

Breathe.

She passed Cottonwood Park, and Fort Richardson, with its safe, cordoned fencing, the military housing that she'd walked away from.

For a good reason.

But sometimes . . .

Breathe.

Farther up the Glenn Highway, she passed the landfill, then the correctional facility, and finally took the Artillery exit over to Eagle River Road.

Passed Eagle River Elementary. With any luck, Hazel would start second grade there in a couple days.

Or she'd be in foster care while her mother went to jail. . . .

Breathe.

Tillie wound her way off Eagle River Road, back to Meadow Creek Drive, a nice name for a nice neighborhood with families and fishing boats and pickups and swing sets in the backyard and friendly Labradors and manicured lawns and sure, probably a few broken families, but for the most part . . . safe. The kind of life that Pearl—and Tillie—had wanted for Hazel.

Pearl had even mentioned, toward the end there, getting a dog. If she hadn't gone so quickly, Tillie might have given in.

Most of the houses sat on half acres with a line of thick evergreen between them, the forest still trying to reclaim the land.

She turned into the driveway of the smallest house in the neighborhood, but in her estimation the prettiest, painted a deep yellow with a blue door—Pearl's idea—and a chain-link fence around the back for the someday dog, and a mostly manicured flowerbed and—

Wait.

She put the car in park, and everything inside her seized.

Smoke drifted, black and thickening, from the backyard.

No—

She threw herself out of the car, rushed to the gate, and let herself inside, ran along the side of the house.

Stopped.

The playset, the homemade swing set that Pearl and Tillie had built for Hazel on her third birthday, threw flames into the twilight sky.

How—

She ran to the patio, where the hose lay curled in the box. She cranked on the water, then sprinted over with the hose, opening up the nozzle as she got close.

The water hit the structure, and the flames sizzled, the smoke cluttering the air, acrid and sharp. She coughed, pulled her shirt up to her nose, and kept spraying. The water filmed back over her, wetting her hair, her shirt, but the flames started to die, spurting now and again to life.

"I figured this would bring you home."

She froze even as she doused the last of the flames. The charred legs still held the second story fort aloft.

She turned, the hose in her hands, and braced herself.

Rigger stood on the patio, the sliding door to her house open. He held a chicken leg, and she didn't want to know how long he'd been living in her house, sleeping in her—or Pearl's—bed, probably ripping the house apart in his search.

She raised her chin, turned off the nozzle. "What are you doing here?"

"I think you know, Steelrose."

"That's not my name."

"That will *always* be your name."

She rolled her eyes.

He took a step toward her, threw away the chicken leg, and wiped his arm on his sleeve. He wore a black nylon muscle shirt, a pair of track pants, kicks. Bald, but a thick black beard scrubbed his chin, and he'd easily put on thirty pounds of muscle in the five years since she'd last seen him.

Now he advanced at her, and she held up the hose.

He laughed. "You think a little water is going to stand between you and what's mine?"

"It'll slow you down."

"Not even a little, honey."

Then he leaped at her. She threw on the water, but like he said, it barely hiccupped his movement. It worked just enough for her to dodge him, though, to get a leg out and trip him. He went spinning into the ash and fire.

She took off for her car.

He rolled, shouted, cursed, and she didn't have to look behind her to know he'd found his feet.

She hit the gate, pulled it shut, heard the latch fall and sprinted toward the Ford. Opened the door, slid in—*C'mon, c'mon!*

The engine whined, refused her, and in a second, he had yanked her door open.

He grabbed her arm, and she reached behind her with the other and got her hand on a book.

A hardbacked copy of *The Black Stallion*, worn and broken and her current read-aloud to Hazel.

As Rigger dragged her from the car, she nailed him on the side of the head.

He shook off the blow, although it did loosen his grip on her.

She rolled away, onto her feet, breathing hard.

It seemed that *somebody* in this nice neighborhood might be calling the police, or the fire department. But then again, that would mean questions.

Still. She pulled her phone from her back pocket, backed away, pressing the emergency button.

"Really?" Rigger advanced on her, ripped the phone from her hand, threw it.

And then, even as she searched for it, he punched her.

Right in the jaw, and her face felt like it might explode. The punch turned her around, slammed her to the ground. Wiped thought from her brain.

Get up. A voice in her head screamed, and she listened, rolling to her knees.

He lunged at her, but she rounded, blocked his blow, put her fist into his face.

Bam! Now he was bloodied too.

It only turned him into a bull, rabid, and she saw it enter his eyes.

This was the look Pearl had warned her about. And of course she knew it—but she'd known him before, too, so—

"Are you really going to kill me? Because you do and you'll never find it. Never find *her*." She backed up toward her car, and in the distance, a siren moaned.

Thank you, Meadow Creek Drive. Even if no one had the courage to come out of their house, someone *had* called the cops. Or her emergency call had gone through—

The siren stalled him, just for a moment. His eyes narrowed. "You can't run from me anymore, Tillie. I want it back—"

"I'll give you the money, Rigger. Just . . . leave. Just leave us be." She held up her hands, and they shook.

His smile ripped a chill through her.

The siren grew louder.

She took off for her car, dove in and shut the door. Locked it even as he slammed his fist on the glass.

Then, *thank you*—her car turned over. She pulled out, spitting up grass as she missed the driveway.

He ran out into the road.

She met his eyes as she floored it.

He spun out of the way.

At the end of the block, a glance into her rearview mirror confirming that no, he wasn't running after the car, she let up on the gas, refusing to drive like a maniac.

Especially as she passed the police on the way out of the subdivision.

Her body shook, but she kept driving through the neighborhoods, the night descending around her. Only when she stopped at a light and spotted the neighboring driver staring at her did she realize she was bleeding. A cut on her face, her lip split open, and probably she wore a black eye too.

Rigger knew how to throw a punch, of course.

She put a hand to her face and turned onto a side road, then searched the backseat for a towel. Nothing.

One thought pressed over her—they needed to leave town. *Now.*

She opened the glovebox, shifted inside it. Her hand closed on a package of travel tissues. As she pulled it out, a piece of paper fluttered out.

She pulled out a tissue and pressed it to her face, then picked up the paper.

Find me if you need me.

The tight, blocky handwriting conjured up the owner. Moose Mulligan. Mr. Tall, Dark, and Handsome, booth two, in the front, chocolate milk, midnight chicken, fries, and the man who'd asked her out.

She'd turned him down.

She hadn't seen him since because he'd fled after she turned him down for a date. But what was she to do?—saying yes meant peeling back her life and . . .

And that would get them all into trouble. At the very least, her secrets were ticking bombs that he'd be better off not knowing.

Still, she'd felt bad, missed his friendship, so she'd sent chicken home with his brother what seemed like years—but might only be weeks—ago, with a note asking him to come back.

Then Rigger had shown up, and she'd forgotten about Moose, what with trying to keep Hazel safe.

But he was a friend. And more importantly, a pilot.

And he'd written his address and phone number on the napkin and . . .

Her eyes filled, her throat burning. *Maybe* . . .

She put her car into drive, and with the sun in her rearview mirror, she headed toward the Glenn Highway.

His address put him east of Eagle River in an upscale community located on the Knik River.

It didn't have to be complicated, just a simple "Moose, can I get a ride?" To where? Juneau? Or even Fairbanks. Just someplace off the map.

Of course, she'd need the money first. But that came after she appeared on Moose's doorstep. . . .

She glanced in the rearview mirror. Not looking like this.

She needed a gas station and then directions to Moose's place.

Pulling into a Speedway, she got out and headed inside to the bathroom. Kept her head down.

No wonder her head throbbed. Rigger, the former MMA boxer, had managed to bloody her nose, blacken her eye, and split her lip with one lousy punch.

Tearing off paper towels, she wet them, then eased the coldness onto her nose, cleaning it off, then pressing into her lip. She held back a groan and then dabbed at it until she didn't look like she'd been dragged across blacktop.

Then she wiped her shirt and zipped up her black jacket. Pulled back her dark hair and took a long breath.

A woman came out of a nearby stall. Middle-aged, she was overweight and wore a sweatshirt with Moose's Pub and Pizza written on the front. Her eyes widened at Tillie.

"I'm fine. Just a little fight with a door."

"Yeah," said the woman, turning on the water. "I hope the door got the worst of it."

Tillie made a face.

"You should report that."

"Thanks," Tillie said and headed outside, her head down. Yeah, she needed to ditch town, and fast, before she left a trail of breadcrumbs.

She got into her car, pulled down the visor, and found a pair of sunglasses. Then she reached for her phone in the console between her seats to grab the GPS to Moose's place.

Stilled.

Her phone lay in the yard.

Worse, Roz's location was still in her phone, her last known position. And sure, she had a password, but it was easily breakable by no one but Rigger. Hazel's birthdate.

She got out of the car and went inside, now wearing her sunglasses, and headed to the checkout counter. "Do you have a phone I can use?"

The young clerk considered her for a moment, then reached under the cash register and pulled up an old landline phone. "You okay?"

"I will be." She dialed Roz's number, grateful for the fact that she'd made Hazel memorize it.

And how sad would Pearl be to know that Hazel was memorizing numbers in case Tillie got arrested and Hazel went into foster care. Some mom she'd turned out to be. She shook her head as the phone rang.

And rang.

And rang.

And then, finally, picked up.

"Roz—it's me. I lost my phone—"

"I know."

Not Roz, and her legs nearly buckled. "Rigger. Listen—"

"You listen. You have one hour. Get the money and get here, or you will never see Hazel again. But I will leave you Roz as a gift to bury."

"Rigger, just don't—"

He hung up.

She pressed her hand to her chest, her breaths coming too fast.

"Ma'am, are you okay?"

She barely saw the kid, even as she hung up and turned away.

"Ma'am?"

Air, she needed . . . *air*. Pushing outside, she gulped in the night, the fragrance of pine and a little diesel and the sense that she was so far out of her element . . .

More than air, she needed rescue.

The woman from the bathroom came out. Stopped. "Honey? Let me help you."

Tillie looked at her, her gaze on her sweatshirt, and then gave a painful, dark laugh. "Seriously?" Her eyes filled. "Can I . . . can I borrow your cell phone?"

The woman frowned.

"I need to look up an address."

The woman pulled out her phone, and Tillie pulled the paper from her pocket and keyed in the address. Read the directions up Highway 1 and over to the Old Glenn Highway.

From there, she would go past Lookout Point, then take a left on River Drive.

She could find it from there. "Thanks." She handed back the phone, dangerously close to unravelling.

"Are you sure you don't want me to call someone?"

"No. I . . . I think, I hope I've figured it out." *Please.*

And yeah, it might be stupid, but the fact was, Moose might be exactly the answer. Get the money, give it to Rigger, then talk Moose into flying her and Hazel far, far away. Off-the-map kind of far away.

Maybe then they'd all live through this.

Maybe. But clearly she was in over her head, and suddenly, the idea of finding Moose simply clung to her. As if he'd somehow materialized out of the night and right into her brain. Or heart. *Whatever.*

She got into her car, closed her eyes as if—praying?—and the stupid Ford turned over, acting as if it hadn't quit on her during her time of need. Pulling out, she imprinted the map in her head and headed toward the highway.

This was not a bad idea.

Moose was her friend. He cared.

See, this was not a bad idea.

He'd come looking for her, for Pete's sake, at the diner, had left his address behind like a calling card. And indeed, it read, *Find me if you need me.*

This was not a bad idea!

She turned off the Glenn Highway just as the sun winked out, leaving a pall over the land. The forest closed in, the river to the east, below the ridge, the road winding along the top, and mountains rising to the west. A wild, untamed land.

A place she could still get lost in, with Hazel.

Please!

She turned left on River Drive and began searching for his house number as the route led her closer to the Knik River.

Beautiful homes back here, some log, some timber-framed, many with green tin roofs, long drives, lamplight along porches, evergreens and golden aspen and red maple trees, the sense of luxury and a life without trouble.

No one hunting these people down, kidnapping—

She brushed away the moisture under her eyes. This was not a bad idea. . . .

A sleek black mailbox with bronze letters listed his address, and she slowed. No gate, but the long gravel driveway suggested it sat on the river's edge, with a view.

This was not . . .

She turned in and found herself pulling up to a magnificent timber house with a large cleared yard, a garage wing and, from what she could see in the fading light, a view of the river.

A porch covered the entrance, up a short, wide flight of stairs, a light over the door, beckoning and . . .

This was a bad idea.

Who was this man? She'd pictured his house as a nice ranch-style house, or even a split-level in a suburban neighborhood, something modest and unassuming, like Moose.

But Moose was a lot more than she thought. He did own and operate a private search and rescue team, and that probably took money. And skills. And sure, she was already a little wowed by that, but . . .

But this . . .

Yep, very bad idea.

She turned her car off and stared at the house. A few other cars sat in the drive—a Jeep, a Nissan Rogue. And as she sat there, she heard music drifting into the night, and laughter and . . .

He had friends. And a life. And she just couldn't bring trouble into it.

Except . . . *Find me if you need me.* And then, for a second, she was sitting in a booth with him, and he was telling her about his cousin who'd gone missing and how he regretted that, and . . .

And then Pearl reached out of heaven and down into her heart and said . . .

"Trust."

Right. For Pearl. For Hazel.

She got out of the car. Headed up the stairs. Stood at the door. Then closed her eyes and pushed the doorbell.

Managed not to run when she heard footsteps.

Bad. Bad idea—

The door opened.

Silence. Moose stood there, a tall, gentle giant, his frame filling the door. He wore a flannel shirt, rolled up at the elbows, and a pair of jeans, and the slightest tousle to his hair, those gray-green eyes pinned on her, and he smelled weirdly delicious, as if he'd been grilling and . . .

No, this was a very—

"Tillie." He stepped out then, and maybe she'd stepped back—probably, because inside she was already running—but he caught her hand. "You're hurt."

She'd completely forgotten about her face, thanks to the horror in her chest, but she nodded, then shook her head and—shoot, now her eyes burned.

"Come in."

He tugged her inside. Shut the door behind her. Then came to stand in front of her, so much concern in his eyes that standing there in the entryway, she knew it would be okay.

Somehow, they would be okay.

Even when she looked up at him and said quietly, "I need your help, Moose. My daughter has been kidnapped."

And it wasn't quite the truth, but close enough.

He just blinked at her, his expression hollow. Probably from the revelation of the fact that she had a daughter. *Oops.* But he said nothing. Just reached out and pulled her against him, his big arms around her, holding her tight. "Okay," he said softly. "Okay."

Oh, she wanted to lean into him, to put her arms around his neck and hold on, to close her eyes, but . . .

But they had no time.

Still, just that moment was enough.

Yes, this might be the best idea she'd ever had.

She pushed away from him.

He caught her arms, then nodded and stepped away. "Let's get some ice on your eye."

She followed him, trying not to be awed by his magnificent kitchen, and in a moment, he was handing her an ice pack. "Stay here."

But he didn't go far, just stuck his head out of the sliding-glass door and said something to whatever guests he was entertaining.

And then she knew. Because of course, the people who followed him in were his Air One team. She knew a few of them—Axel, his brother, of course, and Shep, and Boo, the EMT, London, a fellow pilot. And country music star Oaken Fox. *Huh*, she hadn't expected that.

Finally, another woman, a redhead who came in and stood by Axel.

"Tillie?" Boo said. "What happened?"

Moose stood at the end of the island, gripping it, and she got it—all that cool control went into that grip because a fierceness had entered his expression.

It was exactly that fierceness that gave her the will to swallow, then turn to his team, to Boo, then Shep and Axel, and finally back to Moose. "I'm sorry, but I had no other choice."

Then, because of exactly that reason, she doubled down on her lie. "My daughter has been kidnapped. And I need your help to get her back."

Silence. Moose looked at his crew, and specifically the woman standing with Axel, and finally back to Tillie.

"We'll get her back," he said quietly. "I promise."

And deep down in her soul, she believed him.

THREE

MOOSE DIDN'T EVEN KNOW WHERE TO START with his questions. Like, who had hit Tillie and why, and how did he get his hands on him?

And then—she had a *daughter*? He hadn't even remotely seen that one coming.

The kidnapping part, however, might be the most important, so as she leveled her words at his team, he tried to ignore the shaking in her voice. And the memory of the way she had, ever so briefly, clung to him in the entryway. And just tried to focus on the Most Important Horrible Thing.

Kidnapping. *Right. Focus.*

His team stood, silent, absorbing Tillie's words in his kitchen, the smell of the grilled steaks still lingering in the air. He walked over to the sliding door and shut it, and with that, muted the sound of the river rushing in the darkness and any remnant of joviality around the table just a few minutes prior.

He'd invited the team over for a small, put-the-past-behind-them celebration. His brother, Axel, had finally found the love of his life in Flynn Turnquist, a detective from Minnesota, and country singer Oaken Fox had purchased an A-frame home south of Anchorage, in a posh area overlooking a ski resort, probably to start a life with Boo Kingston, the team EMT. And Moose . . . well, he'd survived being buried alive, so that had felt like a reason to celebrate.

In fact, he'd managed to almost, but not really, put Tillie and her disappearance behind him.

Okay, not at all, but he'd been trying, and that counted.

And then . . . and then the doorbell rang, and now he stood at the edge of what felt like a dark and stirring mess of trouble.

He didn't have a second thought about diving in. And never mind helping Tillie—

"How old is your daughter?" he asked now, cutting through the shock.

"Seven." Tillie set her ice pack on his granite island.

"You need to keep that ice pack on," Boo said, coming up to her. "The eye is pretty swollen." She gave her face a once-over. "Doesn't look like your nose is broken, however."

"I've had a broken nose. I know what it feels like," Tillie said, and Moose had to look away. Good thing he was holding on to the counter.

Seven.

"Start at the beginning." This from Flynn, who currently worked in the Investigative Support Unit of the Anchorage Police Department, her job mostly in the area of hunting down robbery suspects, vehicle hijackers, and, conveniently, kidnappers.

Flynn slid onto a stool at the counter and pulled another out for Tillie, patted it. She kept her voice soft, and it could by why Tillie sat down. Boo picked up the ice pack and handed it to her, and Tillie obeyed.

The small action had everyone breathing again, or so it seemed, because Axel walked over to stand behind Flynn, and Oaken perched on the arm of one of Moose's leather sofas. London stayed by the door, arms folded, Shep standing nearby.

"I ... uh ..." Tillie glanced at Moose, an expression in her beautiful brown eyes that he didn't recognize. She'd always exuded a sort of calm confidence, even the time he'd managed to cajole her into sitting down with him, chatting about their lives.

Um, not a mention of terror in her life. He could hardly breathe through the fist in his chest.

She looked at Flynn. "My sister and I moved here from Florida. Miami. And when we came, we, uh ... we emptied our joint savings account. About a hundred thousand dollars."

"That's a lot of savings," Shep said.

She glanced at him, back to Flynn. "We were running from her ... ex. Who is ... not a great guy, and who thought the money should belong to him."

Moose mentally added that to his list of questions. But really, they had no time. "He followed you here?"

She looked at him. "Yes."

"What happened to the money?" Axel asked.

"It ... some of it went to pay for my sister's cancer treatment. It was ... experimental, and ... it did work, for a while, at least." She looked away, sighed, and when she met Flynn's gaze again, her eyes were glossy. "She passed away three years ago."

More silence.

"I'm sorry," Moose said softly.

Tillie nodded. "Thanks. Um, but now ... I don't have the full amount. And the rest of it is ..."

"In the bank?" Oaken said.

"Under my patio."

Moose raised an eyebrow.

She set the ice pack down again. "Rigger showed up about a month ago at the diner, looking for me. I don't know how he found me—maybe he followed me to work. I panicked and ran. Hazel was staying at a sitter's house, so I grabbed her and . . . hid."

Moose tried not to narrow his eyes, but . . . why?

"I have a friend here—an ex-cop who was down in the lower forty-eight visiting her family. She got back a few days ago, so I brought Hazel there, hoping . . ." She blew out a breath. "We thought if I had the money—what was left of it—then I could offer it to him and he'd . . ."

"Leave?" Flynn said. "Just like that?"

"I don't know! I just know he's . . . he's dangerous."

"He did that to you?" Axel said, pointing to her face.

"Yes."

Moose looked away from her, swallowing hard. He usually had a pretty good handle on his emotions, but . . .

"I don't know if Rigger was waiting for me or what, but when I went to the house, he'd set the playset on fire. We have cameras on the front of the house, so maybe he thought I'd come home."

"Which you did."

"I didn't know he was there—"

"Why didn't you call the police?" Flynn asked.

"What could they do? It all happened so fast. And it's my word against his."

"They could arrest him for assault," Shep said, lifting his chin toward her appearance.

"I hit him too."

Moose drew in a breath. He wanted to say *Attagirl*, but that had probably only made Rigger angrier.

Thank God she hadn't been hurt worse, and with that thought surfaced his prayer two days ago, while trapped in the glacier. *Please. Keep her safe. Bring her help if she needs it.* "How did he get your daughter?"

"I called 911, but he grabbed my phone. I think he must have used it to track Roz's address. When I realized that, I called Roz to warn her. . . . He answered." She drew a breath then, maybe remembering the call, because he saw a sort of horror flit through her eyes.

"And?" Flynn said softly.

"I have an hour to get him the money or he leaves with her."

Moose glanced at the clock. She'd been here a total of fifteen minutes. "Where is he?"

"Anchorage."

Forty minutes away. "We'll never get there in time."

"I could go to Roz's house. Stall him. . . . If someone else can pick up the money." She looked at Moose.

Him? Um, no way was he leaving her. He looked at Shep, who nodded and turned to Tillie. "Where is it, exactly?"

"Under the firepit, under the patio pavers, in a waterproof box."

"Cash?"

"Yes."

Shep frowned.

"I wanted a way to get it, fast. . . ." She swallowed.

More questions, but Moose just walked over to Shep. "I'll text you an address. You go."

He noticed that London followed Shep to the entryway.

"Axel, grab Tillie's address, send it to Shep. Flynn, you should get on the horn to—"

"Dawson. I'm already on it." Flynn had pulled out her phone. "We'll get a negotiator on the scene too."

"Wait!" Tillie's voice stopped him cold.

Flynn looked up from her phone.

"You're a cop?"

Flynn frowned. "Yeah."

Tillie slid off her stool. "Okay. Uh, this was a—" She slid the stool in, held up her hands. "I'll take care of it—"

"Tillie!" Moose didn't mean his tone, but, "What's going on?"

Tillie had turned a little white and now swallowed, met his eyes.

"I . . . It's just that Rigger is dangerous. And if he knows there's cops . . ." She shook her head. "I'm sorry. I shouldn't have come here. This was a bad idea." She turned and headed toward the door.

Moose caught up to her, grabbed her arm.

She turned, stiffening, her eyes wide.

He let her go, hands up. "Listen. Dawson is my cousin. You can trust him." He looked at Flynn. "Right?"

Flynn must have read his look, because she pocketed her phone. "Yeah. Just me and Dawson."

Even he could tell she was making false promises, but if Moose could get there first . . .

That was it. He'd go with her, figure out a way to stall or even talk Rigger away from her kid—and yeah, even to his own ears it sounded half-cocked, but all he had to do was buy them time.

He lowered his hands. "I'm going with you. We'll talk to Rigger. If all he wants is his money, maybe he can be reasoned with." He didn't believe a word of what he said, given the damage to Tillie's face, but it also bought him time with her, to get Flynn and Dawson on site and some SWAT backup. . . .

"No way," Flynn said. "I'm not going to let you walk into a possible kidnapping with an armed felon."

"He's not armed," she said. "And I don't think he'd hurt Hazel."

"Except for the kidnapping part," Flynn said.

"I think . . . I think we can solve this. Without the police." Flynn gave her a look.

"Please. If he sees cops, then . . . then things could get ugly."

"No way I'm letting you walk in there—"

"It's not up to you." Tillie, for the first time, wore an expression on her face that resembled a fight.

"The only one in danger here is me," Tillie said softly. "And I want to keep it that way."

Moose glanced at Flynn, saw fight on her face too, and stepped between the two women. Turned to Tillie. "Then we're going to

ONE LAST PROMISE

go talk to him. And Flynn and Dawson are coming as backup. Any sign that we're in over our heads, we're out."

Moose glanced at Flynn, and she gave him a look that said she didn't much like his plan. She opened her mouth as if to argue, but he held up a hand. "I promise. No one will do anything stupid."

"Call me and turn your phone on speaker. And if he has a weapon, you leave."

He nodded.

But Tillie was shaking her head. "I'm sorry I came here. I panicked, and . . . this was—I was really just hoping to ask you for a ride. A plane ride . . . to anywhere. I didn't expect you to . . . This is too dangerous, Moose. I don't want you getting hurt."

"This is the best thing you could have done," Moose said. He put his hands on her shoulders. "I told you to find me if you needed anything. This guy hurt you, Tillie. And he has your daughter. Let's go talk to him, at least. And if I'm with you, then maybe he won't try anything." His voice lowered. "If it goes south, Flynn and Dawson will be there. It'll be okay. I promise."

Her mouth tightened. He didn't look at Flynn.

"Okay," Tillie said softly.

He reached for his jacket, shrugged it on, and then put on his boots. "Let's go."

Shep and London had already pulled out of the driveway in Shep's Jeep. Now he opened the garage door and grabbed his keys from the hook. Held the door open for Tillie.

She came out, and he led the way off the porch, across the driveway, and to his truck. He spotted her Ford Focus in the driveway, the one with the dented bumper, and it raised more questions.

Too many.

He got in his F-150. She slid into the other side.

"You sure you want to do this?"

"Never been more sure about anything in my life," Moose said as he fired up the truck.

46

He pulled out and spotted Flynn and Axel coming out of the house, followed by Oaken and Boo. He backed into a spot on the drive, then pulled out along his driveway, the motion-detector lights popping on as he headed toward the road.

She sat quietly beside him, her hands in her pockets.

He reached Old Glenn Highway and turned onto it, headed for Highway 1. "Can I ask how—"

"No."

He glanced over at her. "I didn't know you had a daughter."

"How would you?" She looked at him, her expression stoic in the wan dash light. "I'm not in the habit of sharing my personal life with the customers who come into the diner."

He'd sort of thought . . .

But he nodded. He wasn't her boyfriend, and she didn't want him to be—she'd made that pretty clear when she turned him down for a date. And sure, she'd clung to him at the door when he'd embraced her, but he could easily attribute that to fear, or maybe relief.

Now, she sat staring out the front windshield, almost a soldier's expression on her face.

On her *wounded* face.

His entire body burned. Talk. He was just going to *talk* to this guy.

"How'd he find you?"

"I'm not sure—except the house we live in is in my sister's name, so probably that's the connection."

"How does he know your sister?"

She looked out the window. "He got her hooked on heroin in high school." She wiped her cheek. "She got clean, but . . . it probably caused her liver cancer."

That still didn't connect the dots, but when Tillie went quiet, he didn't know what to say.

So he just reached out, across the console, and found her hand. Squeezed it.

She glanced at him then, her jaw tight. "I'm sorry."

"Nope. We'll get your daughter back, and then . . ." He offered a quick smile. "Then we talk."

Her mouth made a tight line, and she looked away.

And the fist in his chest tightened.

"Where in Anchorage are we going?"

"Earthquake Park. It's a little ranch house."

He said nothing as they passed Eagle River and then entered the city limits of Anchorage.

"Turn right on Northern Lights," she said, pointing.

"Is this where you live?"

"No. My house—my sister's house—is in Eagle River."

No wonder Dawson hadn't found her when he'd searched Anchorage for Tillie Young.

They passed Minnesota Drive, all the way to McKenzie, and he took another right.

No sidewalks in this part of town, but the houses were small and on tidy city lots, built after the 1964 'quake. Some had since been remodeled or torn down, creating an eclectic array of styles.

She pointed to a small ranch with a jutting front deck and a trio of birch in the front yard. The closed blinds along the front bay window obscured the view, so no joy on a sniper shot.

"Who is this Roz?"

"She's the ex-cop. She used to work in the gang unit."

"Do I want to ask how you met her?"

"Probably not, but let's just say that Rigger's been on her radar for a while."

Okay. Moose turned off the truck, parking it behind Rigger's car, and got out. Tillie emerged from the other side, and he caught up to her, grabbed her hand. "Stay behind me."

She looked at him. "You stay behind *me*. He sees you and he's going to get rattled."

"Just so we're clear, you're not going in there without me."

Behind him, Flynn and Axel had pulled up across the street. Axel turned off his lights.

Moose dialed Axel's number, then put his phone on speaker and mute and slipped it into his jacket pocket.

Tillie headed toward the door. She knocked, then opened it and stepped inside.

He followed her in.

The entry led to the family room and a kitchen on the back of the house. A hallway led back to the garage, the bedrooms on the opposite side, away from him.

A recliner and a side table sat opposite a sofa.

A man stood in front of a fireplace, his hands on the shoulder of a little girl in a worn nightgown. She was cute—dark hair, like Tillie's, and pretty green eyes, and she bit her lip, her eyes wide, and clutched a stuffed animal to herself.

Seated on the recliner, a bruise to her cheek, was a woman, beefy, with short white hair, wearing leggings and an oversized T-shirt. She sported a shiner too—clearly Rigger's calling card.

"Stop," said Rigger, and Moose caught the storm door as it closed. Stayed in the entry as Tillie took a step onto the faded brown carpet.

"Who's he?" Rigger said.

"A friend," Tillie said.

He looked at Moose. "Get out."

"I'm sorry, Tillie," said the woman.

Tillie held up her hand.

"I can't do that," Moose said quietly. His gaze scanned the room. "And as long as you stay unarmed, this can all end without anyone getting hurt." More hurt. But he didn't want to throw accusations.

He hoped Flynn was listening. *Not armed, Flynn. No shooting.*

"This is none of your business."

Moose said nothing.

"Your money is on the way," Tillie said. "Why don't you let Hazel go."

Hazel made a move then to run to her mother, but Rigger yanked her back. "Now why would I do that?"

"Please, Rigger. You don't want Hazel to go back with you. That's not a life for a little girl."

Rigger's eyes narrowed. "Why not? She's my daughter. She'll live the life I want for her."

The words landed center mass in Moose. He didn't know why, but all this time he'd thought . . . well, he didn't know what he'd thought, because yes, the questions had been circling, but . . .

Rigger was Hazel's father? Her sister's ex? What life had Tillie lived?

And maybe Hazel hadn't known this either, because suddenly she rounded on Rigger and, even as Moose stood stunned, the little girl hit Rigger below the belt with what seemed to be everything inside her. Rigger grunted and bent over, and then—

Then Roz leaped at the man, and Hazel took off for Tillie, and Moose—all Moose saw was fury.

Blind, red fury, the likes of which he'd never tasted before, filled his chest, his throat, his very breath, and he too launched himself at Rigger.

Three steps across the room, and he reached the thug right as Rigger threw Roz away, slamming her against the wall.

She crashed into a coffee table and fell to the floor as Moose tackled the man, his arms clamped around him.

Moose was a good foot taller, twenty pounds heavier, but the guy was all street brawn.

Street brawn and hate.

He thundered back with an elbow jab that speared into Moose's ribs. Moose grunted but held on.

50

Then Rigger sent his fist into Moose's thigh, and something sharp seared through him. His leg buckled and he fell.

Rigger broke free.

Moose glanced at his leg. Blood.

Rigger held a small switchblade in his grip. He shook his head, bouncing away. "Now you did it!"

He turned toward Tillie, who pushed Hazel behind her.

"Run!" Moose shouted, even as he pushed away from the wall.

Rigger dove at Tillie, but she somehow got her hand up and slammed the knife arm away.

Then, in a move that looked practiced and even professional, she swept Rigger's legs out.

The man went down.

Moose dove on him.

Tillie turned and pushed Hazel out the door, running hard after her.

Moose gripped Rigger's wrist with both hands as Rigger and he rolled. Rigger got a knee into his thigh and Moose grunted.

A shot to Moose's chin snapped his head back, and Rigger ripped away from him.

Rigger bounced up, Moose rolling hard to his feet.

Moose hadn't even bloodied him.

Rigger glanced toward the door.

"Stop!"

Moose looked over at the voice.

Roz. She stood in the kitchen, holding a handgun trained on Rigger.

Moose stood between them. "Roz. Put the gun down. Nobody gets shot today."

"He's not going out that door," Roz said, her voice steady. "You stay right here until the police come."

"The police aren't coming," Rigger said, and Moose hoped his phone was still on. Except it if was—why hadn't his team rushed in to help?

Roz took a step toward him. "Get down on your knees."

Rigger laughed at her.

She pulled off a shot that zinged past Moose into the wall behind Rigger. And Moose could almost hear his words again. *"Now you did it."*

Rigger roared and leaped at Roz.

She shot again, and missed him, because he didn't even slow, just tackled her, shoving her back into the kitchen table.

Another shot went off, and Moose found himself in the fray. He yanked Rigger away, but Roz and Rigger fought for the weapon, and Moose got his hand on it too, twisting with them, jamming it down, away from them—

"Rigger, let go!" Roz, shouting.

And then, another shot.

Just like that, Roz went down.

Rigger ripped away.

Moose held the gun.

And then the door slammed open, and Flynn and Dawson and who knew how many SWAT officers stormed into the house. One of them yelled, "Down, get down!"

Moose dropped the weapon and hit his knees beside Roz. She lay on her back, her sweatshirt swimming with blood, and he bent over her. "Where are you hit?"

But she simply writhed, her hands over her body, and he couldn't find the wound.

Hands grabbed him back, threw him to the ground, and he held his hands out. "It's not me! It's not me!"

A knee went into his back, however, and a hand grabbed his wrist, wrenched it behind him.

"C'mon!"

The other wrist, and said hand forced his head down. "Don't move."

"Don't let him get away!" He tried to look for Rigger, but so many legs filled the room, he couldn't see him.

Rigger certainly hadn't been forced to the linoleum.

And behind him, Roz was shouting. "Tillie. Run. Run!" So that didn't help.

But he lay, facedown, hands cuffed, breathing hard, thinking the same thing. *Run, Tillie, run!*

Roz then went painfully quiet. He glanced over at her, but she was lost behind so many shouting bodies.

Flynn's voice—"We need a bus—now!"

And another voice—his cousin Dawson—"He went out the back!"

Aw. Moose closed his eyes, jaw tight. *C'mon!*

Moose rested his forehead on the floor, listened to the thunder of his heartbeat. And tried not to feel the mountain crashing down over him, again.

Shep thought that London left covert life long ago, on the top of a mountain.

Or maybe he just wished it.

Still, as they pulled past Tillie's tiny bungalow in Eagle River, the night dropping down over it like a haze, he realized he probably needed someone who possessed a few sneak-and-grab skills.

Could be he was simply imagining a past for her, given his sketchy information. Although, the girl he'd met as a teenager certainly had a spy-vibe about her. Mysterious and international, even then, back at a summer camp in Montana. And meeting her again on a mountain years later...well, the time and place certainly gave off Sydney Bristow vibes. But maybe he'd just done bad math. . .

"Turn the corner and let's park. See if we've been followed."

He did exactly that, turning his Jeep around in a driveway and then settling it in a shadow under a massive lodgepole pine. "I feel like I'm in a spy movie."

"No. This is a heist movie." She looked over at him, and he couldn't tell if she was kidding.

Then she winked, and it sent a zing right through him, and shoot, they were in an unrequited romantic tragedy.

"Let's just get this over with."

Tillie's place was a little box of a house, tucked away among the trees, with a facade that seemed to have been painted with melted butter. Cute. Sweet. Not at all the kind of place you'd expect to find a cache of money. But then again, people who hid things had a way of painting a pretty exterior.

He glanced at London. She'd said little on the way over here, her jaw set in a hard line, probably reliving Tillie's words about Rigger. Shep was doing the same. The idea of a man hitting a woman the way Rigger had hit Tillie—Shep's gut was a knot.

The least they could do was grab the money and try to untangle her.

He hoped that was the reason for London's pensive vibe.

"The neighbors have a light," London said, pointing to a house next door. "But it seems like they aren't home. The house is dark. I hope nobody has a dog."

As if on cue, a dog barked into the quiet of the night.

Perfect.

"Okay, let's go." London slid out of the car, then crouched by the door, closing it fast.

He grabbed a shovel out of the back seat, then got out and came around the car behind her.

The air held a hint of pine from the surrounding trees. The faint smell of smoke also wafted by, perhaps from a nearby chimney. The hum of the highway murmured in the distance.

"We should call the cops."

"You heard her. She needs this money." London glanced at him. "Don't be a pansy."

His eyes widened and she laughed a little, the sound sneaking through him to take hold, and shoot, but this woman . . .

Maybe it hadn't been the brightest idea to reach out with the offer to join the Air One team, but at the time it had seemed like . . .

Like he'd been saving her life.

Just like she'd saved his.

"Let's go." She took off across the street, walking fast, avoiding the tall streetlight, into the yard of Tillie's home, through the grass, and over to the side of the house without stopping.

He scooted behind her, his heart a hammer.

"I'll bet the neighbors are staring out their windows, watching, dialing 911." He shook his head, then imitated a fictional neighbor. "Elmer, why is that man holding a shovel?"

"Just act normal."

"How is this normal?"

"I mean—act like you belong here."

With her?

She looked back at him, her blue eyes twinkling, and for a moment, he thought she could see inside him, all the way in, where he didn't have a hope of keeping his feelings for her tucked away.

Yeah.

See, this was why he had to tell her the truth. Because a year working with London Brooks had stirred up everything he'd been trying to forget and seeded new hope, a future he could no longer ignore. And didn't want to.

"Ready?" She started to ease out of the shadows.

Just then, a car turned down the street, passed their SUV, and beamed light across the yard.

She whirled around and shoved him back into the shadows, against the house.

He put his arms around her waist and pulled her close as the car motored by.

Her hands gripped his arms, her head against his chest, and he could almost feel her heartbeat. Definitely slower than his.

The car passed. "Okay, let's hurry." She pushed away from him and jogged to the gate, then through it to the back of the house.

He didn't know what to do with the rush of adrenaline that burned through him. One of them clearly had a knack for this sort of thing. . . .

Still, there he went, following her around to the back of the house.

A playset, blackened and still smoking, sat in the shadows of the yard, charring the air.

London was already moving patio furniture. "She said it was under the fire pit, right? Grab that side."

He hustled over and grabbed the edge of a round fire pit, helped her move it aside. Then he dug his shovel into the patio paver. The sand chipped away, and he rocked the shovel as London got on her knees. In the wan light, her golden hair held back in a ponytail, wearing a light canvas jacket, she seemed every bit of the woman he'd met so many years ago.

And for a second, he was back in the chalet in Switzerland, working with her to dig them out of their icy tomb.

"Take this." She'd pried up the square stone paver, and now he bent to grab it and move it aside.

Right. Focus. Not the kind of memory to take out and relive.

But he might never forget the blinding, terrifying moment he'd fallen in love at first sight.

She pried off the next paver, and he loosed another. Soon, they'd cleared a square area covered in sand. When he sank his shovel into it, it hit plastic.

"I think it's a plastic bag, or the ground covering." London had turned her phone light on but put it face down on the ground so only a bit of light pooled out. Still, he made out the hole as he dug, breaking through the plastic.

His shovel thudded on something hard.

"There's a box here." She pulled up another paver, then tore at the plastic covering with her hands.

He cleared out the area.

Indeed, an airtight plastic box, right where Tillie had said.

London sat back, gasped, and then looked up at Shep. "I have to admit, I wasn't sure. I mean . . ."

"Her story was a little wild."

"Yeah. Except she came to Moose. Which said she was serious. You don't involve your friends unless you really need help."

"After disappearing for a month first."

"Yeah, there's that." She shook her head. "Clearly she's desperate to come out of hiding."

"If this guy really has her daughter—which it seems he does—that seems like a good reason."

She leaned forward, brushing sand away. "Yeah. To save someone I loved, I might just give up everything too. Here, I think there's a latch." Picking up her phone, she shone her light on it.

He tried not to be shaken by her words and reached into the dirt. "It's stuck."

"Try the shovel."

He put the shovel's pointy end against the latch, used it as a lever, and the latch popped open.

He dropped the shovel, then knelt again, taking one edge as she took the other. They lifted the lid.

Inside lay another plastic bag. It held a box of some sort.

Shep reached in and took out the bag. Set it on the patio. A twist-tie secured it.

He untwisted it and reached in. Pulled out a hard-sided carry-on-sized suitcase. "Feels pretty light for a suitcase filled with money."

"And it's not locked," London said. "Weird."

"Yeah." He set it on the patio, and she knelt beside him as he found the zipper and unzipped it.

Lifted it open.

And he'd half expected it, but still, the sight of the empty case hit him like a punch.

He swallowed.

"This is bad," London said.

He glanced over at her. She'd picked up her phone and now shed the light on the interior, as if confirming.

"There's a note." She reached in and picked up a folded piece of lined paper. Opened it. Frowned and handed it to Shep.

"It's just a number."

"Five digits, so it's not a phone number," said London. She took the paper back and turned it over. "There's nothing else on it."

Nearby, the dog barked again, and Shep jerked. "Let's get out of here."

She nodded. "Should we put the patio back together?"

A light flicked on across the backyard at the house over the fence, probably someone letting in the dog, but Shep was already on his feet. "Nope. Let's go."

He carried the suitcase, in case they'd missed something, the shovel in the other hand.

London got up, holding the paper. "We'll google it in the car."

Yeah, hopefully a long way from here. "And we need to text Moose an update."

London headed out around the side of the house just as another car came down the street, its lights bathing the front yard.

Shep dropped the shovel and yanked her back, against him in the darkness, his arm going around her waist, holding her there.

For a second, he couldn't breathe, watching the pickup drive by, feeling her molded against him again. Strong, lean, perfect.

And then she laughed.

Laughed.

Which made his stupid heart beat right out of his body.

She turned in his arms. Looked up at him. "What, saving my life again?" She smiled, her eyes twinkling and blue and . . .

Shoot. He couldn't stop himself. Longing simply took over him, grabbed up his common sense, and threw it out into the night. Told him that yes, this was the right thing—that working together for a year had rekindled her feelings too, and that she felt the same way that—

And yeah, he should have asked, but again, his common sense had lit out for the lower forty-eight by now, so he just leaned down and . . .

He kissed her.

Just like that. One hand still around her waist, the other holding the suitcase. Pressed his lips against hers, and for a second, a brief, amazing second, she stilled and her lips softened.

He wouldn't exactly say kissing him back, but not *not* kissing him back either, so—

Aw. She was the night, mysterious, with the scent of fading summer on her skin, the taste of too many unspoken hopes, and he was way down the road into their tomorrows when he felt her hands on his chest.

Oh.

No.

She pressed back, caught her breath. "Shep . . ."

He let her go. "Yeah . . . I . . ."

"I don't, I mean . . ." She swallowed. "I don't think I'm ready."

He didn't want to mention that it had been three years since her fiancé died . . . but maybe a person never let go of their first love. "I get it. I'm sorry—"

"Don't be sorry." She offered a smile, suddenly not the person who'd just led him on a clandestine looting mission, but almost tentative. Even regretful. "I . . . you're . . . I . . ."

"Let's just go," he said. "It's okay."

Then he picked up the shovel and left her there, not looking back, a burn in his throat.

Stupid, *stupid*—

She caught up with him and said nothing as they walked to the car. He unlocked it, threw the shovel and suitcase in the back, and got in.

She was already in the passenger seat, on her phone, googling something. She didn't look at him.

The car felt as cold as the icy tomb where they'd nearly perished, once upon a time. So much for true love.

Or . . . maybe she'd never felt that way about him.

Not now— "Could be a date." He pulled out his keys, started up the car.

"That's six numbers."

"Coordinates?"

"Lat and long?"

"I'd think that needs a decimal point."

He put the car into gear.

She was too pretty, sitting there with the glow of the light on her face. And he'd gone and dropped a bomb between them. "Time-travel parameters?"

She looked up. Smiled. "Not enough digits. Unless the month was just one digit. In that case, you need to send me to May of 2772."

"Why you? I'll go."

Her mouth opened, and for a second, he thought that she might spill out something about her past, about the life she'd once lived.

But then again, he supposedly knew nothing about that life, so . . .

He raised an eyebrow.

Then, softly, "You're right. You go. You were always better at showing up at the right time and place." And she met his eyes with a look that said she remembered everything about how they'd met. And everything that had gone down between them.

"Did I screw everything up?"

"No," she said, her mouth a tight line. "But now isn't the time—"

His phone buzzed on the console. A text. He picked it up, read it. "It's Axel. Things went south." He looked at her, his breath tight. "Roz is shot, Moose is in custody, and Tillie's in the wind."

Perfect. Now she could add car theft to her résumé.

Not that it was long, but still—what had possessed Tillie to jump into Moose's truck, put it in reverse, and pull out of the driveway—

Wait. Probably the *Run, Tillie, run* from Roz. And then gunshot behind her, and she'd simply grabbed Hazel and done just that.

Run.

She'd spotted the truck and just reacted—she'd seen Moose leave the keys in the ignition, and it'd all clicked.

She threw Hazel into Moose's truck, belted her in, ran to the driver's side, and got in.

She had the car in reverse even before she spotted Flynn running through the night, uniformed SWAT on her tail, and one of them tried to stop her—banged on the car—but she floored it.

Barely missed Axel's Yukon, slammed her car into drive, and slammed the gas to the floor.

Didn't look back.

Beside her, Hazel was crying, of course, and she grabbed Hazel's hand, squeezed. "It's okay, Hazelnut; it's okay."

But no, it was far, far from okay, and even Hazel knew that, because she shook her head and pulled her hand away.

Okay, fine, she'd deal with the little girl's emotional breakdown after she got them—

Where?

She didn't have a clue where she might be going. Just pulled out onto Northern Lights Boulevard and merged into traffic.

"Mom—who was that man?"

"That was Moose. My friend."

"No . . . the bad one. The one who said he was my dad."

She glanced at Hazel. Tears reddened her face, and she had pulled her knees up, draping her nightgown over them, her boots on Moose's nice leather seats.

"Honey, he's . . . he's not your father. He's just saying that. Your real father was a good man. A soldier who died fighting for his country. He was a hero."

Hazel snuffled, ran her hand across her face, dragging snot with it. "He hurt Grandma Roz."

Tillie nodded, her chest tight, not wanting to think about what exactly might be going down back there. In her worst nightmare, Moose was dead and—

She should never have gone to his house. *Stupid, stupid!* Her throat burned, and she blinked back heat in her eyes.

She stopped at a light, breathing hard.

"Where are we going?"

She looked over at Hazel. Swallowed. Right now, Shep and London were digging up the money, but if Rigger had gotten away . . .

No, she couldn't go back to the house. "I . . ."

"I have to go to the bathroom," Hazel said.

Right. "Okay, I'll find a gas station."

"And I'm hungry."

Of course she was. "McDonald's?"

Hazel smiled, nodded.

Fine. "One Happy Meal coming up." Except—*shoot*. Her wallet was in her car . . . back at Moose's.

"Sorry, just the potty for now, honey."

She should return his truck too, so as not to be a felon. There was that.

She pulled into a Holiday station and parked between a couple more trucks. Lights beamed down from the tall stanchions, and the odor of diesel and gas followed them into the station. Inside, the smell of greasy chicken fingers under the heat lamps stirred her gut.

She needed a Happy Meal too.

She followed Hazel into the bathroom. Stood at the mirror. *Yikes.* They looked like a couple of homeless people. Or worse. Washing her face, she emerged a little cleaner. Hazel came out, washed her hands, and met her eyes in the mirror. She had Pearl's eyes, a little gold around the irises, a heart-shaped face. A real beauty.

Of course, that had only gotten her sister into trouble.

Tillie took Hazel's hand, and they walked out of the station, got back into the truck. She had the urge to turn around, return to Roz's house, check on . . . everyone. But a police car zoomed by on the road behind her, its siren moaning and . . . *Nope.*

She shouldn't go back to Moose's house either.

"Mom? Are we going?"

She'd been sitting in the car, the engine running, just holding on to the steering wheel. She glanced over. "Yeah. Sorry."

"I want to go home."

"I don't think so, honey."

She put the car into drive.

A hand slammed on her driver's side window, and she jerked, jumped. Hazel screamed.

She stared, and for a second, blinked at the man.

Not. Rigger.

Axel stood by her door, his blue eyes fierce, his mouth set. *Uh-oh.*

Her heart hammered as she lowered the window. "Um—I panicked."

Axel glanced into the truck, then back to her. "You did the right thing."

Just like that, the fist inside her chest loosed. She breathed in. "How's Moose?"

"Dunno."

The shots.

"Was he . . ."

"I don't know. I don't think so, or Flynn would have texted me."

"And Rigger?"

Axel grimaced. "I think he got away."

So, going home was definitely out, then.

"Roz?"

"An ambulance was on the way when I left."

She closed her eyes.

"Who are you?" Hazel, leaning across the console.

He smiled, and Tillie's heartbeat slowed a little. "I'm Axel. Who are you?"

"I'm Hazel."

"Nice to meet you, Hazel." He looked at Tillie. "Did you have a destination or. . ."

"I left my car at Moose's house." Not really an answer, and perhaps he knew it, because he let a beat drop between them.

"I think Moose's house is exactly where you should go." His words emerged gentle. "And stay."

"I don't . . ." She glanced at Hazel, then turned back, and lowered her voice. "I've brought Moose enough trouble for one night."

His voice dropped. "Moose has been worried sick about you for a month. He tried to get Dawson to find you—"

"Dawson?"

"Our cousin. He's a detective with the Anchorage police."

Oh.

64

"Moose cares about you, Tillie. It might be nice if you were there, waiting, when he got back."

He stepped away from the truck. "Or I suppose you could keep driving. Because as much as Moose loves this truck, I think he cares about you more."

And now she couldn't breathe. Axel met her eyes. Then he nodded and walked away. She followed him through the rearview mirror, saw him get into his Yukon. Drive away, back toward Roz's place.

"Mom?"

"Yeah, it's okay, Hazelnut. We're going to be okay."

Funny, that's exactly what Moose had said to her.

She turned the heat up as they got back on the road. Hazel curled up on the seat, putting her head down on the console, and Tillie rubbed her shoulder.

The big truck found its way back to Moose's place almost on its own, and as she pulled in, her decrepit Ford Focus looked pitiful and desperate.

You could keep driving. She got the gist of Axel's words. She could take Moose's truck, and he wouldn't come after her. Wouldn't press charges.

And that made her what kind of person?

"Where are we?" Hazel lifted her head.

"Someplace safe." She parked the truck, then turned it off and went to her car. Inside were Hazel's backpack, her own backpack, and a few supplies she'd picked up over the month—toiletries, foodstuffs, a couple blankets and pillows.

Yeah, definitely homeless.

Hazel had gotten out, come around the car. "This is a really fancy house."

"It is." She handed Hazel her backpack and pillow. "How would you like to stay here for a few . . . days?"

Days?

More like hours.

She sighed as she followed Hazel up the steps and knocked. Nothing.

Axel *had* told her to go here. She opened the front door.

Quiet. Just the hum of the refrigerator in the kitchen.

"Take your shoes off, honey."

"It's so big."

Indeed, Moose's home felt gargantuan, with the vaulted, beamed ceiling and the towering stone fireplace that rose in the great room. She'd noticed his gourmet kitchen before, with the eight-burner stove and the massive, ten-by-six-foot granite countertop, but only now took in the second story that overlooked the great room.

"Where should I put my stuff?" Hazel still held her backpack and pillow.

Tillie felt like she might be in that old movie, the one she'd watched with her sister at Christmastime, about a kid, alone in his house.

"Um, upstairs?" She looked into a room on the main floor—an office with a walnut desk and bookshelves—and then opened another door—the basement. So, "Yes, upstairs we go."

Hazel scampered upstairs, dropping her pillow on the way, and Tillie scooped it up and heard Hazel shouting, "Mom! The bedrooms are huge!"

Of course they were. She found herself on a bridge between two sections. One led to double doors—she guessed that might be the master, so, nope, not that direction.

Hazel had run down the hallway to the other section. A bedroom at the front of the house, and one at the back. Only three bedrooms, but to her seven-year-old who'd only lived in their tiny house, their bedrooms the size of Moose's guest closet, perhaps it did seem huge.

She found Hazel in the front bedroom, standing on a huge

king-sized bed with a homey brown quilt, pure white sheets, and pillows the size of her car.

"Hazel, don't jump on the bed."

Hazel jumped off and ran into the bathroom. "Mom! You have to see this!"

Tillie dropped her blanket and backpack, along with Hazel's pillow, on the bed and followed Hazel into the en suite.

Hazel stood in a whirlpool tub big enough for, well, Moose, or even her entire Marine unit.

And wow, she hadn't thought about that life in years, so neatly putting it behind her, altering nearly everything about herself, at least on the outside.

On the inside, she'd needed the remnants of the marine she'd been to survive the last month. And if she were to go back there, the thought could make her smile, imagining St. Nick and Popeye trying to cram their bodies into the jacuzzi.

"Mom, look!" Hazel pointed up, and Tillie followed her gaze to a skylight. Only then did she realize that under her feet, the tile was warm.

Double sinks, and a shower with a bench, and perhaps this wasn't such a terrible idea. In fact, maybe she could also find a laundry room.

"Do you want to take a bath?"

"Yes, yes, yes, please!"

She laughed. "Okay. Go ahead and run it. Close the door. I'm going out to the car to get our stuff. I'll see if I can find you something clean."

Hazel jumped out of the tub, and as Tillie turned to go, she found small arms giving her waist a squeeze. "Thank you!"

She looked at Hazel through the mirror, the smile on her face. "For what?"

"For not making me sleep in the car."

Her words punched Tillie right in the sternum, even as Hazel rounded back to the tub and started the water.

Oh, Hazelnut.

She closed the door, hearing Pearl's voice. *"Just don't let him find her. Don't let him take her."*

Trying, sis. Why hadn't she been smarter? And now . . .

She couldn't think about Moose, not yet. Not until Hazel was clean and safe and sleeping.

Taking another trip to the car, she unloaded her trunk—clothing she'd purchased over the past month. Not much, really—just a sweatshirt and a jacket and some boots, and clothes for Hazel. But they'd been worn so many times, they smelled lived in, survived in, really.

She brought them back inside, then emptied their backpacks and wadded the entire mess into a couple pillowcases she took from the bed.

Hazel was in the bath, splashing, and Tillie knocked, then spoke through the closed door. "Everything okay?"

"I'm a mermaid!"

"Yeah, you are." She smiled and almost felt a laugh, something foreign and scorched, in her chest. Then she took the clothes in the pillowcases downstairs to the basement.

Nice digs—a sectional sat in front of a massive theater screen, a pool table with the cues in a rack on the wall on the other side. A glass door led somewhere, and when she peeked in, she found a hot tub and a sauna room.

Her thoughts went to Hazel splashing in the tub. She'd die if she saw the hot tub.

Don't get too comfortable. The thought pinged inside Tillie as she headed down the hall. She peeked into one room, and it looked like an office. The next was an expansive bedroom, not unlike upstairs, but clearly occupied, and a little messy.

She found the laundry room at the end of the hallway. Dumping her clothes into the water, she added some soap and shook her head at the way she was diving into Axel's suggestion.

She didn't deserve this. But . . . desperation.

Then she headed upstairs.

She'd brought some food inside—cereal, yogurt, a bag of chips, a few chocolate bars. She'd left any hope of real nutrition behind when Rigger showed up. Now her body craved something substantial. Except, how audacious was it to open his fridge and dive in?

Very. But Hazel was hungry and so was she, so . . .

Steaks. Wrapped in plastic. Along with a salad and broccoli—clearly the dinner he'd left behind. Someone had taken the time to clean up.

She pulled out the salad and the steak. Started to unwrap the plastic when footsteps on the outside stairs stopped her.

She reached for a knife in the block. Because Axel's other words hung in her head too. *"I think he got away."*

She turned off the lights, backed away from the kitchen entrance, hiding.

Please, Hazel, stay upstairs.

Tillie had locked the front door—she'd checked. Still.

She held her breath as the door opened.

Steps, inside, heavy. Then the door closed.

Rigger wouldn't close the door, would he?

The movement stopped. Oh no—

Then steps, down the short hallway, toward the kitchen and—

"Stay back!"

She rounded, the knife up.

"Holy cats!" The light slammed on, and Moose stood in the entry, his eyes wide.

His face bore a scuff on his whiskered chin, and blood crusted his jeans, and just like that, his hand grabbed her wrist. "Let it go, Tillie. I'm not going to hurt you."

She nodded. And he let go. She yanked her hand away and set the knife on the counter.

"What are you doing here?"

He blinked at her. "I *live* here."

"I thought—" She was shaking now, stepping away from him, terribly aware of the look on his face, a little angry, a little relieved—honestly, she couldn't place it. "Are you okay? I was afraid they were going to arrest you."

"They did arrest me! Or tried to—long enough for the media to come by and get a great shot of me handcuffed against a cruiser. So yeah, that will be a big help to my lawsuit."

Lawsuit?

He took a breath. Closed his eyes. "Okay. Sorry. I am usually a little more reined in."

Yes. She knew that. She'd seen him after the rescues while he processed . . . usually with a milkshake rather than a stiff shot of whiskey. Which was at the least, interesting. Definitely telling about the kind of man he was.

That probably accounted for why she stood in his kitchen, the knife on the counter, feeling more chagrined than afraid.

Probably accounted for why she'd too easily gone to him for help.

"I'm so sorry, Moose."

He opened his eyes. Sighed. "No, Tillie. I'm sorry. Are you okay?"

"Yes." She nodded, just to confirm. "And Hazel is taking a bath in your swimming pool upstairs."

He blinked at her a moment, then let out a laugh. "Right. Okay."

And just hearing him laugh made her want to weep, a rush of light and warmth through her.

Maybe they would be okay after all.

The door opened then, and Axel came in. She glanced at him.

"Good," he said, and sat on the bench to unlace his boots.

Good?

"He said I could come here," she said to Moose, as if in explanation.

Moose nodded, glanced back at his brother. "Yep. That was a good call."

"Was it? Because Rigger is still out there, and—"

"And I have lights everywhere and a security system. The guy who used to own this place was . . . he was a little paranoid. Not sure why, but I don't hate it."

For some reason, the fact that Moose wasn't the original owner, hadn't built this place felt . . .

Well, a little like he wasn't *completely* out of her league.

What? No, she was just tired. And unwound and . . .

"Moose, your leg."

He looked down. "Yeah. That was unfortunate. As it turns out, just a flesh wound. But it's messy."

"Your entire pant leg is bloody."

"I need a shower." He glanced at Axel. "How about heating up the grill? I'd like a redo on those steaks."

"On it," Axel said and winked at her as he walked past.

What? She didn't know why, but she turned to Moose to tamp down her overwhelming sense of relief.

Because this was still a bad idea. Desperate and temporary at best. "I won't be in your hair long, and I promise to stay out of the way—"

"Oh no, you don't."

Moose walked over to the counter and pulled out a stool. "Sit down. And don't move until I come back. Because I need to know exactly what is going on."

And this time he didn't smile.

FOUR

MAYBE HE DIDN'T WANT TO KNOW.
Moose had pulled on a pair of shorts and run the towel over his head, and stood in his bathroom, the haze of his hot shower still settling on his bare shoulders, his wet, dark hair, as he stared into the mirror and tried to get his brain around the last three hours of his life.

He ran his hand over his wrist where the SWAT guy had grabbed it, wrenched the cuff too tight. Left a mark there, but it was nothing compared to the open wound on his thigh.

He lifted the hem of his shorts, got a better look. For such a small wound, it had really bled. They'd butterflied it closed after he refused to go to the hospital, although it needed a couple stitches, given the depth of the two-inch slice.

But his wounds were minor in comparison to the haunted expression Tillie wore when he'd left her in the kitchen.

An expression that had him wondering if he should just . . . leave it. Let her keep her story secret. They weren't in a relationship, and sure, he'd practically dived headfirst into her problems, but that's what he did.

He was a rescuer. That didn't mean they had some sort of romance in front of them. And maybe he didn't want a romance with someone with so much baggage.

Aw, that wasn't fair. Everyone had baggage.

Everyone could start over.

Besides, he had a few scars, both inside and out.

He ran his hand over his chin, decided not to shave, given the scuff on his chin, and hung his towel on the rack.

Then he scooped up his torn, bloody pants and shirt and came out of the bathroom. Night pressed against his bedroom windows, and the steam followed him out.

A knock sounded and he threw the clothes in the hamper in his closet, then opened the door.

Tillie stood in the hallway. She held up a tube of superglue. "Let's take a look at that wound."

It felt weird to have her here, in his home. All his daydreams suddenly front and center. But in those daydreams, she was here for dinner, on the patio, or watching a movie in the theater, or even watching a game of hockey on the flatscreen in the great room....

Never running from her ex—

Whatever. Because he refused to wrap his head around the idea that a thug like Rigger could be the *father* of her child.

Her child.

Yep, he might be in way over his head. *Back away, back away now*.

Instead, "Okay."

Her gaze landed on his shirtless torso.

"Just a sec. I'll meet you downstairs." He walked over to his dresser and pulled out a black T-shirt, pulling it over his head as he came out into the hallway and shut his door.

Axel stood at the stove, frying up some potatoes that had gone cold. The scent of butter and garlic suddenly landed in Moose's empty stomach, twisted.

Tillie stood by a stool in the kitchen. "With all that blood, I thought I should take a look."

He sat and rolled up his shorts. She pulled up another stool and bent to examine the wound.

"What are you, a doctor too?"

She laughed. "No. But I've been in my share of scrapes."

He wanted to ask, but there were too many questions.

Frankly, he didn't know where to start.

Her fingers probed the skin on either side of the cut. "It's a pretty clean slice. I'm concerned that the knife wasn't clean, but we'll put some antibacterial on it." She glanced over at Axel, who'd turned, folded his arms, and leaned against the counter, watching.

Moose wanted to fist-bump his brother for directing her here, because in his darkest nightmares, she was out there, alone and scared.

"I'm going to pinch this closed, then glue it. It'll take a couple seconds to set up, but it should work. Axel, do you have any bandages, some ointment?"

His brother turned the heat off the cast-iron skillet. "Do you want Batman or Spider-Man Band-Aids for the superhero?"

Moose gave him a look, and Axel raised his hand. But okay, they'd probably gone through more superhero Band-Aids than the average kids, growing up in the woods at their homestead outside Copper Mountain.

"This'll hurt," she said.

He said nothing as she drew the edges of his wound together, then applied the glue. Held the wound closed, then continued to the next section. "You're lucky he didn't get the knife straight in. This could have been a deep wound."

"Providence, not luck."

She glanced up at him, shook her head, then went back to work, finishing up. Axel appeared, holding a gauze cloth and some medical tape, along with a tube of ointment. "No Band-Aids."

"I don't need that, either."

"Just long enough for the ointment to stick," she said and finished doctoring the wound. Then she stood back. "I can't believe they didn't make you go to the hospital."

"They tried," Axel said, back at the stove. "He ditched them."

"The media was already on the scene. The last thing I wanted was questions. We already have trouble because of the media."

Axel glanced over as he plated the potatoes, frowned. *Oops.* Moose hadn't told his brother—hadn't told *anyone*—about the lawsuit.

He didn't need anyone worrying but himself.

"Because of the show?" Tillie said. "I saw a couple of the episodes. They even had a scene at the diner. . . ." Her eyes widened. "That's it. That's how Rigger found me."

"Wait—what?"

"They caught me on screen, just in the background of the Skyport Diner. Maybe they didn't even realize it—after all, I didn't sign a release. But I saw it, and it was so brief I didn't think anything of it. But with all the play the show has gotten . . ." She sank onto the stool. "It kept bugging me. I left no trail, or at least I thought so. And Roz wouldn't betray me, so . . ."

"The *show* caused this?" *That stupid show—*

She held up her hand. "I don't know. I mean . . . but . . ."

He shook his head. "Worst idea I ever had."

"It helped catch a killer," Axel said, pulling plates from the cupboard. "If Flynn hadn't seen the show, she wouldn't have followed up on the Midnight Sun Killer, and he'd still be out there." Axel set the plates on the island. "I'll grab the steaks."

"I'm sorry I got you into this," Tillie said quietly, sitting on the stool.

"I think I got you into this," Moose said, his gut tight. "But I'm not exactly sure what *this* is." He didn't want to ask, but . . . "Who is Rigger, really?"

A beat, and she sighed, then nodded. "He's—"

"Mommy?"

The voice jolted through him, sweet and high. He turned, looked up.

Tillie's little girl stood on the bridge that overlooked the great room, her dark hair wet and in tangles, plastered to her head. She wore pink sweatpants and a misshapen shirt with a Disney princess on the front.

"Hazel." Tillie slid off the stool. "Come downstairs, and I'll brush your hair."

"I can do it."

Tillie held up a hand. "Of course. Do you want something to eat?"

Hazel nodded.

Tillie looked at Moose. "I don't suppose you have anything besides steak and salad?"

"Axel keeps a supply of junk food in the pantry," he said and got up. "He's thirteen years old on the inside." Indeed, he found a box of macaroni and cheese and brought it out.

"A thirteen-year-old who makes killer macaroni and cheese," Axel said, setting the plate of steaks on the counter. "Give me that." He looked at Hazel, who'd come downstairs. "Hey, kiddo. Do you like tuna?"

She nodded.

"One tuna mac coming right up." Axel grabbed a pot from the drawer next to the stove, twirled it by the handle, then filled it up with water.

The ham.

Hazel climbed up on a stool, her little legs dangling, her feet bare.

The temps were dropping into the low fifties at night.

Moose got up and headed to his fireplace, opened the screen and grabbed wood from the rack next to the hearth.

Yes, he was procrastinating because . . .

Because if Rigger was Hazel's father, that meant . . . what? He was Tillie's ex too?

Nope, not going there. He stacked a couple logs, added kindling and some crumpled paper, then stood and grabbed the container of fireplace matches.

"That's a long match."

He glanced over his shoulder to where Hazel had come to stand behind him. She ran her brush haphazardly through her hair, working it into a knot at the ends.

"It's a fireplace match. Wanna help?"

He glanced at Tillie, who'd stayed at the counter, and she shrugged.

Hazel stepped up and he lit the match, then held out the end for her. She took it, and he pulled her closer, put his hand over hers. "Put the flame on the paper—like this." He lit some of the crumpled paper in front. "Then over here, we'll light the birch bark." He moved her hand with the match and ignited the old, dried curls of birch bark he'd picked up in the yard.

The fire began to flame to life, and he helped her shake out the match. "Good job."

She grinned.

She was missing her bottom incisors. But her top front teeth were in, big in her mouth. Wow, she was a cutie.

At the stove, Axel poured the noodles into the boiling water.

Meanwhile, Tillie had plated the steaks and set the table, like they might be at the Skyport for dinner.

So many questions.

Like how'd she ended up in Alaska, and . . . and how about that crazy move she'd done on Rigger, sweeping out his feet? Reminded him a little of how she'd taken Moose down a few months ago when he'd accidently surprised her in a wintery parking lot.

He watched her as she took the brush from Hazel, then held

the ends of Hazel's hair and worked out the snarls. Hazel scowled even as Tillie made an effort to minimize the pulling.

"Where have you two been the past month?" He didn't know why he started there. It seemed easier than the questions about Rigger. Especially in front of Hazel.

"In our car," Hazel said.

His eyes widened. Tillie sighed. "Just for the last week."

"A week. *In your car?*"

"We were camping," Hazel said. "With sleeping bags."

"We stayed at a few parks around the city. Kincaid. Earthquake. There are a lot of parks around."

Camping.

"This looks amazing." Tillie pulled her plate toward herself. "You want some salad, Hazelnut?"

"Gross."

"Macaroni and cheese in five," Axel said.

Moose piled salad and some squash on his plate. Maybe food would help him unsnarl his brain, because now he was stuck on an image of Hazel and Tillie sleeping in their car as the nights got colder.

Yeah, no, that wasn't happening again.

"For the record, we also stayed at a few hotels," Tillie said softly. "I just ran out of money."

The money. She seemed to connect with that thought the same time he did. "Where are London and Shep?"

Right.

He'd left his phone in his jacket and now slid off the stool—

"I got it, bro," Axel said, already dialing. He put it on speaker, then grabbed the pot of noodles and dumped the water out into the sink, holding onto the lid.

The call rang and rang, then went to Shep's voicemail.

Axel put the noodles back on the stove, then hung up, no message.

"That's not good," Moose said.

"Let's try London." Axel dialed her number, then added the cheese mix and retrieved milk from the refrigerator as the call rang.

Again, no answer and it went to voicemail.

Axel hung up, then added the milk and stirred. Silence.

"Okay, now I'm worried," Moose said. He looked at Tillie. "You think your friend Rigger went back to your house . . ."

"He's not my friend," she said, a little flash to her eyes.

He looked at Axel, who was opening the tuna can.

"Eat," said Axel. "Then worry. Besides, Shep and London can take care of themselves. You don't have to rescue everyone."

Really? Because it felt like it.

Axel poured Hazel some milk, then gave her a bowl of hot macaroni and cheese.

"I love macaroni and cheese!" Hazel put down her milk, leaving a mustache of cream on her lip.

"Doesn't everybody?" Axel said and winked.

Hazel picked up her spoon and dug into her dinner. Moose poured himself a glass of milk and offered one to Tillie, but she declined, preferring water. Then he sat at the island and ate a perfectly decent, but a little overdone, steak, trying to do exactly what Axel said.

But . . . he had to know. Not in front of Hazel, however, so he started with, "Where'd you learn the superglue trick?"

Tillie had cut up her salad. "The Marines."

He raised an eyebrow.

"Staff Sergeant Tillie Young, reporting for duty." She winked, popping a bite of steak into her mouth.

"Wow. Staff Sergeant. Four years, then?"

"Straight out of high school. Was going to be career. I was in for six."

"Why the Marines?"

"My dad was a marine." She lifted a shoulder. "Semper Fi."

Right. "And then?"

She sighed. "Then my sister got sick and she needed medical care, so . . ." She glanced at Hazel. "We moved to Anchorage."

Yeah, there were a few empty spots in that answer. But maybe that's all she wanted Hazel to know.

Axel had fixed himself a plate, too, and now ate at the end of the island, scrolling through his phone. Maybe sending Flynn a message. Hopefully.

His thoughts returned to Shep and London. The last thing Moose wanted was for them to get tangled up with Rigger.

He didn't care what Axel said. Of course they were his responsibility.

"Bro."

Moose looked up from where he'd sopped his steak in ranch dressing.

Axel slid his phone across the island, and Moose picked it up, looked at the screen, his chest knotting.

"What?" Tillie asked.

"Local Anchorage media has picked up the altercation at the house." He set the phone down. "Got a great shot of me getting arrested."

Her mouth tightened.

"They listed my name. And Air One Rescue." He slid the phone back to Axel.

Silence as Axel met his gaze. It wouldn't be hard for Rigger to track down Moose's home address.

Which meant whatever had been started back at Roz's house might get finished here. And sure, he had security, but the first rule of defense was to not get caught in the first place.

He didn't need to know all the reasons why they were in this situation.

He just needed to know Tillie and Hazel were safe.

He put down his fork. "How would you guys like to go on a road trip?"

Hazel had finished her mac and cheese and now put her glass down, really cementing that milk mustache.

"Where?" Tillie asked.

"Do you trust me?"

She swallowed, then nodded.

"Good. Get your stuff. We leave in ten."

He got up from the stool.

Axel came around to grab his plate. "Tell Mom hi."

Moose had brought her to his home.

His. Home.

With his father and mother. And a dog named Kip and a huge yard, with a slide and fresh air and a river she'd warned Hazel not to get close to, and fresh-made cinnamon rolls and . . .

Peace.

Or at least a ceasefire between the guilt and shame in her soul.

Guilt that she'd dragged Moose into her problems. Shame that she hadn't been smarter, kept Hazel safe.

Kept the promise to Pearl.

But here, as Tillie stood in a pair of leggings and an oversized sweatshirt, nursing a cup of coffee on Moose's deck, watching Hazel throw a stick for Kip in the yard . . . she simply breathed.

In. Out. Fresh air. Safety.

Overhead, to the west, a few dark low-hanging clouds suggested a storm, but around them, the sky arched blue and beautiful, the majestic Alaska Range jutting through the clouds, triumphant, some of the peaks glistening a glorious white.

And the air. Piney, with the wind stirring up a tangy, delicious fall scent. The river at the far end of the property rushed, a distant applause to the day.

"There you are."

Moose came out of the door to the main floor of his parents' A-frame home. An apron deck wrapped around the sides and front and jutted out over a lower floor that opened up into the yard.

She and Hazel had slept in a guest room on the lower floor, snuggled together in a way-too-comfortable queen bed, one she hadn't really wanted to leave this morning. But the scent of cinnamon rolls and sizzling bacon, along with Hazel's persistent nudges, had drawn her out from under the comforter. She'd braided her long hair, then found her way up the stairs to the main floor where Moose's mother, May, had been pulling a tray of fresh cinnamon rolls from the oven.

May had smiled at the mother and daughter headed up the stairs. "Moose said he'd brought home guests last night. I'll bet you're hungry. Sit down. Do you like eggs?"

"Love them." Tillie pulled out a chair for Hazel, who still wore her sweatpants from last night, her dark hair tousled with sleep. "Is Moose up yet?"

"Yes. For hours. He's helping his dad in the barn, working on the snowplow assembly." May wore an apron over her curvy body, her salt-and-pepper hair pulled back into a bun. Gray-green eyes like Moose, along with his smile, and her entire demeanor seemed to spill out into the room—homey, calm, generous.

Tillie could stay here forever.

Another one of her bad ideas. But as Moose and his father, Ace, came into the kitchen for breakfast, she soaked in the rapport between them, the way they sorted out some sort of problem with the plow together. She guessed that Moose had filled them in on her situation, because his parents asked no questions, just looped her into the breakfast as if she belonged.

His mother even doted on Hazel, making her chocolate milk

from a homemade mix on the counter. It left a mustache on Hazel, who seemed to have shed her trauma from last night.

The sound of whining at the gate across a nearby room made Hazel slide out of her chair and walk over to a boxer puppy. She knelt and stuck her fingers through the gate. "What's his name?"

"Kip," Moose's dad answered. "It was too quiet around here, so May asked that I get her a dog."

"*Please*. The dog is for him," May said and got up. "More coffee, Tillie?"

Tillie held out her mug—it bore the words *Last Frontier Bakery* on the side.

May filled it. "I think Kip needs to go out. Maybe Hazel wants to go with him?"

And that's how Tillie ended up on the deck, watching her daughter play, wondering how long the magic, this perfect bubble, might last.

She turned to Moose as he stepped out of the house, and by the look on his face, the answer was . . . not much longer. He wore a blue thermal shirt that outlined his muscled frame, a pair of faded jeans, and worn boots, laced up. He hadn't shaved, so a couple days of dark whiskers layered his chin, his hair tousled and tucked behind his ears.

She knew he was handsome—any girl with eyes could see that. And she knew he had to be heroic, given the stories she saw of him on the news, rescuing people, or even the few times he'd talked about a rescue at the Skyport, during one of his late-night stop-ins.

In fact, he'd always been a little bigger than life to her.

Now, he came over to her, stood beside her, and his shadow cast over her, tall and bold, and he even smelled good, as if he'd showered. . . . Perhaps coming here had been a bad idea after all.

The last thing she could do was start to lean on Moose, or anyone, really. Not with Rigger on her tail.

But what if Rigger wasn't in the picture?

Not even then, given the risks.

Moose looked out into the yard. "She's cute."

"The dog?"

"No. Kip is a monster. He eats everything he can chew on. Including my Sorels. I mean Hazel." He looked at Tillie. "She has your smile."

She swallowed, then nodded, and hated the lie of omission. But she'd made that decision long ago, hadn't she? It hadn't mattered until now, really.

She took a sip of her coffee. "Thanks."

"And a bit of fearlessness that she must get from you too." He turned to her.

She wanted to say that no, that was all Pearl, but maybe not, so she looked over to him and smiled. "I don't know. I'm still pretty unraveled, on the inside."

"You're safe here, Tillie. This place is off the map."

"Rigger won't be able to track you down here?"

"He'll have to work for it. In the meantime, I talked with my cousin Dawson, with the Anchorage PD—"

"I remember."

"And Flynn is hunting down Rigger too. We'll lay low here and let them do their job."

She drew in a long, pine-scented breath. "I don't want any of your family to get hurt."

Moose gave her a grim smile. "Me either."

"Mom, watch! He can fetch!" Hazel threw a stick, and Kip went bounding after it, bringing it back. She tried to wrestle it from his mouth, and a tug-of-war started.

"He's a sweet dog."

Moose rolled his eyes.

"What? You don't like dogs?"

"I like dogs. I just like well-behaved dogs."

"They don't get there without a lot of love and supervision."

SUSAN MAY WARREN

"Like children, I guess."

She raised a shoulder.

Silence fell between them. She finally looked over. "You aren't going to ask?"

"Not if you don't want to tell me."

Oh.

"I know I came in with both barrels last night, but I did a lot of thinking during the drive up."

"While I was sleeping."

"You were tired. You both were. I was still pretty lit up."

"You have questions."

"Thousands. But I've decided that I can live without answers." He turned to her. "You need my help. That's enough for me. No reasons why. Just . . . because."

Her throat tightened. "Shoot, Moose. It's not supposed to be like this."

"What?"

"I'm supposed to be the one who listens. Gives you milkshakes in your dark hours."

He laughed, and the sound of it was a balm to her clearly still-frayed nerves.

"What?"

"Nothing. Just . . . you do know that I only ordered the milk-shakes because you made them. And pie."

"You love pie."

"I do. But not at midnight."

She smiled. "So you just came in to see me?"

"Seriously, for a whole year I only came into the diner during your shift."

Yes, she'd known he liked her—he'd asked her out. But . . .

"Did you turn me down for a date because of Hazel?"

"I felt like it was too complicated."

"I'm a helicopter pilot. We can do complicated."

She turned away before this all got out of hand. "Not my kind of complicated."

Silence again, and she decided not to fill it.

But maybe he got it.

He finally took another sip of coffee, then tossed the rest out into the yard. "I have to go to town to get a part for the plow and some groceries for Mom. Want to come with me?"

"Sure. I'll get Hazel—"

"Hazel is fine here with my mom. She's going to make cookies. I'll bet Hazel would enjoy learning how to make them. Mom's recipe is world—or at least Alaska—famous."

"I don't know. . . ."

"She'll be fine."

Laughter from the yard below suggested that Tillie might have a fight on her hands ripping Hazel away from Kip. "Okay. Let me tell her, then I'll change and meet you." She finished her coffee, then while Moose went into the house, she walked down the steps to talk to Hazel.

"You sure you want to stay?"

"Forever!" Hazel threw her arms around her mom. "Can we get a puppy?"

"No." Tillie unwrapped Hazel's embrace. "I will come back. In the meantime, obey Mrs. Mulligan."

"Yes, Mom."

Mom. Another lie, of sorts, but Tillie just nodded.

Some guilt she'd determined to live with.

An hour later, she walked down the sidewalk of Copper Mountain, Moose's hometown, heading toward the hardware shop.

"Your family owns this?" She spotted the words *Ace's Hardware* drawn on the window.

"For eighty years. My grandfather before him." A tiny bell jingled as they came inside the old wooden building. She felt like she'd stepped back in time with shelving along the perimeter and, like a card catalogue in a vintage library, rows of wooden shelving that contained small drawers, all labeled. The place smelled of history and wisdom. A couple of faded pictures in frames hung near the wooden counter, one with a man standing in front of a 1960s Ford truck, another with three generations, four people—two men, two teenage boys—crouching in front of a moose, clearly hunted.

"That's my grandpop, Arlo," Moose said.

"His namesake," said Ace, who stood at the counter. An older version of Moose, he bore Moose's girth and height, and dark brown hair. He wore a pair of Carhartt overalls, his name on the upper chest.

"Namesake?" Tillie asked.

"Got that part, Dad?"

Ace pointed to a box on the counter and grinned.

Moose looked at it. "This is all we need to fix the tripping system?"

"Four springs. Had them special ordered." Ace stuck his hands in his pockets, sat on a high stool, smiled at Tillie. "So, you're the waitress."

"Dad—"

"Axel told me about you." He winked.

Moose closed his eyes, shook his head.

"Moose needs a friend who isn't in the rescue business. You're welcome as long as you'd like to stay."

And another ball filled her throat.

Moose picked up the box and headed outside. "Sorry. That's what happens when you're single too long."

She glanced at him. "You've been single too long?"

He put the box into the bed of his truck, then grabbed a mesh bag. "I've always been single. By choice. We need to stop at Gigi's."

He walked down the sidewalk toward a cabin-turned-store just down the street from the pizza place. The scent of roasted tomato sauce lifted into the air as they passed.

Her stomach growled.

"Really?"

"It's just a reflex. I love pizza."

"Noted." He turned into the store. The grocery store had once been a cabin with many small rooms, all of them like mini departments now. Moose headed toward the fresh produce and picked through a bin of potatoes.

"Mom's making a roast tonight." He put the potatoes into a bag, grabbed a bunch of carrots, a bag of onions.

She went quiet behind him, all the way until he paid and walked out onto the street.

"You okay?"

"I just . . . you make it all feel so normal."

"What?"

"This. Me landing on your doorstep. Your mom, making breakfast, a roast for dinner. Who are you?"

He glanced over at her. "I don't know what you mean."

"I guess I mean . . . thank you."

His eyebrow went up, but he smiled and turned to her. "For a year, Tillie, you've been serving me chicken, making me shakes, and listening to my post-rescue rants. Thank *you*."

Okay, sure. Yes. Of course all of this was just about friendship, and maybe that was for the best.

Definitely for the best.

Besides, *"I've always been single. By choice."*

Interesting. Especially in light of his late-night chicken commitment.

Except, perhaps she had been single too long too, and read into this more than it was.

He dropped the food into the bed of his truck. "Listen, it's too early for pizza, but how about a cup of cocoa at the coffee shop? They make an amazing spiced nutmeg hot cocoa."

"It's the last week of August."

"In Alaska."

"Good point."

The street wasn't busy, but she still thought it sweet when he held out an arm, as if to protect her as they crossed the street in front of Denali Sports. They passed the Forest Service office, then Bowie Mountain Gear. He held the door open for her at the Last Frontier Bakery.

Inside, a few people sat in worn leather chairs, their coffees sitting on side tables made from rough-hewn pine. That same pine covered the lofted ceiling and walls, and the place smelled richly of the north woods and coffee.

"Hey, Moose," said a woman over the sound of milk frothing.

Tillie followed the greeting and spotted a young woman who appeared in her late teens. She wore her dark curly hair in front cornrows, tufted and free in the back, and a black apron with the store emblem on the front.

"Hey, Cally. How about a snowflake cocoa?"

"Milk, white, or dark chocolate?"

"Dark, and—" He looked at Tillie.

"White."

"On it." Cally disappeared behind the array of machines at the counter.

A man in the corner called a greeting, and Moose walked over and shook hands.

The local sheriff, by the looks of it. Good-looking, early thirties, brown hair, a gaze that flicked over to her.

"Deke. How are you?"

"You know. The usual. Broke up a party over at the Copper Mountain campground last night. Caught a speeder out on the highway. And there've been reports of a moose in the area, wandered into a few yards."

"It's not breeding season yet."

"No, but it's gone from hot to chilly quickly. Could be messing with their rutting season."

"I'll keep an eye out."

"Cocoa's up," said Cally.

Tillie had listened to it all from across the room as she read posters of past and upcoming events. Like the big summer breakup and the fall bluegrass festival, held over Labor Day. Pinned to the board were advertisements for houses for rent, pizza delivery from Northstar Pizza, an event at the library that involved an out-of-town author, and a call for participants for classes at a nearby art center.

Moose walked up to her holding the cups of cocoa.

She took hers. "This is a cute town."

He lifted a shoulder. "Sometimes."

"Please." She took a sip of cocoa as they pushed through the door into the sunshine. "Oh, wow. This is—"

"Told you."

Yeah. The sun hung high overhead, peeling away the slight chill that scurried in around the fir trees that hugged the buildings. The entire town seemed about three blocks large, with one main street and a few off-streets. Quaint.

The kind of town she wouldn't mind raising Hazel in.

"This looks like a great little town to be from."

"It is. But it's also suffocating. Everyone knows everyone. And everything."

Right. They'd started walking down the street, toward the river that flowed at the edge of town.

"So, not a great place to hide, then," she said.

He glanced at her. "Oh, um . . ."

"I'm kidding. I noticed you didn't introduce me."

"Did you want—"

"Nope."

He nodded. And didn't ask.

And suddenly, the fact that he didn't ask, didn't want to know—

And that just felt unfair. To him. And honestly, a big part of her wanted to let him in.

He deserved the truth, at the very least.

"Okay, ask me what you want."

A few tourists roamed the streets, and Bowie Mountain Gear had put out a sale rack of clothing. A wolf-looking dog stood with a woman with brown hair, dressed in a lightweight puffer, jeans, and boots. She perused the rack of clothing, but at her dog's alert, she looked up.

"Moose!"

Beside Tillie, Moose slowed. "Stormi?"

The dog whined and Moose knelt. Stormi let his leash go, and the animal came over to Moose, hunkered down, whining. Moose rubbed his ears, and the dog rolled over, exposed his belly.

"Apparently, you two bonded during our epic rescue," Stormi said, coming over to him. "Rome, c'mon, buddy, don't make a fool out of yourself."

Moose laughed, rubbed Rome's chest. "What are you doing up here?"

"Rome and I trained at a school in Montana, and the instructor was from Copper Mountain—Jericho Bowie?"

Moose stood up, and Rome flipped to his feet, nudging his hand for more. "Yeah, Jericho and I are old friends. He was here earlier this summer with his dog Orlando."

"Great tracking dog." She motioned to Rome to sit, and the dog obeyed. "We're going to do some mild training. Ridge is planning to hide in the woods, let Rome find him. He's over at the Northstar grabbing a pizza for his arduous wait."

"And your sister?"

"She's out on a charter flight over Denali."

"Sky King tours?"

"Yeah. I suppose you know everyone around here."

Moose glanced at Tillie, back at Stormi. "Yep."

Rome barked as a man came out of Northstar Pizza. Moose lifted his hand, and the man waved back. He held a pizza box and headed toward a Bronco.

"Where are you guys staying?"

"A little bed and breakfast in the area."

"The Samsons'?"

"Good guess."

"There aren't that many, and Beau and Nan Samsons' place is popular. They're only here during the summer, but they're always booked."

"She makes an amazing fry bread with homemade blueberry jam."

"You should try her suaasat soup. It's made with seal meat."

Stormi wrinkled her nose. "I'll stick to pizza."

He laughed. "Good to see you." He gave her a hug as Rome sat and wagged his tail.

They continued down the street, and Tillie hated the tiny twinge inside at the way Stormi had looked at him with so much warmth in her gaze.

Of course she had. Because that's what Moose did—he rescued people.

Which meant that really, Tillie wasn't anyone special, was she? Aw, that wasn't fair.

Her insecurities should probably just pipe down. Moose was here. With her. And that meant *something*.

They came to a park at the end of the street, where she saw an amphitheater and a boardwalk running along the edge of the river all the way to a lookout three blocks to the south.

Moose turned to her. "Tell me about how you managed to take down Rigger at the house. You have skills . . ."

That's right. She'd offered. But that question she hadn't expected. He could have asked about Rigger. Or the money. Even the question she was dreading about Rigger being Hazel's father, although there wasn't much to explain there.

But this . . . this was easy. "I mentioned being a marine, right?"

"They don't teach that kind of hand-to-hand combat in the Marines. That's an MMA move. Picked that up from Rigger."

Right.

They'd reached the edge of the block, ventured out onto the boardwalk. Ten feet below, the river frothed over rocks near the shore. A mist rose in the air, fine and cool.

"I was training to be an MMA fighter when I got out."

He stilled, turned to her. "What?"

She shrugged. "Let me back up to the fact that I didn't really have any real skills. I enlisted when I was seventeen, joined full-time when I was eighteen, and did four years, and by that time, I was back Stateside, and they offered me another two years, so I re-enlisted and Pearl came to live with me."

And shoot, now she had to start lying. But she'd tell most of it.

"Rigger kept coming around, and he'd changed a little, at least back then. He thought I had the skills to be an MMA fighter, so he started training me at a local gym when I was off-duty. I learned the sweep from him."

Moose nodded, took another sip. Then, "Seriously, that's the very last thing I expected to hear."

"I know. I wasn't me back then, not really." Or rather, a part of herself that she didn't want to remember.

"Did you ever fight?" His eyes held what looked like horror.

She shook her head. "I went into the ring once, but . . . no."

He nodded again.

"But I did become an Iron Maiden."

She liked the surprise that flitted over his face. "Really? That's what—the all-female version of American Ninja Warrior, right?" And right then, his gaze moved over her body.

"I might have been in better shape back then."

"You're in fine shape now."

A beat. And her face might have been heating, and his eyes sort of widened—"I mean—"

She laughed. "Being a waitress is it's own form of workout."

"It is," he said, smiling.

"Anyway, yes. The difference between an Iron Maiden and ANW is there is no distinction between men and women in ANW. So the organizations wanted to make a female competition. I started in ANW and won the Miami City competition two years in a row. Went to nationals in Vegas both years. Made it to stage two the second year—fell on the crisscross salmon ladder. Then I went to the Iron Maiden championship and . . ."

He waited.

She smiled.

"You *won*?"

She shrugged. "Not bad for a waitress."

"*Whatever*. You won." There was a hint of pride in his voice. It swept through her, found her bones.

"Yeah. Nearly fell on the Power Tower though. I was never much of a heights person. Just don't look down, right?"

"Right. So . . ." His smile dimmed. "Is that the money Rigger wants?"

He'd put that together pretty easily. "Yes. There was a pretty nice cash prize of a hundred grand. He thought he was entitled to the money since he'd sort of trained me."

"Sounds like you spent a lot of time taking care of your sister."

"I was all she had." She finished her cocoa. "I shouldn't have abandoned her."

"How did you abandon her?"

"I left her for the military, just like my dad did. And . . ." She lifted a shoulder. "Anyway, we were happy for a while in Anchorage. And now I'm all Hazel has."

The wind whipped up around them as they reached the end of

the boardwalk. She turned and stared out at the river. Blue and sparkling under the sunlight, beautiful and lethal at the same time.

"You're not alone anymore, Tillie."

His voice nudged under her skin, found soil. But even with the tenderness, she fought not to flinch.

No. She sighed, turning to correct him, but he'd turned to the rail.

"You know, the worst day of my life happened here. Or one of them."

She looked up at him, but his gaze seemed far away.

"My brother, Axel, was about ten years old. We were in town, goofing around. It was hot—summertime—and a bunch of people were hanging out by the shore throwing rocks, a few wading. I was hanging out with my friends—Hudson Bowie, and Deke Starr, who you met—and we were, I don't know . . . throwing a football around, I think. Anyway, I heard shouts and saw my stupid brother jumping into this river."

"He jumped into this? It's so dangerous."

"A little kid had gone in and got swept up by the river, and he went in after him. By the time I got over there, Axel had grabbed the kid but had hit the rocks and broken his arm. Took three guys to get them out of the river, and by then, both of them were nearly drowned."

"That's terrifying."

"Yeah." He went silent for a moment. "I was supposed to be watching my brother."

And that, right there, explained everything. Why Moose ran the rescue team, why he hovered, why he never gave up on someone if they needed him.

"The thing is, I do realize that Axel has his own mind. He does what he wants, and I'm finally starting to get that. But it doesn't make it any easier to watch. I can't help but want to step in when someone I care about is in over their head."

He looked away from her, upriver, and a muscle clenched in his jaw.

Oh, Moose. He deserved better than lies. She put her hand on his arm. "Moose, I need to tell you something—"

His cell phone buzzed in his pocket, and he pulled it out. "It's my mom." Swiping it open, he put it to his ear.

Tillie could hear his mother's panicked voice over the line— "Moose, you have to come home. Hazel's missing."

FIVE

AS IF EVEN THE WEATHER JUDGED HIM FOR his empty assurance to Tillie that Hazel would be safe at his parents' home, of course Hazel had to go missing under a looming Alaskan storm.

Overhead, the clouds that had parked over the Alaska Range for most of the morning had trucked east on a chilly wind and now took up position over the Mulligan homestead. The wipers on his truck barely kept up with the deluge, the wind casting leaves onto the dirt road.

Beside him, Tillie gripped the door handle as if she might leap from the truck. She'd gone painfully, heart-wrenchingly quiet at the phone call, looking at him with wide eyes when he told his mother they'd be right home.

ASAP.

Which meant that most of the groceries were probably destroyed in the back of the truck, given the way he'd peeled out of town.

The last thing he cared about right now was his mother's roast.

His pickup spat mud as he turned onto the dirt road to the

house. He glanced at Tillie, her whitened hand, her even whiter countenance. "We'll find her."

She gave him a tight-lipped nod, and it just about speared him through. Why, again, had he thought it a good idea to leave a seven-year-old alone with his mom while a stalker was on the loose? He wanted to slam his hand on the steering wheel, but that might only jar Tillie.

Tuck it in, bro. Keep it together. Words he'd said to Axel plenty of times.

He blew out a breath and managed not to skid as he stopped in front of the house. The rain pelleted down, soaking him through as he got out and headed through the sopping yard.

His mother stood on the deck, dressed in a raincoat, holding two flashlights and a whistle.

He took a flashlight and the whistle. "What happened?"

Poor woman looked stricken. "We made cookies. I knew it was about to storm, so when she asked to take Kip out, I told her to let him do his business and come right back. I took a load of laundry out, then the cookies from the oven, and ten minutes passed before I realized she hadn't returned. I went outside and called for her. Nothing." Her eyes reddened. "I'm sorry, Tillie. I think Kip ran off—and she went after him."

Tillie had taken the other flashlight. Water plastered her hair to her face.

"She loves dogs."

Right. Not what either of them was thinking, but maybe she didn't want to panic his mother. He seemed to be managing that for the both of them. His hand settled on his mom's shoulder. "You stay here in case she comes back."

Tillie had already scrambled down the stairs into the yard, calling for Hazel.

"I'm so sorry, Moose—"

"Mom. I'm sure she's close. Could be hiding under a tree until the storm passes."

His mother swallowed, nodded, but when she cast her gaze to the river and back, he felt it too.

His chest tight, he went down the stairs and into the massive yard. Most of it had been cleared, scrub grass and a few weeds making up the greenery, the space edged on both sides by thick forest. Deer paths ran into the woods in both directions, and Tillie headed down one, her light on, no care for the storm.

He headed to the river.

The storm turned the water a deep bullet gray, frothy and violent as it rushed over boulders, rocks, and debris, a churning, roiling mess. The storm pounded against it, raking up a haze, the waves pummeling the shoreline.

Hazel, where are you?

As he stood, a branch cracked upriver, probably torn by the pull of the water, and tumbled into the turbulent water. It bobbed, hitting rocks, its leaves shredding off in the boil, turning it bare. It hung up on a cluster of boulders just beyond the shoreline, the river rising over it, forcing it down. And for a second, it disappeared under the water.

He was turning away when he spotted it bouncing back to the surface farther downstream in the frothy wash, then vanishing as it rode the clutter of waves. *Resilient.*

"I took the deer path all the way to the neighbors' house." Tillie, breathing hard, her voice shaking. "I didn't see her."

He glanced past her, downriver to the Shulls' house. With their eleven children, it seemed possible that Hazel could have found a friend there.

Or . . .

He glanced upriver. "Let's go." He held out his hand.

Tillie took it and gripped it hard before she let go and followed him into the woods. He took off at a jog through the hazy forest. "Hazel!"

The deer path wasn't wide, and he held out his arm, pushing away tree limbs and brush. The river roared to his left, the rain a barrage of pellets on the leaves. "Hazel!"

"Where is the next homestead?" Tillie asked, breathing hard behind him.

"Ten miles north we'll hit the Starr family lodge. But nothing between here and there except . . ." *Oops.*

Silence.

"Except?"

He slowed, his strides long. "Except a gorge where a tributary cuts down from the mountain into the river."

"Certainly she wouldn't try to cross that."

Certainly. But he heard the tremor in her voice.

Thunder rolled above, and he hunched his shoulders, the rain spurring a chill through him. They walked on spongy loam, the forest so thick he could barely see the river now. But a little girl chasing a puppy could have easily run under the canopy of branches.

And then there were the other dangers, things he didn't want to say out loud.

Like the moose Deke had seen. Or bears. Or wolves.

He probably shouldn't think about them either. "Hazel!" He shone his light into the woods. Tille, too, called out, her light bright.

And then they reached the gorge. Twenty feet down, it dropped into the tributary, which was nothing more than a stream at the height of summer, but the rain had filled it, turned it into a fast-rushing creek.

She searched it, breathing hard.

"I should have brought my walkie. Maybe she came home."

Tillie looked at him, her eyes wide, stricken.

"We'll find her," he said, turning to her, and then he couldn't stop from pulling her to himself.

She wrapped her arms around him, and her entire body trembled. If he wasn't careful, they'd both get too cold, and this search party would become an advanced rescue op.

"I have an idea." He held her away from him. "C'mon. We need to get back to the house."

"I'm not going back without Hazel!" She backed away from him and nearly stepped off the cliff. He grabbed her arm, yanked her back.

She righted herself, her eyes fierce.

"You need a change of clothes, decent footwear, a terrain map, and a walkie. Even some overnight gear."

"Overnight gear?"

He met her eyes. "We will find her, Tillie. But the fact that she's not on either trail says we need to regroup, think through our strategy. Time is fading, and we only have eight hours of daylight left, so we need to use it well. Do you trust me?"

He realized he was repeating the words he'd said to her before, in the yard, and grimaced.

But she nodded, quickly, as if committing before she could change her mind.

"Okay, one more shout, then we're heading back to the house."

He stood there for a long moment as she called Hazel's name, the sound dissipating in the rain.

Then he took her hand. "I'm going to run. Shout if you're falling too far behind."

She nodded, a grit to her jaw, and he suddenly saw the strength and determination that had made her an Iron Maiden.

Then he took off down the path. It was slippery, but he wore boots, so his feet found purchase, although the branches slowed him down. One of them hit him across the face, and his mouth burned, tasted tinny.

Behind him, Tillie's breath came hard.

But she kept up.

They arrived at the yard, and he spotted his mother on the deck, still in her gear, and the fact that Hazel hadn't returned felt like a punch to the sternum. But he didn't slow and thundered his way up the stairs.

"Nothing?"

He shook his head, and his mother covered her mouth with her hands.

Tillie came up behind her.

"Mom, get Tillie some rain gear and boots."

His mother nodded, and his command seemed to embolden her. She headed toward the house, Tillie behind her.

He followed, then pulled off his boots in the entryway and headed up the stairs. On the way, he pulled out his phone and checked the cell service. Finally back in range.

Then he reached for Ridge White's card on his dresser and dialed, setting it on speaker. He was digging out dry clothes when the man answered.

"Ridge. It's Moose."

"Moose! Hey, man, how—"

"Is Stormi around?"

A beat. "Yeah, right here."

Stormi came on the line, clearly on speaker. "What's going on?"

"I have a missing girl. You think Rome can help find her?"

Another beat. "Absolutely. Where?"

"I'll have my dad pick you up. Be ready in five."

He pulled on a dry thermal shirt and Gore-Tex pants as he called his father.

"I'm already closing the shop," his dad said. "I'll swing by the Samsons."

"Perfect. And hurry."

By the time he was downstairs, Tillie had changed, her hair back in a ponytail and under a wool cap. She sat on a chair, pulling on Gore-Tex pants. His mother had piled a bright yellow jacket on the table and a pair of wool socks and gloves.

Now she closed the closet near the door and set a bag on the table—flares, a space blanket, a couple power bars, matches, and a candle.

"It's our winter bag," she said.

Moose grabbed it and shoved it into a backpack near the door. Then he went to the walkie set charging on a stand. "Mom always made us take these when we went out to play." He turned one on, then another, and checked them. Gave one to Tillie, and put the other on a hook in his jacket pocket.

"Mom, you have the third, and when dad gets here, you give Stormi the last one."

"Stormi?" his mom said.

"The woman with the dog?" Tillie asked.

"Yes," Moose said. "She's on her way with Dad. Rome is a tracking dog. Do you have anything of Hazel's—"

"Of course." Tillie had pulled on the pants and wool socks and now headed down the stairs. She returned with an old, ratty stuffed dog.

"Perfect," his mother said and pulled it to herself. Closed her eyes.

Praying, probably.

Tillie took a breath and sat, pulling on the boots near her chair. His mother's hiking boots.

She then grabbed the jacket and the walkie. "Shouldn't we bring a jacket for Hazel?"

"I'll wrap her in the blanket and carry her," Moose said, reaching for the door. "Mom, I'm going to check in every fifteen minutes. You don't hear from me, you call Axel."

She gave him a look of chagrin. "I already did that."

Well, okay then.

He looked at Tillie. "Let's find Hazel." Then he headed out the door.

"Great view, huh?" Oaken came up behind him, and Shep turned and took the proffered cup of coffee.

Shep stood at the massive two-story A-frame window of Oaken's new chalet-style home, staring out at the jewel-colored mountains around him. In the distance, the ski resort with its wide, green slopes, a few peaks at the top chilled with a fresh layer of snow, almost called his name. Ski lifts hung as if frozen, waiting for the first layer of crisp white snow.

How he loved autumn, the sense of anticipation stirring inside him as he waited for the first snowfall. He could already hear the swish of his skis slicing through the snow echoing inside him.

"Thanks for being willing to keep an eye on the place." Oaken grabbed his own mug of coffee.

"Sacrifices. It's a tough gig, but someone needs to do it." Shep held out his mug to Oaken for a toast. "You do know that I'll have to use the sauna and hot tub."

"Knock yourself out." Oaken wore a pair of faded jeans, a flannel shirt, and wool socks. A real Alaskan, apparently, despite his only-recent move north. "I'm glad you told me about this place."

"Drove by it every day last winter. Seemed perfect for you, and I knew the view would be worth every penny. I'm glad it was still on the market." He turned back to the window. Glanced at the dark clouds over Denali in the distance, then tried to see if he could spot his place down the road, along the highway. A modern, boxy townhome that sat with other boxes on the side of a mountain. He'd gotten it in foreclosure, gutted it, and remodeled it into something he liked coming home to.

Most of the time.

"Better than living out of a motorhome."

Oaken looked at him.

"My parents were ski bums in the winter, park guides and climbers in the summer. Well, sort of. My dad was a street preacher too. But we lived an unrooted life, traveling where God led them. It was just me and my older sister. Homeschooled, although I'd call it more like unschooled. We learned a lot about life, though."

Oaken took a sip of coffee. "Sounds cool. Where are your parents now?"

"The last text I got, they were headed to Snowbasin, in Ogden, Utah."

"How long have you been with the team? I never asked." Oaken set his cup down on a nearby glass table. A local interior-design place had furnished the digs. The place had a mix of modern and woodsy, with glass-and-black iron-side tables, deep brown leather sofas, a mix of furry bearskins on the wooden floor, and an oversized coffee table made from the trunk of a redwood, and it all sat in front of a soaring whitewashed stone fireplace.

A couple of contemporary Alaskan animal prints—moose and bear—hung on either side of the fireplace. Oaken picked up the remote control and aimed it at the hearth, causing it to flash into perfectly contained flames.

"Two years. Spent a year on a rescue team in Montana before moving here. Had a cousin who recommended Moose's team to me. We have relatives that live in Montana."

Oaken walked over to the kitchen, where a massive leathered black granite island held enough chairs for the first line of a hockey team, and opened the two-door Sub-Zero. "I have some fresh blueberry pie from the Skyport Diner." He pulled out a box. "Boo and I ate there last night. Want a piece?"

Shep had eaten alone last night at the Tooth after working out, also alone, and trying not to let himself believe that London might be avoiding him.

That was after, of course, getting Axel's text that Moose was out of the clink and back at home. Shep had given London a ride to the Tooth to pick up her car, then watched her drive away.

No pie for them.

Sheesh, why had he kissed her?

"Yeah, sure," he said to Oaken's offer and came over to the island. Oaken pulled out a couple plates from his walnut cupboards and set them on the counter.

"Have you heard from Moose?" Oaken asked. "I haven't heard anything since Axel texted and said he was going to Copper Mountain."

"He called, but I was working out. I tried calling him back, but you know how sketchy it is up there—and with the rain—"

"He has a landline at his house."

"A landline—what's that?"

Oaken laughed as he opened the box. "I have a pretty full tour schedule this fall, but I'll be back in January. I can't wait to get back up here and do some skiing too."

"Dude. The beginning of winter is not the greatest time to come to Alaska."

"I'm not here to sightsee," Oaken said, and winked.

"You two getting serious?" Shep settled onto a stool.

"I've always been serious. But yeah, when you find the one, you know, right? I'm just trying to figure out . . . well, she's not quite ready to tour with me, so I need to figure out how it's going to work."

"You just gotta dive in and make it work. And figure it out as you go." He didn't have a clue where that'd come from. He took the pie Oaken shoved at him.

"Dive in, huh?" Oaken said.

Right then, his crazy kiss with London decided to flash in front of his eyes. "Um . . . okay, don't listen to me. What do I know? I've been single so long I've forgotten what love feels like."

"I doubt that. Besides, you're beginning to sound like a country song."

Shep was all sorts of lying today, because ... "Okay, but you don't see me buying a house to live near the woman I love, so you're way beyond my life experience."

"Please." Oaken dished up his own pie.

"What? Oh, this is good." Shep washed down his blueberry pie with coffee.

"I know. And you know what I mean—"

Shep raised an eyebrow.

"For the love—do you seriously think we're all blind to you and London?"

Shep set his fork down. "There is nothing going on between me and London."

Oaken brought his pie around, sat down on a stool.

"Fine. Maybe ... once upon a time there was ... we ..."

Oaken cocked his head.

"It was sort of a brief, traumatic meeting. We were caught in an avalanche together for three days."

Now Oaken put down his fork. "What?"

"It was in the Alps, in Switzerland—long story. The ice nearly won—we were close to dying of hypothermia before they found us. But, yeah, she made ... an impression."

"And now she's here, working with you." Oaken took his own sip of coffee. Then, "I'm listening."

Shep shook his head. "Nothing to tell. We were rescued and she went her way, I went mine, and ..."

"And then she ended up in Alaska with you? C'mon, Shep—"

Yeah, okay, even he wasn't buying his flimsy story. "Okay, we sort of kept in touch. Texting now and again. I heard she was ... between jobs. So I suggested she come here. She did. No biggie."

Oaken had taken another bite and now nodded. "Mm-hmm."

"Really. We're colleagues, nothing more."

Shep could choke on his own lies, but perhaps they were just lies from his viewpoint. Maybe that really was all London wanted.

A guy should probably pay attention to that, start feeding himself some honesty.

Silence, and finally Shep looked up to see Oaken studying him. "What?"

"You okay?"

"Yep." *Nope*. He sighed. Because suddenly her words to him returned. *"I don't think I'm ready."* "Actually, London lost someone she loved in the avalanche. So I'm not sure she has any room in her heart for anyone else."

Oaken said nothing, just nodded. "I get that. But the truth is, you think you don't have room, and then, suddenly, the right person comes along, and you'll do anything to make room for that person."

Maybe he wasn't the right person. But Shep didn't say that. Still, it was time to put space between them.

He finished off his pie, then washed off his plate and put it in the dishwasher.

"Thanks," Oaken said. "I'm taking off for a quick trip to Montana to meet with my producer, but I'll be back in a couple days. You have the code for the door?"

"I do. Thanks."

Oaken got up just as Shep's phone buzzed on the counter.

Shep picked it up.

Of course—London.

LONDON
_____

I figured out the five-letter code.

Meet me at the hospital.

He pocketed the phone. "I'm heading to meet London. I'll see you when you get back."

"Just friends, huh?" Oaken grinned, pointed at him.

Shep lifted a hand and headed for the door. *Yes. Just friends.*

Under an hour later, he pulled into the parking lot of Alaska Regional Hospital. The clouds had darkened over the far mountains, and a slight wind bullied him as he got out. Winter, pushing into the autumn already.

He found London in the lobby. She wore a pair of leggings, runners, and a pullover. "Hey," she said.

"Hey," he said. "What did you find?"

"I did some searching, and I think this is a badge number." She held out her phone. "I finally tracked it down—it's a number to a retired Miami police detective named Rosalind Turner."

"Tillie's friend."

"Yeah. I got ahold of Axel, and he thought Roz was still in ICU, but when I got here and asked, she'd been moved. I got us passes." She handed him a sticker with his name.

"Wow. No covert op?"

She frowned. And again he had to check himself. One of these days the gig would be up.

"What's with you and covert ops?"

"I don't know, this all seems so . . . like an episode of *Chuck*."

She frowned. Then, "I remember that show. That's a flashback. So, who am I? Sarah Walker?"

"Maybe."

She laughed. "Okay. Great show. Hated the ending. Let's go, Chuck." She hit the elevator button. "Or would you prefer Casey, her ex-partner?"

The doors opened.

"No. I'm the other guy—"

She walked in, cocked her head at him. "John Casey?"

"No. What floor?"

"Three. And—wait. Do you think . . . you're Captain Awesome?"

He grinned.

She shook her head as the doors opened. But just like that, the weirdness had vanished.

Except for the fact that he had a suspicion that she *was* Sarah Walker, or had been . . .

She walked out and down the hallway, flashing her badge at the nurse guarding the station.

Shep followed and they stopped at a room where she knocked, then pushed the door open. "Rosalind Turner?"

A woman lay on the bed, short white bedhead hair, an IV in her arm, pale and half asleep. She roused at London's voice, her eyes widening.

"We're friends of Tillie's," London said. "She calls you Roz?"

The woman's features relaxed and she nodded. Reached for the remote and moved her bed to a sitting position.

"I'm Shep. We both work with Moose on the Air One Rescue team."

"How—" She swallowed and reached for a cup, but London had already grabbed it, pointing the straw toward her. Roz took a sip, and the blankets dropped to her waist.

She winced. Only then did Shep see the massive dressing around her abdomen.

London placed Roz's cup back on the tray. "Can we get you anything?"

"Is she okay?" Roz managed.

"Yes," Shep said. "Tillie and Hazel are with Moose. And they're safe."

She shuddered. Then she closed her eyes and pressed her hands against her face. Her shoulders shook.

"It's okay, ma'am," London said, pulling up a chair to sit by the bed. "They're going to be fine."

Roz shook her head.

London grabbed a tissue and held it out to her. Roz took it, wiped her eyes. "And Rigger?"

"He's gone," said London. "Our friend Flynn is looking for him."

Shep hadn't heard that.

"Tillie needs to leave town. And keep running."

Roz's words hung in the silence of the room. Finally, London asked, "Why?"

Roz shook her head.

London pursed her lips, then dug out the piece of paper. Opened it. "We found this in the suitcase."

Roz's eyes widened. "You found the suitcase."

"We did. What does this mean, Roz? I know it's your badge number."

Roz's jaw tightened, and for a second, she looked exactly like the toughened cop she might have been. "I can only talk to Tillie."

London sighed and folded up the paper. "We're just trying to help."

Roz shook her head. "I don't think anyone can help." She reached for the remote and started to lower her bed down, her expression set.

London got up. "We'll figure this out, I promise." Then she gave Roz a smile.

Shep knew that look. The look that said she'd keep her word.

The same one he'd worn when Colt had come to him a year ago with a request.

The same one he glimpsed in the bathroom mirror as they walked out of the room.

Truth was, he'd made promises too. In short, where London went, he went.

And Captain Awesome wasn't going to let anyone down. "C'mon," he said as he pulled out his phone.

"Where are we going?" London asked.

"We're going to your place to get your stuff." He walked down the hall and pressed the elevator button.

"Why?"

"Because we're taking a road trip to Copper Mountain."

So many promises broken, Tillie didn't know where to start apologizing to Pearl.

I'm sorry, sis. I'm so sorry—

The words kept searing through her as Tillie followed Moose into the tangled nightmare that was the Alaskan boreal forest. They'd taken the deer path again, shining their lights through the mess of branches as they walked, scanning for any sign that Hazel had left the path.

A quarter mile from the house, just before they reached the gorge, Moose found a swath of broken branches, trampled grass, and another deer path veering off along the rim of the cliff.

Tillie wanted to weep with relief. Until—

"Look," Moose said as they came out to the edge. "Is that Kip's tug?"

She looked, and she simply wanted to break free and wail at the sight of the purple tug Hazel had used to play with Kip. It hung from a tree branch caught in the bramble along the edge of the gorge, trees and brush growing from the rugged sides.

They stood high on the cliffside, fifty feet above the turbulent, rising creek, and now she moved to the edge, her knees nearly buckling, save for Moose's hand on her arm.

"It doesn't mean she's in the water, Til. Just breathe."

But breathing felt like the last thing she should be doing. Oh, she'd made such a mess of all this.

No, God had made a mess of it all. He'd chosen the wrong mother to raise Hazel.

"C'mon. Let's keep following the deer path."

But she couldn't move from the edge of the cliff, shining her light into the flood, bracing herself to find Hazel's body flowing downriver or caught on a boulder or a downed tree or—

"Tillie. She's not in the river."

She rounded on him. "How do you know that, Moose? What, do you have X-ray vision that can see to the bottom? Or psychic powers? How do you know she hasn't slipped off the cliff and—"

"I don't." His gaze came down hard on hers. "You're right. But I do have hope. And right now, in the middle of the storm, that's all I've got, so I'm going to hold—"

A dog barking in the distance made him jerk. Her too.

"Do you hear that?"

"Yes. Let me call it in. See if Stormi is anywhere near us." He lifted the radio. "Stormi? Come in, this is Moose."

Crackling. Then, "Moose. Sorry I haven't checked in. Rome is working the scent in the yard. It's pretty messy—"

"It's not Rome," Tillie said and took off toward the barking.

"Tillie!"

She kept moving, listening, her heart thundering, shaking away Moose's words.

She didn't believe in hope. She believed in action. In not letting life career out of your control, and if it did, then you probably deserved it.

She probably deserved it.

Hazel, however, did not. She called out Hazel's name, the sound eaten by the rain and the roar of the creek below.

The deer trail moved away from the river, and she followed it, the voice of the dog obscured by the tangled woods.

Why had she agreed to come to Moose's house? She should have just taken his truck and . . . and . . .

Aw, it didn't matter how many crimes she committed, as long as Hazel was safe.

"Hazel!" Moose's voice thundered, his footsteps hammering up behind Tillie. She glanced at him. "I told Stormi where we were, but I'm not sure if we're on the right track, so I told her to let Rome work."

Whatever.

More barking. She froze. Turned. Put a hand out to Moose to stop him.

He stood, breathing hard, the rain pinging around them, dripping off the rim of his raincoat hood.

Another bark.

"It's back toward the river," Moose said, pointing through the forest. And then he left the trail and plowed through the bramble, breaking a trail like, well, a moose. Except a moose actually might be more graceful. He left a swath of destruction, pushing away branches, trampling downed logs, crunching brush beneath his massive boots.

Tillie followed the path, nearly pushing him.

He picked up his pace as daylight opened ahead of them, the world a mist of gray, dour shadow. But the barking grew louder. The rushing creek sounded closer too.

And then the sound of crying rippled up into the storm.

Tillie pushed past Moose, running. "Hazel!"

Just like that, the forest stopped. She tried to pull up, but the land had slid down, and with one slippery step, she stepped into midair.

Went over the edge.

Mudslide. The entire cliff had given way, fallen toward the river, a slope of trees and debris that ended in a yawn at the bottom.

She fought the descent, clawing at anything to slow herself, but the rain was a river that caught her up, shot her down the mountainside. She rolled over and snagged herself on a jutting log just before her momentum would have plummeted her over.

She hung, half in, half out of the mouth of a drop.

And when she looked down, there, some twenty feet into the well of the cave, on a ledge, sat Hazel, her knees drawn up, Kip struggling out of her arms to get to the intruder, barking wildly.

Mist rose from the depths below, and a rumble suggested the creek, angry and rising, flowing at the base.

"Hazel!"

"Mom!"

Just as she might have slung her leg up and found purchase, something hit her hold hard and dislodged her.

She dropped like a rock into the cavern, through the mist.

Water closed over her as she splashed down, a thousand icicles spearing her body. She clamped her mouth shut to stifle a scream, then kicked hard.

She didn't surface—instead, her head banged on a rock, so hard it nearly knocked the breath from her. She put her hands up, fighting, the current yanking her—

A tunnel. Or a channel. Under the walls of the cavern, tumbling her out into the river, away from Hazel.

No! She kicked, fought, twisted, her hands fighting for a hold on the rock, but the current turned hungry, wedging her into a gnarled, rocky egress—

Then a grip closed around her wrist and yanked.

It forced her against the current, and when another hand grabbed her jacket and pulled, she broke the surface.

She heaved in hot, razor breaths.

"Breathe, Tillie. You're okay."

Air. It smelled of dirt and moss and decay.

Moose had pulled her against him and now put his arm around her waist, kicking to tread water, his other hand gripping the cave wall. Blood trickled from a wound on his temple. Her own head throbbed.

She finally caught her breath. "You nearly killed me!"

His eyes widened.

115

"You came down on me—"

"You pushed me!"

Her mouth opened. But he was right.

"It's okay," he said, his tone clipped back, calmer. "We're okay—"

"Mom!"

She looked up, and Hazel peered over from the cliff, ten feet above.

"Hazel. Are you okay?"

She nodded, her lips tight, the expression of someone trying not to cry. *Good girl.*

"I'll get up to you, I promise."

Although, how?

Moose seemed to already be asking that question. Tillie had dropped her flashlight in the fall, and apparently, so had he, but enough daylight remained for her to make out their predicament.

"It's a sink hole. The mudslide only made it bigger. I'll bet that tunnel under the rock leads out to the main creek." He hadn't let her go, and heaven help her, she didn't move away from him.

He was solid and strong and everything she needed to cling to as the dark water swirled around them. "It's not big enough to get through. It got tighter the more the current pulled me down."

"I think I can boost you up onto the ledge. Then you can climb the rest of the way."

"I got this." She pushed off from him, swimming hard to the ledge wall. Hazel leaned over from above. She appeared soggy, but not injured, but Tillie wouldn't know until she scaled the ledge.

Moose came up behind her. "I'm going to plant myself here. You climb on my shoulders, see if you can grab the edge."

She accidentally dunked him on her first go, her foot slamming him into the water before he had his hold. He came up sputtering.

"Sorry."

"My bad. Give me a second."

He wedged one fist into a fissure in the rock, the other hand on a lip, his feet finding holds below the waterline.

She found handholds and managed to get her knees on his shoulders, then used the rock to steady herself. He grunted, and his body shook a little.

"You got this?"

"Can you reach?"

She stretched up, but her fingertips landed six inches from the top.

"You gotta do something quick, Tillie. I'm slipping."

Right. "Hold on tight, Moose. I need leverage." Then she crouched and sprang up hard.

One hand caught the ledge, slippery and rough, just long enough to get her other hand on it.

Then she kicked her way up the cliff, Moose's hand catching her foot to push a moment before he went back into the water.

It gave her enough to get one elbow up, then the other, and she leaned in and edged herself on, rolling onto the cliff.

Hazel launched herself forward. "Mom! *Mom!*"

Tillie closed her arms around her, clutching Hazel's body to hers, shaking, trying not to weep, but, "Hazel. You scared me. You really scared me."

Hazel leaned up, wiped her face—which really meant adding another layer of mud—her tears thick. "I'm sorry—Kip ran off, and I kept chasing him, and I think he thought we were still playing. And then I fell and he fell too and—I landed on this ledge. I hurt my leg. . . ." She showed off a tear in her pants. "I called and called for you."

"I'm here now, baby. I'm here now." She sat up.

Moose. She scrambled over to the edge. "Moose!"

She couldn't find him in the darkness. "Moose!"

"Over here."

She wished she could make him out more, but he seemed a hulk, clinging to the edge of the rock.

"Current got me."

"You okay?"

A beat.

"Moose?"

"I will be. I need to figure out how to get up there."

"You still have your pack?"

"I do."

"What about that space blanket? I'll find something to secure it to. You could pull yourself up."

"It'll rip. It's not strong enough. But the pack is." He swam over. "If I throw it up, can you secure one of the arms to something? I'll use the other arm strap for leverage."

See, this was why he was the rescuer. "Yeah. There's a lip here—I think that could work."

He swam over, then shucked off the pack. "Please catch this."

She stood on the edge.

"Without going back in."

"Thanks. I wasn't sure."

A chuckle deep inside the cavern, and it found her bones, heated them.

Wow, he had a way of making her feel less afraid, less alone. Probably why she'd longed for his late-night visits at the diner. Such a quiet, lonely place late at night, and then he'd come in, and suddenly her entire world would feel easier.

They just might survive this.

He threw the pack, and she grabbed it out of the air. Then she hooked one side on the edge of the lip, held it there, and dangled the other side down. It covered three feet, but if he jumped . . .

He found a ledge under the water and leaped for it.

Missed, and splashed back into the water. She refused to panic, but it took a chunk out of her, waiting for him to surface.

"The current is getting stronger," he said, swimming to the edge. "Try to grab on this time."

"Thanks for that." But he smiled, and she smiled back. And that smile rooted inside her. Gave her exactly what she needed when he grabbed the pack on the second lunge and struggled up the edge. She hunkered down on her end, then grabbed his hand and helped haul him over.

He scrambled onto the ledge on his hands and knees, breathing hard. "Thanks."

She nodded, also scrambling back.

And that's when her foot slipped out. It kicked the pack.

Which splashed down into the cauldron, sinking.

Silence.

Moose sat down. Rubbed his hand over his mouth. "That adds an element of difficulty to this season of Iron Maiden, Alaska Edition."

She just stared at him. Then he smiled, and *oh*, he was handsome. Waterlogged, bleeding, mud in his whiskers, and soggy, but those gray-green eyes latched onto hers, and she simply couldn't think.

What was this man doing with her? Never mind the cave. Or the mud. Or the fact that they probably had no way out. What was he doing with *her*, with all her drama and trouble and—

"I'm sorry, Moose."

"You're sorry? *I'm* sorry." He wrapped his arms around her.

And right then, she didn't care why. . . . All she knew was that Moose was here.

And if Moose was here, maybe hope was too.

SIX

AT LEAST IT HAD STOPPED RAINING.

Moose sat with his back against the ledge—an eight-foot hangover that seemed like it had once been the bottom of the cave until the mudslide had broken off the rest.

He wanted to keep the memory of being swept under the rocks into the cauldron of the creek wedged there, forever away from his brain.

Not how he wanted to die, thank you.

Although, hypothermia wasn't top of his list, either.

Tillie sat on the ledge next to him, her arms around Hazel, who wasn't sopping wet, thank the Lord, but still shivered.

He himself fought a bone-deep chill. Too bad the pack had gone soaring off the edge. . . .

And it was a ridiculous thought, but the memory of the avalanche on the glacier reached out and tugged on him. Back in the belly of the whale.

The cave even smelled like a rank sea creature, the mud rife with an earthy, almost dead, scent. Water trickled down the walls, and below, the churning river filled the cavern, almost deafening, a ringing in his ears.

Whatever message God might be trying to send, Moose was listening.

"I'm hungry, Mom," said Hazel, tucking her knees up to herself. "And I'm cold."

"I know, honey." Tillie cast a look at Moose. "I could try to climb out."

"The walls are concave and slippery, and even if you got to the top, the mudslide would send you back down." He had caught Kip and now ran his hands through the puppy's fur. The animal lay between his legs, filthy, but warm and sleeping.

Tillie shivered then, and oh, he wanted to put his arm around her. She'd clung to him after he'd ripped her out of the mouth of the current, so he edged closer to her, his leg against hers, and put his arm around her. "Reminds me of Navy boot camp."

"Whatever. Your most difficult boot-camp experience was probably trying not to fall asleep in the chow line. Or doing the fifty required daily push-ups. Try running the Marines' Crucible and then come talk to me."

"The Crucible? I've heard of that. Is it as terrible as they make it sound?"

"Forty-five pounds of gear, not including my M16, forty-eight miles of marching, fifty-four hours with three MREs—mine were chicken a la king—and four hours of sleep. Not to mention the thirty-some warrior-readiness stations."

"What are MREs?" Hazel said.

"Meals Rejected by Everyone," Moose said, cutting in on Tillie's response.

She looked over at him and held up a fist. He bumped it.

"I've heard about those Marine readiness stations."

"Iron Maiden would love them—we crawl through barbed-wire trenches, cross logs on cables, climb over walls, transport pretend wounded over a battlefield, swing on ropes over a pit, and carry water and ammunition over every obstacle they can think of. . . ."

"Good training, then."

"And it all ends with a massive pugil-stick bout, and that's super fun when you're dog tired."

"Okay, you win."

"Oorah." She looked at him, grinned. "Sorry, Navy. I know you guys aren't pansies. The Navy corpsmen deploy with the Marines, so there's that."

"Thanks. Except I was a chopper pilot, so I didn't have to dodge any bullets."

"On the ground. I'll bet you dodged a few in the air."

"I did a tour in Afghanistan, so yes. Managed mostly to not get shot down."

Shoot, he should have said that differently, because—

"*Mostly?*"

Her body warmed his, and he wasn't shivering as much. "We got a call that a couple spec ops guys were wounded. I flew in to evac them and ended up getting grounded."

Silence.

She turned, looked at him.

He glanced at Hazel.

"She's heard my stories. She knows about war."

Not the war he'd seen. He drew in a breath. "I was transporting the wounded out when I got shot down. I managed to get out and took one of the guys with me, but my chopper was blown up, and I spent four days hoofing it to safe ground, carrying my soldier to safety."

"Through enemy territory."

"Pretty much, yes." He had done a great job of keeping the memories out of his head, at least the last few years. But sometimes . . .

"So you're a hero."

"No. I screwed up. It was my job to rescue him—"

"Wow. Savior complex much?"

He looked at her, stiffened. "I—"

"Moose. It was war. You do what you can, and you keep going."

His mouth tightened. "I'm not a savior. But I had a job—"

"Okay, Navy, you need to let that go."

He looked back at her. "*I* had to be rescued."

Her mouth opened, then closed. "I get it. You can do the rescuing, but getting in over your head . . . that's not the Moose way."

"I could try to climb out."

"Calm down, Moose. I get it." She kissed the top of Hazel's head. Looked back at him. "I've spent most of my life trying to make sure that everyone is okay. Pearl. Hazel." She lifted a shoulder. "If anyone understands the guilt—it's me."

Oh.

"Is that why you left the Navy?"

He swallowed, his chest suddenly tight. "The man I carried out reminded me a lot of Axel, and I . . . I started having nightmares. And then . . ." He sighed. "I just needed a change."

"So you came home and started a rescue service."

"Not exactly." He looked at her, debating, then, "I started a flight service. I could already fly planes—learned how to fly in high school. I bought a little bush plane and started flying hunters and fishermen out into the bush. Transporting locals and even a few tourists who wanted to see Denali."

"So where did the rescue bit come in?"

He took a breath. He'd skim over the brutal parts. "There was this hunter who had a fly-in cabin. I was ferrying him, along with a couple other passengers who wanted to see Denali, when an ice storm forced us down. We were stranded and ended up needing to hike out. The short of it is that I ended up carrying the man out after he broke his ankle. He was so grateful, he gave me the money for Air One."

"You do that a lot?"

"What?"

"Carry people out of danger."

He looked at her. "I've never thought of it that way, but I guess."

"Like Superman," Hazel said and lifted her arm, zooming her hand into the air. "In your helicopter."

He smiled. "Okay, that's a little overstated but—"

"Superman. I like it." Tillie looked over at him. She'd relaxed a little, her body moving into his. Tucking herself against him.

"That's not all." And he didn't know why he suddenly had the urge to speak them aloud, the promises he hadn't kept, but here he was again, trapped in a cave, so . . . "Pike was pretty wealthy but very alone. His son had walked away from him after Pike's divorce, and they'd lost touch. It took us three days to get back to civilization, and during that time, we talked, a lot. Pike wanted to find his son, tell him some things. When Pike died, he gave me his home."

Silence.

"The thing is, I made him a promise during that long hike back to civilization that, if anything happened to him, I'd find his son and tell him . . . stuff. Things Pike said to me."

"And you haven't."

"No. And . . . every time I walk in my front door, I think about that, and how I've let Pike down."

"Did you try to find his son?"

"I don't even have his name."

"What about his lawyer? Does he know him?"

"I asked, but apparently he can't find him either, so . . ." Moose shook his head, as if angry with himself. "But it . . . it's there, right? That promise. And . . ." He indicated the cave with the rotation of his finger. "Feels a lot like the story of Jonah, right? Trapped in a whale? Maybe God is trying to get my attention."

"Maybe."

"You agree?"

"It worked, right?"

Huh. "You really think that?"

"I don't know, Moose. You're the one always talking about hope. God is . . . I mean, do I believe in God? Yes, I think. But I've never . . ." She pulled Hazel back against herself. "Trusting is harder. All my life people have told me to trust them. My mom. My dad . . . and he never came back."

Right. "How old were you when your dad left?"

"The last time? Twelve. He was deployed."

"You mentioned that. Was he killed in the war?"

"Nope. And not listed missing either." She glanced at him. "I think he went AWOL."

He raised an eyebrow.

"Yeah, so, we lived with a foster family for a while. Anyway . . . like I said, I'm not real good at trusting." She took a breath. "I trust in what I can do, what I can see. I trust in my love for Hazel. And . . . I guess now I trust you. Or I'm trying to."

She looked over at him, and he couldn't speak. Because, *oh,* he didn't want to let her down. Because she *could* trust him. More, she could trust God, if she let herself.

His prayer back in the ice cave stirred inside him. *Please. Keep her safe. Bring her help if she needs it.*

Softly, "You can trust me, Tillie."

She looked over at him, her eyes wide, so much on her face he didn't know what to do with it.

"And as for God, you can trust him too." Maybe too much, but he couldn't stop himself.

She gave him a tight smile, then looked down at her daughter. Hazel had turned, snuggled into Tillie, Tillie's arms around the little girl. Such a pretty girl, with dark hair and pretty green eyes.

Green eyes.

Tillie had brown eyes.

And Rigger had been as Aryan as the Hitler Youth. Blond hair, blue eyes.

Wait—

Blued-eyed and brown-eyed parents couldn't have green-eyed children. Or at least, his biology class in high school had suggested that it was rare. So, he could be wrong, but with the thought, his chest simply released, and he took a full breath.

Of course Rigger wasn't the father. Because Tillie would never be with a man like Rigger. She was . . . honest. And sweet and kind and . . . frankly, he didn't want to think of her with *anyone.*

Anyone but him. And that thought just sort of lodged there, refusing to budge. In fact, it had been tooling around his head for a long time. He just hadn't wanted to acknowledge it.

But here she was, suddenly in his life, needing him and . . .

Still, who— He nearly opened his mouth to ask when her words hit him: *"Now I trust you. Or I'm trying to."* Okay, so he wouldn't ask. And it didn't matter. She was here now, with him.

"And I promise, I will keep you safe." He kept his voice low, his arm still around her, but her gaze shifted, and she looked up at him, nodded.

Hazel had closed her eyes, and he glanced down at her and back to Tillie.

She still looked at him, her gaze in his, those beautiful brown eyes barely visible in the fading sunlight. But even in her bedraggled, sodden state, her hair plastered to her head, blood on her scalp—he had checked, and she had whacked it good—she still possessed a breathtaking beauty, born from grit and perseverance and even, even if she didn't believe in it, hope.

Because people who hoped kept fighting. Kept staying the course. Kept reaching out with their whole hearts.

That was called faith.

And maybe he was here to help her see it.

"Tillie. You don't have to trust God. Yet. But I think he's trying to get your attention too. To show you that, even when life seems to pull out from under you, you're not alone."

He lifted his hand, touched her face. Ran his thumb down her cheek.

"I'm sorry I got you into this mess," she said quietly.

"It *is* your fault, so . . ." He lifted a shoulder.

Her eyes widened.

"Aw, Til, I was just kidd—"

She kissed him. Just leaned up and pressed her lips to his, soft and yet sudden and sure.

And okay, it startled him, and sure, he'd been single for nearly forever, but he didn't need any help figuring out how to respond. Sheesh, he'd been quietly dreaming—no, *hoping*—for this moment for the better part of a year. So he kissed her back, moving his hand behind her neck to return her touch. Softly, perfectly.

Even while his heart nearly exploded.

Hazel shifted in Tillie's arms, and he lifted his head. Met Tillie's eyes.

She swallowed. "Um . . ."

Kip got up, started to bark, and outside, voices and barking, and then light swept into the cave.

Then, of course, his brother hung over the edge like a crazy man and waved. "Hey, bro. You okay?"

"Yep."

Axel grinned. "So, this is going to be a thing?"

"Just get us out of here."

But as he looked at Tillie, Moose wanted to say yes. Yes, this was going to be a thing.

One minute Tillie was wet and cold and stuck in a cave.

The next she was out, wrapped in a blanket, aboard a chopper that arched away from the hole in the earth, Hazel held tight to herself, buckled in across from Moose, who was grimy but looking at her with a fierceness that reinforced his words. *"And I promise, I will keep you safe."*

Oh boy, she believed him. Really believed him. And that scared her as much as the fact that she'd kissed him.

Clearly she'd lost her mind. But he'd looked down at her with such emotion in his eyes, and it'd sort of . . . indeed, she'd lost her mind. Just given into the moment.

I'm sorry, Moose.

The chopper hummed so loudly she couldn't talk to him anyway. Axel had strapped in beside Moose, and Shep sat on the other side of Hazel, who held Kip, wiggling in her arms.

She didn't recognize the man with dark hair at the controls. London sat in the copilot seat.

Outside, night crept over the land, the sun gone, the sky arching dark with pinpricks of starlight. Beneath them, she spotted the Copper River, a glistening silvery snake that wound around the mountain and the rocky shoreline.

They veered away and skimmed over the forest, populated here and there with lights from houses, and in the distance, the gleam of the town of Copper Mountain lit up the night like a beacon.

They touched down at the Copper Mountain airport, and Axel unbuckled and threw open the door. Another man ran out onto the tarmac and met them.

"Colt! What are you doing here?" Axel grabbed his hand as he got out.

"Tae and I came to visit the baby, and we'd just gotten into town when Dodge radioed that you were coming in. Thought we'd hitch a ride back to the ranch."

Axel turned to pick up Hazel, who winced, her leg clearly injured. Moose had also unbuckled and held out a hand to help Tillie.

She took it, unable to stop herself.

"You look tan," Moose said to Colt as he hopped out.

"All that Florida sunshine," Colt said. He shook the hand of the pilot, who'd climbed out. They pulled each other in for a back slap. "Dodge. Congrats on the baby."

Dodge grinned, and a weird pain speared through Tillie.

Nothing like the joy of a newborn. She remembered it like it was yesterday. Yeah, they'd been happy then, at least for a minute.

"What happened?" Colt said to Moose. Shep joined him, London disembarking last.

"Got trapped in a mudslide," Moose said.

"Colt Kingston?" London came up to them. "I can't believe it."

Colt seemed nonplussed to see London, his mouth opening, and she gave him a hug. "So, you did survive Nigeria."

What was that about?

Moose turned to Axel, who still carried Hazel, who carried the puppy. "I want to take her to the hospital." He reached for the puppy.

"No!" Hazel jerked the dog away, holding on.

Moose looked at her. "Hazel, let's trade. You give the little troublemaker to my brother. He'll bring him home. And I'll take you to the hospital for a look-see on that leg."

"He's hungry."

"Of course he is," Moose said and finally eased the pup from her arms. Tillie pulled Hazel from Axel's arms.

"We're also going to get Tillie's head wound looked at."

Axel took the puppy from Moose. "I'm going to check in with Flynn. I'll tell Mom to make up a couple beds for Shep and London."

"I have a room at the Samsons," London said. "We were already driving up when Axel radioed in that you'd gone down the sinkhole, and I figured we'd be here overnight, so I called them."

"That's also when we realized we needed a chopper and called Dodge at Sky King Ranch," Shep said.

"Thanks," Moose said, and shook Dodge's hand.

"We left a car here," Shep said. "We'll give you a ride to the hospital."

"I'll call Dad to pick me up," Axel said, crouching to attach a leash to Kip. He glanced at Moose. "Got the lead from Stormi. Good call, by the way. Rome did a good job tracking you down."

"We left a path the size of a grizzly, so . . ."

"Still." Axel stood up. "There's a future there with K9 SAR." He pulled out his phone and walked away.

Hazel shivered and Tillie kissed her forehead. "We'll be warm soon."

Tillie's head had really started to throb. She'd knocked her brain around good when she hit that rock.

As if reading her mind, Moose turned to her. "I can carry Hazel."

"Are you sure?"

Moose looked at Hazel. "Can I carry you?"

Hazel nodded, and Moose took her. "Let's go."

Watching Moose carry little Hazel had Tillie's chest all knotted, her throat tight.

He buckled her into Shep's Jeep, then sat on one side, Tillie on the other as they drove to the hospital.

Hazel leaned against Moose, his big arm over her, keeping her warm.

Then he carried her into the hospital and right into the ER. And while a male intern sutured Tillie's wound—yes, it needed stitches—Moose waged a thumb war with Hazel and played I Spy and told her a story of the time he'd gotten stitches and how brave she'd been to save Kip, and the entire time, Tillie wished for a different life.

A life that wasn't riddled with mistakes and hiding and lies and . . .

But then she wouldn't have Hazel, and it didn't help to try to rewrite her mistakes, so—

"You okay, Tillie?"

She looked over from where she lay on the table to see London standing nearby.

Behind her, Shep carried a takeout box from Northstar Pizza. "Anyone hungry?"

"Starved," said Moose, who also wore a bandage on his forehead. He walked over to Tillie. "They want to get X-rays of Hazel's leg, see if there is any structural damage."

Oh. Uh. "I don't . . . I don't have insurance information for her," Tillie said. Or, for that matter, insurance.

Moose nodded. "I get that. Because of all the accidents that happen here in the summertime, the hospital has a flat fee for standard exams, including X-rays. But I can see if they can waive—"

"No. I can pay. I just . . . I'll figure it out."

"I think we can give you the Air One medical grant," London said, and Moose's eyebrows rose.

"There's an Air One grant?"

"There is now," London said, and winked at Tillie.

"Go ahead with those X-rays," Moose said to the intern.

Tillie drew in a breath but nodded.

"The doctor would like to admit you too," said the intern as he dropped his suture tools onto a tray. "You didn't pass the concussion protocol, and he wants to keep an eye on you."

"No, that's not necessary." Although, if she were to guess, yes, she had a concussion, given the thrum in her head. "Hazel and I will be fine." Except, really, she didn't have a place to stay, unless . . .

"My mom has probably baked cookies for us all," Moose said, his gaze on Tillie.

She nodded.

The intern walked over to a wheelchair. "Hazel, want to go for a ride?"

Hazel climbed into the wheelchair.

Hazel glanced at Tillie.

"I'll be here when you get back."

"Thanks, Bear," said Moose and clamped the intern on the shoulder. "Great to see you back here."

"Good to be back." Bear wheeled Hazel down the hall.

"You can wait in the family area," said a nurse. She patted the intern as he walked by with Hazel, a sort of motherly gesture. "I'll bet that pizza is getting cold."

Moose helped Tillie off the table, and she needed it because the world spun, just a little.

Or a lot.

They walked down to the family waiting area, a small room with an orange faux-leather sofa and a table and a television on the wall, set on some news station.

She settled onto the sofa while Shep opened the pizza box. "I hope you like pepperoni and onions. This was an extra that Levi had in the back."

"It's pizza," Moose said and took a piece. "Tillie?"

"I might throw it up," she said.

He sat down next to her. "Are you sure you don't need to be admitted?"

"I don't know. Probably not. Just a headache . . . probably from the stress."

"Or a concussion. I think you should get checked out."

"I'll get you some soda." Shep left the room, probably on that errand.

She leaned her head back.

"Don't sleep," Moose said.

"I have an elephant stomping on my head. I am not going to fall asleep."

"Then we need to talk about something," London said softly.

Tillie looked over at the woman. Pretty, her blonde hair back in a ponytail, tall, some curves, she wore a red Air One jumpsuit, zipped halfway down to reveal a black shirt underneath.

"The money wasn't there."

Tillie just blinked at her for a long moment. Then she sat up.

Bad idea because the room took a fast curve. She reached out, and Moose's hand caught hers.

"Do you need a bucket?"

"Not yet." But maybe. "What do you mean it wasn't there?"

"Shep and I lifted the patio pavers under the fire pit just like you said and—"

"Did you look in the wrong place?"

London pulled out a molded white vinyl chair and sat down, then leaned forward, her elbows on her knees. "No, we looked in the right place. The waterproof box was there. The suitcase was gone."

And now Tillie couldn't breathe. "It was gone."

"Did Rigger find it?"

She glanced at Moose. Nodded, then winced.

"So maybe it's over?" Moose said softly. "If he has the money, he could have left Alaska."

Tillie cocked her head. They didn't know Rigger like she did. And could be that Moose read her mind, because he gave her a look of frustration.

Then he spoke the words she dreaded. "Tillie, what aren't you telling us?"

She swallowed.

Suddenly his attention left her, and he glanced past her, his gaze on the television. He frowned, and she turned to look at the flatscreen.

Her entire body hollowed.

Rigger, except *not* Rigger but in his true persona as Julian Richer, dressed in a neat blue suit, standing outside the grounds of the Alaska State Fair, smiling and talking with a local reporter. The closed captions on the screen caught the tail end of their interview.

. . . JUST ON VACATION. THE FAMILY LOVES ALASKA

**AND WE WANTED TO SEE THE LAST GREAT WILDER-
NESS BEFORE MY POLITICAL CAMPAIGN REALLY
HEATS UP THIS FALL.**

What?

And then the camera panned to a woman who waved. She held the hands of two boys—one looked the same age as Hazel.

And now she got it. She shook her head.

"Tillie. Is that—"

"Yeah. That's Rigger. Or rather, Julian Richer. Rigger was his MMA name." The reporter was winding up her segment with a few facts about Julian—his two championships in the light heavy-weight division, his success as the entrepreneur of a line of MMA gyms across the country, and his current run for mayor in a suburb north of Miami.

They didn't mention his criminal record, his history of drug use, his humble beginning, or even the former questionable profession of his wife, Courtney Baker.

And of course, they wouldn't add anything about Pearl, the woman before all the fame.

Tillie sat back, her arms folded. And only then realized the room had gone silent.

"That can't be the same man I fought with in Roz's house. He's . . . so cleaned up."

"He's a businessman on the outside, fighter on the inside. He's always been a chameleon. The world has no idea."

"I thought he was a small-time thug," said Moose quietly.

"No. He's powerful. Has money and judges in his back pocket and—"

"Dangerous." Moose finished.

"Why would he come to Alaska for money if he's rich?" London said softly.

Tillie looked at her. Frowned. "I don't know. What if he was here for the fair like he said, and saw the reality show and decided he wanted his cash?"

Shep came back into the room holding a Sprite. He opened it and handed it to Tillie, along with a package of crackers. Looked at London. "What did I miss?"

"I told her about the missing money."

"And then we saw the guy on television," Moose said. "I'm trying to wrap my head around the fact that the guy we saw hold a gun on your friend and you is Mr. Clean and Shiny on television."

Her too.

And then silence.

"Listen. My sister was in love with him, and I couldn't stand him, but we needed money. So I let him train me, especially for the Iron Maiden."

"The Ninja Warrior event?"

"She won," Moose said.

London's eyes widened. "You won?"

"Two years."

"Moose—"

"I'm just saying." Moose looked at her. Smiled, with something that looked almost like respect.

And shoot, just when she thought she could tell him everything, she saw the person she wanted to be in his eyes. "That was a long time ago," Tillie said softly. "I've tried really hard to be someone else, to start over. I'm not that person anymore."

She took a sip of the soda and a bite of cracker, and it helped. "A month ago, I was a waitress. How did I get here?"

"In a chopper," Shep said.

She looked at him.

"Oh, you meant . . . that was metaphorical." He reached for a pizza. "I'll just eat my pizza."

London looked at him and grinned, her eyes warm. Then back to Tillie. "The answer is you got here one step at a time."

One stupid mistake at a time, but Tillie didn't say that. "I'm sorry for all of it. For dragging you all into this mess."

Moose covered her hand. "This is where we want to be."

London nodded. "And by the way, we checked on your friend Roz. She's recovering at Alaska Regional. Said for you to come see her."

Roz. She hadn't even thought of Roz since . . . *hold the phone*. "How did you know about Roz? You weren't at the house."

London looked at Shep, then shrugged. "She needs to know." Then she turned back to Tillie. "There was a number left in the case, written on a piece of paper, so we did some sleuthing."

Shep finished his slice of pizza. "It was a badge number, from Miami."

"Roz's number," Tillie said.

"Yeah. We went to talk to her, but she said she needed to talk to you. Only you."

Oh.

"Tomorrow, we'll go back to Anchorage and figure out what is going on," Moose said. "And if we have to, we'll have another chat with Rigger."

"I can't believe the police haven't arrested him," said London.

"Clearly, they haven't put the man who shot Roz and this guy together as the same person," said Shep.

"We'll fix that," Moose said, and the way he said it made her heart lurch. Memories nearly made her open her mouth. *No, Moose—*

A knock sounded at the door, and Bear stuck his head in. "All done. The doctor took a look—no fracture, just some bruising. So you're good to go, although—"

"No, we're going," said Tillie, standing up.

The room tilted again, and she slammed her hand on the table.

Bear gave her a look.

"Just a headache."

He narrowed his eyes.

"I'll keep an eye on her," Moose said, and slipped his hand under her elbow.

Apparently, he meant it, because when they got back to his parents' home, and after she'd put Hazel to bed, she found him, changed, showered, dressed in a pair of flannel pajama bottoms and a T-shirt, carrying a blanket and a bucket of popcorn.

"What's that for?"

"How's your head?"

She'd taken a couple pain meds with the soda and . . . "Better."

"Good. There's a *Downton Abbey* marathon that has our name on it."

"*Downton Abbey?*"

"Would you prefer *The Crown?*"

She laughed. "I have never seen either of them. But . . . you seem more like a *Deadliest Catch* kind of guy."

She followed him up the stairs and into the main room. The door to the office was shut. She'd seen Shep head in there when they arrived to a home that smelled like freshly baked bread and the beef roast that had survived Moose's crazy drive home.

And, of course, cookies. Which sat under a glass topper in a pile in the center of the table.

"Naw. I'm all about the manners and the upstairs-downstairs rules, and most of all . . . I'm a goner for the Dowager, Violet Crawley."

"Who's she—some hot blonde?"

"I like brunettes, and not quite." He sat on the sofa, and she sat next to him and couldn't help but compare it to the feeling she'd had in the cave.

No, he wasn't going anywhere.

And frankly, she didn't want to either. There was a chance that Rigger would finally leave her and Hazel alone—now that he had the money.

So maybe, yes, there were fresh starts.

Moose picked up the remote and turned on the television, queued up the first season of *Downton*. "No sleeping."

She leaned against him. "You do know that's not a thing, right?"

He grinned at her.

And she grinned back.

Yeah, well, no promises. Because she'd very much like to think that tomorrow she'd wake up to a happy ending.

SEVEN

MOOSE'S JAW HURT FROM READING THROUGH Rigger's bio, the one he had dug up on his computer, propped at the kitchen table.

A bio that didn't even come close to matching what Tillie had told him. And Moose didn't know what to do with the gap.

He sat in his pajamas and a white T-shirt, feeling frowzy and unkempt, a little grumpy, his black coffee unable to cut through his mood.

Something didn't add up, and the information on the screen only confirmed it. Someone was lying.

Please, let it not be Tillie.

"Moose. You're up early."

Shep came walking out of the family office-slash-guest room, wearing a pair of jeans and a flannel shirt—the attire he'd worn yesterday under his jumpsuit—his brown hair askew, looking like he'd slept poorly on the lumpy pullout. He carried a toothbrush and paste, probably from the toiletries kit he kept in his car. "Tillie in bed?"

"We were ten minutes into the first episode of *Downton* and she was out. I woke her up at the start of episode two, and that lasted about five minutes. I finally woke her up to go to bed halfway through episode three."

"As long as she didn't seem confused or ill . . ."

"Nope. But I'm a little confused and a little sick after reading up on this Rigger guy." He turned the computer toward Shep. The screen showed a picture of a bald fighter flexing his arms down, teeth gritted, on the cover of *The Ultimate Fight*, a decade ago.

"That's the guy?" Shep gave him a side eye. "You went mano a mano with him?"

Moose turned the computer back. "I held my own, but yeah. His ring name was Rigger, real name Julian Richer, out of Florida. Married, with two children, ages seven and nine. He won two MMA light heavyweight championships when he was younger—ten and eight years ago. He also founded a series of MMA-specialty gyms and started a franchise that put his net worth in the millions. He's running for mayor in Hollywood, north of Miami."

"And he kidnapped Hazel."

"I wouldn't call it kidnapping. More of a threat, with some hostage thrown in. But yes, that was him."

"Seems like a strange side gig while on vacation to Alaska with his family."

"Right?" Moose finished his coffee. "And he's got money. So why would he be after some prize money that legally doesn't even belong to him?"

Shep nodded.

"Unless he's here for his daughter." The voice came from Axel, who'd come down the stairs from the loft. He wore a pair of jeans, his hair still shower wet, and he'd shaved. He walked over and looked at the screen. "Oof. He's pretty."

Moose nodded. He didn't even for a little want his brain to wander over to the connection between Rigger and Tillie.

Especially since the easy math said that Hazel's birthday landed after the man's marriage to—"He's married to a former exotic model, too. Courtney Baker."

Axel moved into the kitchen, grabbed the coffeepot. "So, now what?" He poured the coffee.

Moose sat back. "I don't know, Axel. Who puts their daughter in jeopardy like he did?"

"None of it adds up," Shep said, reaching for a cookie. "Let's just hope it's over."

"You know, you could just let Flynn and Daws handle it," Axel said. "Flynn is pretty good at tracking people down. She could get to the bottom of this."

Moose nodded, his arms folded over his chest. "Yeah. The police might at least know if he's left town. Can you text her?"

Axel smiled, then picked up his coffee and headed to the door. "With pleasure."

Moose laughed, then got up and looked at Shep. "You heading back to Anchorage this morning?"

"Yeah. Picking up London on the way." Shep poured himself a cup of coffee.

"So . . . it's none of my business, but . . . is there anything going on between you two?"

Shep stilled, then glanced at Moose. "Nope." But he said it quickly and didn't quite meet Moose's eyes.

Moose sighed. "Okay." But it put a fist in his gut. The whole night had, and he was just feeling dark.

"Listen," Shep said quietly. "London and I have history. I should have told you that, but . . . anyway, we're working through it. So no, nothing's going on. Now."

Moose had gotten up and stood by the stairs. "Thanks. Let me know if anything changes."

Shep nodded. Gave him a grim smile.

He understood that expression. Had worn the same smile for

the better part of the last year, trying to figure out how to sort out his feelings for Tillie.

Maybe he shouldn't have kissed her.

Maybe he shouldn't have promised her that he'd keep her safe.

Maybe . . . well, maybe he'd gotten himself in over his head, again.

He showered and shaved, trying to figure out why his gut roiled inside him.

What he hated most was the feeling that he'd never quite catch up to all the promises in his life.

Like Grace Benton, the woman who'd died in a blizzard last spring after he'd made promises to her father.

Or like his promise to Boo not to drag her into the public eye.

And Axel, nearly dying twice this summer after Moose had made a lifelong promise to protect him.

And now Tillie, and Hazel . . .

He stared into the mirror, and for a moment, Pike Maguire stared back. *"The only regret I have is that I didn't try harder to keep my word."*

Yeah, he'd lived with that echo in his head for three years now. Kept him awake sometimes.

Sorry, Pike. Moose didn't have a clue how to keep that promise.

He wiped his face, hung up his towel, and wished that he didn't start every day with failure.

Then he headed downstairs to where Hazel and Tillie sat at the table. His mother stood at the stove, making pancakes, the smell of maple syrup spicing the air.

Axel had left, evidenced by the absence of his Yukon in the yard.

Shep came out of the office cleaned up, having used the main-floor bathroom. "I'll see you back at the Tooth," Shep said.

"What's the Tooth?" Hazel asked.

Moose walked over to the coffee maker for cup number eight

thousand fifty-three. "It's what we call our office down in Anchorage."

"Are we going back to Anchorage?" Tillie sat in a pair of sweatpants and an oversized T-shirt, one leg up, her dark hair back.

He turned, nodded. "I think so. How's the noggin?"

She touched her head, winced. "Tender."

"I'll bet. No more spinning?"

She met his eyes. "Not in the way you mean."

Huh.

His mother set a plate in front of Tillie, then patted his chest. "Sit. Eat."

He pulled up a chair and let her set a stack of pancakes in front of him. "I'd be just fine with cookies." He winked at Hazel.

"I'm sure you would," his mother said. "I'll send some on the road with you."

Only then did he notice Tillie's pallor. She seemed to have gone white. He wanted to ask, but she looked up and offered a tight smile, then glanced at Hazel, and somehow he picked up a vibe that now wasn't the time.

Still. "Tillie, should we stay?"

She looked at his mom. "Forever? Sure." Then she smiled at him, and the haunted look seemed to vanish. "But maybe it's time we got back to our lives."

Hmm. Okay then.

But two hours later, she seemed painfully silent as they turned off Highway 3.

"I need to get my car," Tillie said quietly.

Right.

He couldn't get past the feeling that something might be slipping out of his grip. "You should stay at my house—"

"Yes! Please!" Hazel, from the back seat. She'd begged to take Kip with her, too, so she'd been sulking most of the trip, making do with a seen-better-days stuffed dog. Seeing her smile turned his heart.

"No, Hazelnut. Your school already started. And . . . I need to try to get my job back."

He looked over at her. "They have someone else working night shift. She's not nearly as good as you."

"I can't work night shift with Roz in the hospital and recovering. She's my sitter."

Right. "I . . . I could watch her." And there he went, again making promises he couldn't keep.

Tillie reached across the console and touched his arm. "No. You've done enough."

And there it went again, the tiniest clinch in his chest telling him that something wasn't right. That all was not as it seemed.

He swallowed it back, though, and headed home.

Tillie's car sat in the driveway, a wreck that probably shouldn't be on the road. And it occurred to him then that she should have used some of that prize money to buy a car.

Why hadn't she?

But before he could ask, she got out. And what did it matter, anyway?

He turned off the truck and helped her with her bags. His mother had given her an extra suitcase and the Sorels, along with a hat and mittens for Hazel, and now Tillie shoved them all into her back seat.

He noticed that they joined a blanket and some pillows. "You are going to your house, right?"

Hazel climbed into the back seat, barely enough room there. He gave her a tight smile. She held on to her stuffed puppy, then barked at him.

"Okay, Kip. I'll see you soon." He petted the stuffed animal. Hazel grinned. Everything inside him hurt.

Which made no sense because he very much planned on checking in with Tillie. Tomorrow. Or tonight or—"Are you sure you don't want to stay? I mean . . ."

She had rounded to the driver's side. "Moose. You've done so much—"

"I made you a promise."

She cocked her head, a warmth in her eyes. "I know. Thank you. We'll be fine." Then her eyes seemed to turn glossy. And that was just *it*.

"What is going on?" He didn't mean his tone to be so rough, but—"You are acting weird. Like I'm never going to see you again or—"

"You're not."

He stilled.

She glanced inside the car, then shut the door and spoke over the top of it. "I'm leaving, Moose. I'm going to stop by and see Roz and then . . . I have to leave."

He felt punched. "Why? What does this guy have on you that makes you need to run? I don't get it. If you're scared, stay with me. Axel is here. Tillie, I don't understand."

Her mouth closed, her eyes bright. And she just shook her head.

He looked away, back to her. "Then what was that kiss about? I thought—I care about you."

"I care about you too, Moose." Her words emerged so achingly soft his throat simply closed. "A lot. But this . . . this is bigger than you, or your promises. And I have to choose Hazel. Always Hazel. Rigger won't stop looking for us—even if he has the money."

"Why?" He didn't mean for his voice to thunder or to scare that look into her eyes. But—"He has a family. And a home. And money. Why does he want you?"

"Because I can destroy it all."

His phone vibrated in his pocket. He yanked it out. Axel. Moose growled as he opened the call. "What?"

"Hey, bro. Uh . . . we have a callout. Sorry. The state police called—the glacier dam at Skilak Lake down in Kenai broke. There's flooding all along the river—people trapped. Sorry, it's urgent."

Moose looked at Tillie, watched her swallow, her mouth tight.

"I'll be right there. Get the chopper ready." He hung up. Met her eyes. "Please, please, stay."

She drew in a breath.

"Please be here when I get back."

And then he got into his truck and left his heart in two pieces as he turned and headed out of the driveway into yet another promise.

"Mommy, are you crying?"

Hazel's voice emerged from the back seat, and Tillie blinked hard and looked away, hating that Hazel could probably see her in the rearview mirror.

"I'm just tired, honey. I didn't get a lot of sleep last night."

She'd dropped like a stone on the sofa, barely remembering when Moose roused her the first time and no recollection at all of going downstairs until she woke, nearly screaming, hot and clammy from the nightmare.

No, the memory.

The. *Memory.*

She blew out a breath. This was why she had to get as far away as she could from Rigger.

Please let him have taken the money and left. But her gut—and her nightmares, apparently—didn't believe that.

She wiped a hand across her cheek. "I'm fine, honey. I . . . Listen, when we get to the house, I want you to grab your favorite shirts, five of them, and just a couple pants, and don't forget your winter jacket, okay?"

Silence. She glanced up. Hazel's gaze hit her hard through the rearview mirror.

"No."

She glanced over her shoulder. Hazel folded her arms, crossed her legs.

"No, I'm not going anywhere. I wanna go back to Moose's house."

Tillie drew in a breath and tightened her hands around the steering wheel as she turned off the highway, toward Eagle River. She shook her head. "That's not possible."

"It is possible. He said we could stay—I heard him."

"Yes. But we can't."

"Why not?"

"Because . . ." She gritted her teeth. Because eventually her sins would catch up to them, and Moose would get caught in the fight. Because she could only take care of one person in her life. Because—"Because it's just you and me, honey. That's the way it has to be."

"I don't like that way."

Neither did Tillie, and she tightened her jaw as she pulled onto their road, then into the driveway.

No fire, no car in the driveway, no evidence that Rigger had been here to terrorize her. She would bet that he'd called his family to fly here as soon as Roz was injured, giving himself a new identity, a way to throw off the detectives.

She put the car into park, turned it off, unbuckled.

Hazel didn't move.

"I'm going in to get some things. And then we're leaving. If you want anything, you should go now."

Then she got out and didn't look back. *Reality.* She'd learned the hard way, and it was time for Hazel to figure it out too. She couldn't look after her forever, and—

"I hate you!"

She turned, and Hazel had gotten out, rounded the car, and now picked up a rock as if to throw it. Tillie didn't move.

Tears raked down Hazel's face and she shook. "I . . . I don't want to live in the car anymore. And I don't want to . . . I don't want to . . ."

"Hazel." Tillie strode over, dropped to her knees, and pulled Hazel to herself. "I know. I know."

Hazel buried her face in Tillie's neck. "I miss Grandma Roz. And I . . . just want everything to go back to the way it was."

Her too. Only, even then . . .

No, Tillie wanted better, for both of them.

She held Hazel away from her. Met her eyes. "Hazelnut. That man that was in Roz's house—he is a bad man. A very bad man. And I don't want him to—"

"Is he my father?"

Tillie drew in a breath. "We talked about this."

"He said he was, and I keep having this nightmare . . ."

"What nightmare, honey?"

"I don't know." Hazel ran her hands over her cheeks. "There's shouting, and then you're there, and you're fighting with him."

Oh. No. That couldn't be—

"And I'm so scared, I'm hiding under a table, and then he's trying to grab my feet, and I can't get away—"

Okay, that part wasn't real. She held Hazel's face in her hands. "That's not going to happen. That will *never* happen."

"Promise me you'll never leave me, Mommy."

"I promise, with everything inside me. Never."

Hazel nodded and Tillie again pulled her close. "C'mon. We're going to go see Grandma Roz as soon as we're packed." She met Hazel's eyes, and Hazel smiled, then wiped more tears and took off for the house. Hazel knew the code at the door and was inside and in her room by the time Tillie went through the house to the patio.

Indeed, the pavers had been moved, the waterproof box opened, the space emptied.

She knelt beside the space a moment; then her gaze went to the charred playset. She'd steer Hazel clear of that sight.

But how had he figured out their hiding space?

She got up and went to Pearl's old room, opened the closet, and pulled down a small duffel bag from the hidden rafter space above.

Passports, *thank you, Hecktor*, and cash—just a couple thousand. She should have grabbed it all before, probably, but . . .

But she hadn't wanted to believe that she'd have to leave her life behind.

She opened a drawer and took out Pearl's diary—for Hazel someday—and then shoved it all into a backpack, along with a fleece jacket. She shoved a ball cap on and headed to her room.

Hazel was there, her Nanea American Girl doll sticking out from the top of her backpack, along with two *Ella Diaries* books and a book of stickers.

Right. Tillie grabbed the locket on the dresser, stuck that in her pocket, then pulled her fleece from her closet, as well as a sweatshirt and a pair of jeans. "Let's go."

Hazel grabbed her backpack, zipping it as she headed for the door.

And weirdly, as if a piece of her past rose to take possession, it felt like they might be running out into a war zone, her sergeant in her ear. *"Remember your training. Improvise. Adapt. Overcome. Oorah."*

Tillie pulled Hazel back. "Stay with me."

"Mom, you're hurting me." Hazel pulled out of her grip, then headed toward the car.

In Tillie's wildest nightmare, Rigger emerged from the woods on either side of the house, charged, and grabbed Hazel. Threw her in his car. Then it would be all over, wouldn't it?

But no. Hazel got in, and Tillie climbed into the front. "Buckle up." Then she pulled out and tried not to floor it, her heart in her throat.

Sheesh, she'd worked herself into a downright lather. Probably over nothing. Probably, Rigger was on a plane back to Florida with his family.

Probably.

She blew out a breath at the stop sign, another at the light, and by the time she hit the freeway, she'd left the nightmare in her rearview mirror.

Turning on the radio, she glanced at Hazel. She'd pulled out Nanea and had her seated on her lap, talking to her in low tones. Oh, she was so much like Pearl. Sometimes it took Tillie's breath away, seared her, right through to her bones.

Don't worry, Pearl. I got this.

She got off onto Airport Heights Road and determined not to cast a look at the Air One Headquarters, located off Merrill Field, as she drove to the hospital.

She managed almost all the way to the light and then sat there and glanced over.

The red chopper was gone, Moose already on his way to rescue another soul. His truck sat parked alongside Axel's Yukon, along with a Nissan Rogue, an orange Subaru, and a hard-sided Jeep. The lineup of his team.

Her throat burned as the light changed, and she turned back to the road, to the hospital. The car turned in as if it knew the way, and out of habit, she parked in the same place, near the ER and the Ivy Infusion center.

"Leave Nanea here, honey. We'll be back as soon as we see Grandma Roz."

Hazel put the doll in her backpack and picked up her stuffed dog.

Tillie caught Hazel's hand as she came around, and found the locket with her other grip. She pulled it out and handed it to Hazel.

Then they headed inside.

She shook away the memories and managed a smile for the woman seated at the information counter—midfifties, dark brown hair, a look of efficiency about her.

"I'm a friend of Rosalind Turner. Can I see her?"

The information woman—her tag said Mary—turned to a computer. "I'll call up. Your name?"

Tillie glanced at Hazel and then handed over their names.

She wouldn't be here long. But Roz deserved a goodbye, and besides, she'd asked them to come by.

And there was the question of her badge number in the box, or at least, that's what Shep and London had said. Another message from Rigger, that no one she loved was safe?

"Room 312." Mary issued them name stickers, and Tillie took Hazel's hand as they headed up the elevator to the third floor.

It was quiet here, a half-staffed nurses' desk and the muffled sound of a few televisions on in the rooms as they walked down the hallway to room 312.

The door was ajar, and she knocked, then pushed it open.

Roz lay in the bed, half sitting up, eyes closed, a thin oxygen cannula under her nose, an IV in her arm. Beyond her, a window opened up to a view of the mountains to the north. Tillie shook away the trauma of the last day and walked over to the bed.

"Grandma Roz, wake up!"

A pause, during which Tillie might have panicked, and then Roz opened her eyes. She blinked, then, "Oh. Oh my. Oh, *my girls*. I was so worried." She reached out on either side and took Tillie's hand, then Hazel's. "This is good news."

Not that good, but Tillie didn't say anything.

"Grandma Roz, we went to a big house, and they had a bathtub big enough for three people. Or four. And then there was a puppy named Kip, and he fell down a hole and so did I, and then Mom came and so did Moose, and we flew in a helicopter. And I got cookies and pancakes for breakfast."

Roz had always reminded Tillie of that old Cagney and Lacey television show her foster mother had watched. Roz playing the role of Lacey, with her dark, now white hair, her solid body.

Now it seemed she'd simply sunk into herself, thin and pale, and she looked . . . old. And even frail as she smiled at Hazel. "That is an adventure."

Tillie put a hand on her arm. "It's a long story."

Her gaze turned to Tillie. "I met your friends. Or maybe they're not friends, but . . . they were at the house. They know."

Tillie's breath caught. "They . . . know? What do you mean—"

"They know that the . . . package isn't there."

Hazel had gone over to the window, pushed her forehead to it. "What package?"

"Don't play that game with me, Tillie. I know about the . . . cookies."

"Cookies?" Hazel asked, turning.

"For the love, Roz." Tillie spoke to Hazel. "No, not cookies."

She looked again at Roz, cut her voice low. "How do you know that?"

"Your sister. She was worried. Under the patio is a terrible place to hide a hundred thousand . . . cookies. She said it numerous times. So . . . we moved it."

Tillie's mouth opened.

"You remember when you bought the playset? And put pavers on the patio?"

"Yes. That's when Pearl buried the suitcase."

"And I deposited the money. In a safe deposit box."

Of all the things that might have issued from Roz's mouth—"What? A safe deposit box?"

"Yes. C'mon, Tillie. You don't leave that kind of"—she dropped her voice low—"money under your fire pit."

"You do if you can't go to a bank and get it!" She shook her head. "How do I even find it?"

"It's under the name Alicia Torre."

The name she'd used to escape to Alaska. Alicia Torre, and her sister, Henrika, and her daughter, Aurora. "How do you know that name?"

"Please. I was the one who directed you to Hecktor to get new passports. I made him tell me."

Right.

"Okay, so . . . what bank?"

"Northern Skies."

Tillie didn't know what to do with the rush of feelings. Rigger *hadn't* found the money. Which meant that Rigger *hadn't found the money*. Which meant he was still out there.

See, this was why she needed to run.

"Okay. So, how do I get it?"

"There's a key in my house. It's on the lawn mower key chain."

"That's safe."

Roz lifted a shoulder. "Hiding in plain sight, right?"

Tillie shook her head.

"And by the way, the phone is there too."

The what? "What are you talking about?"

"Pearl gave me a secret phone. I think it was her old one, from Florida. Told me to keep it safe—that if anything happened to you or if Rigger showed up, I was supposed to give it to you."

"Pearl had a secret phone?"

Roz wore her cop face. "Yes. Your sister wasn't always . . . well, she had some smarts."

"My sister was brilliant. But she didn't know who to love . . . and who to walk away from."

"Seems to me you don't either."

Tillie recoiled. "What?"

"What happened to the man who came with you to the house? The one who tussled with Rigger while you got away."

"He's . . . I . . . You know what? I can't have anyone else in my life who could get hurt. Like you."

"I'm going to be fine. But you keep making decisions that lead you away from what you really want."

"What I really want is . . ." She looked at Hazel, back to Roz, her voice low. "I want Hazel to be safe from Rigger. I want her to grow up happy, with a mother who loves her."

Roz shook her head, and Tillie had to take a breath, step back. Gather herself.

So much pain in all of that. "I'll get the key. And the money. And the phone." Her eyes filled. "And . . . thank you, Roz. You've been . . . everything to me."

Aw, she didn't mean for it to end like this. Sheesh, she was a marine, made of tougher stuff than dissolving on the floor at a goodbye.

And Roz was too, although now her eyes filled, and a tear dripped down her wrinkled cheek. She looked at Hazel. "Hey, Nut, come give Grandma Roz a hug."

Hazel ran over and flung herself into Roz's arms. Roz grunted but just closed her eyes and held on.

Tillie took another step back. Those two deserved this moment.

The door opened behind her and she turned. "We'll be done in a moment—Flynn?"

The woman she'd met a few nights ago stood in the doorway. Auburn hair pulled back, she wore black pants, a gray shirt, a leather jacket, open, and around her neck, a police badge.

A man walked in behind her.

"Hey, Tillie," Flynn said.

The man walked past her over to Hazel, who'd stood up. He crouched in front of the little girl. "Hi, Hazel. My name is Dawson.

I'm a friend of your friend Moose, and he asked me to come here and see if you wanted some ice cream."

What—

Hazel looked at her mom, back to Dawson, and her expression said she didn't believe him either.

Tillie turned to Flynn. "What's going on?"

Flynn's mouth pinched. "I think you know."

For a second, the slightest brilliant second, the word *Run!* flashed through her mind. The second after that, she saw herself restrained and cuffed and dragged away while Hazel watched, scarred for life.

So Tillie didn't run. She simply looked at Roz, who sat stricken in the bed, then at Hazel and smiled. "It's okay, Hazelnut. You go with Dawson and get that ice cream, and Mommy will be with you as soon as she can, okay?"

Dawson held out his hand, and with everything inside her, she wanted to leap across the bed and kick him in the chin. Land and follow with a spinning punch and—yeah, it all flashed through her head as Hazel reached up and met his grip.

Tillie forced a smile as Hazel walked past her, her breath cutting off as Hazel looked back at her.

Just like Pearl had when they'd taken her away that first time.

Then the door closed, and Tillie looked at Flynn.

"Tillie Young, there's a warrant out for your arrest under Florida Statute 787.03, interfering with parental custody and kidnapping of a minor."

"You don't understand—"

"You need to come in so you can formally sort this out with a lawyer—"

"You don't understand!"

"Tillie—"

And then, against the backdrop of Roz's gasps, one bad decision led to the next and then the next, and suddenly Tillie was out in the hallway, Flynn in the room behind her on the floor—not dead, and probably not unconscious, but definitely incapacitated.

Leaving Tillie to run, and run, and run.

EIGHT

DISTRACTED DRIVING ONLY GOT PEOPLE killed. And distracted flying—

Never. Moose had been there, done that, and right now, he needed his entire focus on holding the bird steady as Axel worked to pluck a family out of the swollen Skilak River.

Some three miles upstream, the dam made of glacial boulders had broken free in the freezing autumn rain, and the river rushed through, overflowing banks, uprooting houses from their foundations, and sweeping away vehicles. All along the shoreline, families evacuated houses that perched on the precipice of the shoreline. They'd already rescued one family from their rooftop after a tributary swept over their property and surrounded the house in glacial ice and debris.

Now the swollen, raging waters had swept a bridge from its moorings, taking a caravan filled with a family—mom, dad, two children under the age of ten—along with it. It lay on its side, half submerged, caught on the debris of the bridge, the family clinging to the vehicle while the frigid, churning, slate-gray water swept over it.

"Ten feet from the car. Almost there." Shep's voice, giving Moose the play-by-play as Axel went down on the line, accompanied by the basket. The wind from the storm had died, so the chopper wasn't pitching, but if the basket caught in the rapids, it would jerk the bird. Moose kept his eyes on the instruments, the terrain in front of him, listening, seeing the rescue in his mind's eye.

"He's at the car," Shep said.

"Axel, don't you dare unclip from the line." Boo's voice, as the EMT leaned over the chopper door, watching.

Good try, Boo, but Axel had his own mind, although yes, he knew safety protocol. And since he'd nearly drowned in a sinking charter boat this summer, he'd been markedly safer.

Somewhat.

Okay, maybe not.

In a moment, Axel's voice came through the radio. "I've got the kids in the basket and jackets on the parents. I'm coming up with the basket."

Which meant the snarl in Moose's chest could ease now, just a little. But the fight with Tillie still sat in the back of his brain, and three hours later, he just couldn't shake the feeling that she was still in danger.

Of *course* she was in danger. Not only because of her words— *"Because I can destroy it all"*—but he'd met Rigger. The man might clean up well, but Moose knew the substance of what lurked under that semi-clean-cut demeanor. His leg still burned with the knife wound along his thigh.

The man had something on Tillie, some reason he couldn't let go and—

"Moose, you're drifting!" This from London, who looked over at him.

He glanced at the directional gyros and moved the chopper back into position. Axel swung on the basket line, along with the kids.

"Hey, not on a joyride here, Cap," Axel said.

Moose said nothing, just tightened his jaw. *Focus.* He could do nothing for Tillie right now except pray. Pray and hope she did what he'd asked.

His chest hurt with the truth he couldn't face.

Shep drew Axel aboard, and Boo pulled the kids out, wrapped them in blankets, and strapped them into seats as Shep sent the basket back out, Axel still affixed to the hoist.

"Ten degrees to the south, Moose," Shep said, and Moose corrected.

London looked out the window. "You're spot on. Hold here."

Easier said than done, but he made the tiny adjustments with the cyclic to keep it in place, and Axel loaded the parents onto the basket.

"We're in. Bring us up!" Axel to Shep, and he winched up the line.

Moose moved the collective and increased the pitch angle on the blades, and the chopper rose, just in case one of the houses teetering upstream on the edge of the washed-away bank took a plunge. He'd already watched one house go in, crumbling away from its moorings, into the flood, to be swept into the dirty, frozen river.

He held the chopper steady now as Shep and Boo helped pull the basket into the deck and the two parents piled out, shivering, sopping wet, probably a little hypothermic.

Axel, dressed in his thermal jumpsuit, also climbed into the bird. He unhooked and held on to the basket while Shep closed the door.

"Back to the CESS," London said, picking up the radio to update the Central Emergency Services Station about their approach. The fire station already had units out, rescuing people in more accessible areas.

Twenty minutes later, they touched down in the parking lot,

the area cleared and cordoned off for Moose's chopper. He turned off the rotors before Shep opened the door. A couple firemen ran out to help, but Boo had given the family a check over—no major injuries. Still, the hospital in Soldotna would confirm.

"Any more callouts?" He looked at London, who was on the radio with the local rescue coordinator. He could hear their conversation, but again . . .

Tillie still crept around his head and—

"Nope. We're clear. And we're nearly at Bingo, so . . . "

"Roger. Shep, get us tucked in back there. We're leaving in five."

Although he'd done his preflight check before taking off, he gave everything a once-over as Shep and Axel secured the basket and Boo finished handing off the family to the EMS. Fuel gauges, instruments and radio, altimeter, trim—it kept his mind off what he might find back at his house.

As in, Tillie, gone.

Boo climbed back in, and Moose waited until everyone was strapped in, then lifted the Bell 429 into the air.

The sun hung low, just above the mountains, which cast deep shadows into the basin of the Alaska Range. The rains had churned up the waters of the Cook Inlet, frothy and dark, and the lights of Anchorage glittered in the distance.

He called in clearance to Merrill Field as they drew closer, then set down on the tarmac, near the Air One garage.

Shep opened the door and they piled out; then he and London shut down the bird. Axel and Shep strapped the chopper down, and Moose got out and checked their work.

The sun had fallen, the sky turning bruised and dark as Moose headed into the Tooth, located in a separate building away from the Quonset hangar that housed their vehicles, the four-wheelers, the snowmobiles, the rescue truck, and, tied down nearby, his Cessna, caught in the shadows of the night.

Boo and London had already flipped on the lights, their voices emerging from the locker room past the main area.

Home. Not really, but his timber home on the river always felt . . . borrowed. He hadn't earned it. Hadn't built it. Didn't deserve it. And perhaps he didn't deserve Air One, either, but Moose had designed the Tooth, from the parachute hanger in the back to the workout room, the bunk room, the lavatories, the locker room, his office, and the main area, all focused around team building and function. He'd overseen the construction, painted the walls, purchased the secondhand leather sofas that faced the flatscreen, installed the kitchen cupboards, designed the massive island, and found the long table that served as their meeting area. He'd tacked the maps of Alaska on the walls and purchased the lockers and benches in the locker room from an old school. Found preowned weight equipment. And poured everything he had into building this place.

Building his legacy.

Strangely, he hadn't given a thought to the lawsuit since Tillie had shown up at his doorstep, but now, as he headed into the office, the manilla envelope still sitting on his desk, a sickness pooled in his gut.

He couldn't lose this place. In a way, he knew how Tillie felt—he'd do anything to protect what he loved. His team. His family.

Tillie and Hazel? He didn't know what to do with the churn of feelings.

Savior complex? No. He didn't have to save someone to feel complete. He just needed to know he hadn't failed them.

He waited until the women walked out of the locker room, then followed Axel and Shep in and changed out of his jumpsuit and into his street clothes. He'd shower at home.

Axel had changed too and now pulled his phone from the top of his locker. "I have five missed calls from Flynn." He turned on his voicemail.

Moose sat on the bench, lacing up his boots. Stopped at the expression on Axel's face.

Shep shut his locker door, and Moose flinched, clearly on edge. He slowly stood up.

Axel lowered the phone. Took a breath. Looked at Moose, his face stricken. "Moose, I think you should sit back down."

"Just tell me." And suddenly, yes, he should sit down, because if Rigger had found Tillie and Hazel while he was out—

"Tillie has a warrant out against her for kidnapping."

Moose stared at Axel.

"While we were back in Copper Mountain, I called Flynn to check on Rigger. She did and discovered that just recently, a judge awarded him custody of Hazel. He swore out a complaint against Tillie for taking Hazel out of state. Flynn went to talk to her—"

"To *arrest* her?"

"To bring her in." He held up a hand. "Just so they could figure out what was going on and—"

"So Tillie is in *jail*? Where is Hazel?"

"I don't know, but Tillie's not in jail." Axel glanced at Shep. "Brace yourself, because she resisted arrest, attacked Flynn, and ran."

Moose sat down. "Tillie took Hazel to protect her."

"No doubt," Axel said. "But if she's noncustodial parent."

"But Rigger isn't her father, so how ... how did he get custody?"

"Unless he *is* her father," Axel said softly.

Silence around him. He met Axel's eyes. "It doesn't matter. It doesn't matter. Tillie is her mother, and something feels off, very off here. Is Flynn hurt?"

"No," Axel said. "Or, she didn't say. But Tillie's clearly in trouble—"

Moose nodded. "Okay. Listen, you check on Flynn. I'm going to try to find Tillie. I'm sure that this can be figured out."

Axel nodded, his mouth tight, what seemed like a little disbelief in his expression.

"I refuse to believe that Tillie is the criminal here. Sorry, but I met Rigger. This is not right." He hit his feet.

"It doesn't have to be right, Moose. But it's the law." Shep's voice stayed calm, quiet.

Moose looked at him. "What's better—to be on the side of the law, or to do what is right?"

"Let's get all the facts first," Axel said, stepping in. "I'll find Flynn and we'll do some digging."

"Let me know if I can do anything," Shep said.

Moose shut his locker, his gut churning. No wonder she hadn't wanted to tell him the truth.

Boo had already left with London, and now Shep grabbed his backpack and headed out the door.

Axel was on the phone with Flynn. Moose walked into his office, glanced at the envelope, then picked up his truck keys and phone. No missed calls.

Tillie hadn't even tried to get ahold of him.

"I'm heading over to Flynn's place," Axel said, pulling on his jacket. He paused. "I know you care about Tillie, but this is more trouble than you want. Just sayin'—you have a lot on your plate—"

"I made her a promise."

Axel sighed. "I know. But your promises are going to get you into trouble. You can't save everyone. That's not your job."

"You don't understand—"

"I think I do, big bro. The fact is, you think you're responsible for everything. And everyone. And I get that that's the way you were made, but I think it's more than that. I think you believe that if you don't, then somehow you're ... I don't know ... failing. Or letting God down or ..."

Ungrateful. Moose didn't say it, but the word lodged inside even as his jaw tightened. "I've been given a lot, Axel. I just want to honor that."

Axel took a step toward him. "I know. But there is your portion, and there is God's portion, and it seems like you're having a hard time figuring out the difference."

Moose's shoulders rose and fell.

"It would be better for you to break your word than to get into bigger trouble trying to keep it."

"Says the guy who went down with a ship that wasn't his."

Axel held up his hands. "I just care about you. And Tillie is great . . . but she's also got baggage—"

"We all have baggage," Shep said.

Axel raised an eyebrow.

"I have baggage." Moose drew in a breath. "The kind of baggage that makes me grateful for a second chance. The kind of chance that Tillie deserves."

"Someday we're going to talk about that baggage," Axel said as his phone rang again. "For now, don't do anything stupid." He answered the phone on the way out. "No, she's not here." He pushed out the door.

Not here.

It hadn't occurred to Moose that Tillie might come *here*. Did she even know where he worked? His mind had put her at the Skyport Diner.

But the cops would have checked there.

No, she wouldn't be any place Flynn would know to check. Shoot, he didn't have a clue where or how to find her.

He picked up his jacket, pulled it on, shoved his phone into his back pocket, and fisted his keys, his prayer back on his lips. *Please. Keep her safe. Bring her help if she needs it.*

He headed to his pickup, leaving the Tooth unlocked for Shep, who was still in the locker room. Axel had already pulled out, was turning onto the highway.

He was taking out his fob to unlock the doors when he heard shuffling, then a voice. "Stop."

He froze. Glanced over to the plane. And spotted a figure standing there, her outline easy to recognize

She held a pistol.

His *bear* pistol, the one he usually kept locked in his office. He'd left it in his plane the last time he'd flown—*aw* . . . "Tillie, just breathe."

"I need your keys, Moose." Her voice wavered.

"Yeah, no. This is . . . c'mon, this is crazy. We can figure—"

"Why, Moose? Why?" She stepped out from the shadow of the plane, still mostly obscured, but he could make out her face, the anguish on it, and from the way her voice shook—*oh*, she'd been crying.

Now it mixed with a sort of fury, given the texture of her expression. "Why did you betray me?"

He frowned. Then, "What?"

"You told them where I was."

He did what? "No—what? No, Tillie, I didn't—"

"How did Flynn know about me? Or where I was—you told Dawson that Hazel likes ice cream! Talk about manipulative—"

"I didn't say anything! I was out on a rescue—"

Her mouth tightened.

And then—"Hold on. I told Axel to ask Flynn to look into Rigger—and that's how she found the kidnapping charge, but I swear to you, I didn't talk to Dawson or whatever it is you're accusing me of."

"She knew I was at the hospital."

He had nothing. Wait . . . "Shep told you about Roz. Axel was there—maybe *he* told Flynn that you were going to the hospital. . . . And hello, but what kid doesn't like ice cream? I don't know, Tillie. I just know that you need to take a breath here. Calm down—"

"Calm. *Down*?" Her voice wavered again. "Did you not catch

the news brief? I'm wanted—and now a fugitive—and Hazel is probably going to foster care!" Her hands shook, and if she came one step closer, he could close the distance, get the gun from her.

Not that he believed she'd actually shoot him. *Probably not.*

"Do you know what it feels like to be ripped away from your family, to live in foster care?"

"No. But I do know there are many foster care families—"

"It's not about foster care! It's about the fact that you have no control over your life. That in a second, your entire world could implode. It's about being seven years old—or twelve—and having to sleep in a foreign bed with strange people telling you to call them Mom and . . ." She shook her head. "I told Pearl I'd never let that happen to Hazel. *Never.*"

His voice fell. "Okay. But—listen. We can figure this out. As her mother, you have rights, even if Rigger does have custody—"

"But I'm *not* her mother." The words emerged soft, almost as if wrenched from deep inside.

He stilled. His heart, his brain, his breath. *What?*

She looked wrecked, her voice broken. "I'm not her mother. Pearl was. I'm her aunt. And the only one she has."

Oh. The words shook through him.

And then, somehow, deep inside, the words released the terrible knot he'd been fighting for three days. "You didn't have an affair with Rigger."

Her mouth pinched. "I was a different person back then, but not that different. And I would never have betrayed my sister."

The sadness in her tone made him ache. But honestly, "You can't blame me, Tillie. You didn't tell me *anything.* This entire time, you've been acting like you're her mom—"

"I *am* her mom."

Right. He sighed. "Okay. But do you have legal custody of her?"

She swallowed, her mouth tightening. "I should. Pearl wrote a letter to the court, but . . . I couldn't . . . we couldn't . . ."

"So after your sister died, you just . . . kept her."

"What would you have done, Moose? Given her back to Rigger?"

And that's what didn't make sense. "No, probably not, but . . . that's the thing. Why does Rigger even want her? He has a family, a wife, and a home and . . . I don't understand."

"He got the judge to issue a kidnapping warrant on me so he could track me down. He doesn't want her. He wants *me*."

The night had sprinkled a few stars above, and they illuminated her face, stony but broken, and her words in the driveway returned to him.

"Because you could destroy him."

She nodded. "I could testify against him. I should have testified against him."

"For what?"

"For . . . so much. But mostly, murder."

He froze. "What?"

"It's a long story."

"Okay. What if you told it to me without a gun pointing at me."

She winced. "Moose, I'm . . . I . . ."

"You can trust me, Tillie."

Her face crumbled. "Yeah. No. I—"

He took a step toward her. Then another until the gun nearly pressed to his chest. Softly. "You can trust me. I will help you."

And yes, Axel was right—his promises were going to get him into trouble. But right now . . . "Tillie, I . . . I think I love you. Or I want to. Ever since you first served me pie and told me that you'd make me a milkshake and then sat with me and made me feel like I wasn't . . . I don't know . . . that I didn't have to . . ."

"Moose." She lowered the gun. "I'm so scared."

He reached out for her then and pulled her to himself and held on. Because, yeah. "Me too."

She wrapped her arms around his waist and buried her head against his chest. "I'm sorry. I'm so sorry."

He closed his eyes. "No more sorries. We're going to figure this out."

And of course, he added, "I promise."

Shep had hoped that the rescue would flush the shock of seeing Colt out of his system.

He pulled up to the Tooth, the place dark and quiet, and let himself in. The big refrigerator hummed, but night bathed the place in shadow.

Shep set a jar of pickles and a ham sandwich on the counter, opened the jar, and didn't bother to turn on the lights as he ate, thinking about Colt and his meeting that morning, which, given the rescue op, felt like a couple years in the rearview mirror.

The man had nearly blown everything when he'd texted Shep at Moose's, asking him to meet in Copper Mountain before Shep picked up London and drove them back to Anchorage. The last thing Shep needed was London walking into the Last Frontier Bakery and discovering that his asking her to join Air One Rescue hadn't simply been a friendly request.

He didn't understand all of it, but Colt's words this morning had stuck with him the entire drive down, and during the rescue, and had even followed him back to the Tooth.

"We got word from our operative in Europe that the Petrov Bratva is still looking for her."

Colt had kept his voice low, and really, Shep didn't understand quite what he meant, but he got the gist of it.

Danger. For London. Because of who she'd been.

And even that he didn't have a full picture of, but she'd been important enough in her circles for people to want her dead. Which was why a year ago, Colt had given Shep her contact information and told him to reach out to her. She'd been working with a missionary group in Nigeria, so that was a surprise. But yes, reach out to the woman he couldn't forget? No problem.

He should have asked more questions.

"Still ice climbing?" Colt had asked today in the bakery, grinning over his cup of coffee and cinnamon roll as if they might be old friends.

Shep recognized the roll as one from Moose's mother's kitchen.

"Nope. Nearly dying with you was enough." Shep finished his coffee. "I need to bring her into the loop."

Colt's grin vanished. "Yeah. And then what? You tell her that all this time you've been spying on her—"

"Not spying. *Protecting*."

Colt held up his hands. "She can take care of herself. What we asked you to do was definitely in the realm of spying."

"And this conversation is over." Shep got up.

But Colt also got up. And suddenly wore the look of a former Army Ranger. "Listen, if she gets spooked, she'll vanish again. It took my people two years to find her after the avalanche. She'd changed her name, again, and if it hadn't been for her showing up at a humanitarian base I happened to be working security at, we never would have found her."

"Why don't you bring her in if she's that valuable?"

Colt drew in a breath, his mouth pinching at the corners. "The more she believes that she's started over, that she's safe, that no one knows what she's done and who she is, the more she relaxes. And then, maybe we get lucky."

"Are you telling me you *want* someone to find her?"

"No. But we do want someone to make a move. We've been trying to figure out who might be behind some events that happened globally. And she's the key to that."

"Silence.

"Not going to fill me in?"

"I don't even know everything. But I do know that she can't go missing. And if she does, then we're back at ground zero. So keep her close."

"I don't want to keep lying to her."

Colt picked up his cup. "Listen. I get it. No one likes to keep secrets from someone they care about. Believe me—my fiancée, Tae, kept so many secrets from me she nearly got my family killed. But she thought she was keeping us safe."

"That's a terrible excuse."

"Look. She's already been betrayed once. If you tell her, it's over. And she's in the wind." He finished his coffee. "You see anything out of order, or she starts to act strangely, you tell us."

The whole conversation had left a pit in Shep's stomach, especially when he picked London up from the Samsons' B and B and drove to Anchorage.

They'd talked about Hazel and Tillie, and then Moose had called them about the rescue, and by the time they reached the Tooth, London had downloaded the weather report and the wind report and gone quiet, in the zone, ready to fly.

He always returned from a rescue a little buzzed on adrenaline, tired and yet wired, needing to work out the knots of his rescues, and sometimes, he hit the gym in the Tooth.

Especially tonight. After they'd gotten back to the Tooth, Shep had watched London leave with Boo, and she'd been friendly enough.

Because, *hello*, that's all they were. Friends. And that's probably all they would ever be. Even with Oaken's words in his head. *"When you find the one, you know, right?"*

If he could, Shep would go back to the moment he'd invited

her to Anchorage and tell her the truth. Or instead, he'd return to that day on the mountain three years ago and not let her leave.

As if he had had a choice, but . . .

He finished his sandwich, grabbed a pickle, ate it, and put the jar in the fridge.

Then he went into the locker room, changed clothes, and came out in workout gear. Moose hadn't exactly built a full gym, but the workout room contained mirrored walls, a weight set, a Nordic track, a treadmill, and an elliptical.

He got on the elliptical and turned on the flatscreen.

Oh, perfect, the finale of their stupid show, and this one had the scene with Oaken returning to greet Mike Grizz and his happy family.

Never mind the fact that someone Mike had trusted had tried to kill him.

Shep turned up the resistance. The fact was, he'd never wanted to be her babysitter. But he owed Colt. And shoot, of course he cared for London.

Colt's words in his head burned through him. *"The more she believes that she's started over, that she's safe, that no one knows what she's done and who she is, the more she relaxes. And then, maybe we get lucky."*

Get lucky how? Someone would try to kill her?

Yeah, Shep wanted out. Or at least, he wanted to tell her the truth.

"I thought I'd find you here."

He looked over his shoulder.

London stood in the doorway, her hair pulled back, dressed in workout gear.

"Hey." Did he sound guilty? He felt like he sounded guilty. He slowed the elliptical. He hadn't broken a sweat yet, but his heart thundered.

"Are you here to work out?"

"Nope."

The elliptical stopped. He got off, grabbed a towel. At least he didn't smell. He wiped his face.

She stood there, arms folded. "We need to talk."

Oh? And suddenly—*oh no*, had she figured him out? Their conversation from the elevator yesterday rushed back at him. Sarah Walker. Chuck.

Captain Awesome. *Whatever.*

"I can't stop thinking about . . ."

And here it came—

"The kiss."

Right. *That.*

"I know that . . . you probably thought that my hesitation was about Tomas, and losing him, but it wasn't. I . . . there's something you don't know—"

He held up his hand. "We don't need to go back there, London. It's in the past. I know you need time."

She stepped up to him. "Actually, that's the thing. I don't need time. I . . . I don't know why I thought I wasn't ready, but . . . I am ready."

He blinked at her. *Oh—*

She stepped closer, touched his arm. "You were amazing today. As always. You always know what to say, what to do, and you're the most . . . honest, real man I've ever met." She smiled, shook her head. "Trust me, I've known plenty of jerks. But with you, what you see is what you get, and that's . . . refreshing. And super sexy. And . . ." She caught her lip, then looked up, searching his face. "You should give kissing me another go."

He stilled. *No, no—*

But what was he going to do? She was right there, stepping up to him, lifting her face to his.

And again, his brain got up and walked out the door, down the hall, and sat down on the sofa while his arms went around her, while she curled hers around his neck, and while he lowered his mouth to hers.

No, no—

Yes. Because she tasted sweet, her body warm and strong against his, and somehow it felt right and good to simply hold her.

Finally.

And then the wanting started. Deep inside, it curled through him, a desire that he'd banked for a long, long time, so long he'd forgotten the power of it.

Oaken's voice tiptoed into his head. *"When you find the one, you know, right?"*

Yes.

Except, Colt was there too . . . *"She's already been betrayed once. . . ."*

He lifted his head. "London, stop. Stop."

Even as the words emerged, he winced. What was he *doing*? But he couldn't kiss this amazing woman and keep secrets from her.

Not when he knew how secrets destroyed.

She stepped back. "What?"

"London." He caught her hand. "Listen . . ." The confusion in her beautiful eyes just locked him right up. "I need to tell you something. You don't know everything about me. I'm not . . . all . . . you think."

She made a face then, a sort of incredulous look and shook her head. "What kind of secrets do you have? Seriously."

He took a breath. "Okay, but first, I need to tell *you* something."

She narrowed her eyes.

Then, "I know you were a spy."

And that stopped her cold. She drew in a breath. "What?"

"I know you did covert ops . . . and I know that something terrible happened on that mountain three years ago. Something more than an avalanche and your fiancé dying."

"I think that was enough."

He held up his hand. "Terrible enough for you to change your name and go into hiding as a so-called missionary in Nigeria."

Her eyes widened. "I wasn't hiding—"

"I know all this because . . . Colt is my friend too."

A beat.

"Colt? You're friends—since when?"

"We served together."

"Before or after he was captured by Boko Haram? Because that's how I know him—he was in Nigeria working private security for a doctor at a refugee camp in Nigeria and got kidnapped."

"Before. I was with the Tenth Mountain Division and got seconded to Colt's Ranger team, as a medic. But most importantly, Colt . . . he asked me to keep an eye on you."

She looked at him and then . . . laughed. *Laughed?*

"Seriously?"

"Yes—"

"Okay, yes, I can see that. And that makes sense. He always thought I was a CIA agent or something." She shook her head. "Colt is wrong. I was never a CIA agent. But I was definitely Agent Walker." Then she winked.

And just like that, the world froze, cracking.

The fact was, despite everything, London had never actually *lied* to him. Omitted, yes. Kept her past a blank slate, of course.

But lied to him straight out?

Never.

Until now.

"See, that wasn't so hard, was it?" Then she cupped his face. "No more secrets."

Yeah, whatever. He caught her wrists, pulled her hands away. "No. Colt asked me *a year ago* to watch over you."

"What?" She shook from his grip.

Aw. Because now he remembered the rest of Colt's words. *"If you tell her, it's over."*

But the fact was, one of them had to stop lying.

"He told me you were in trouble. And that you needed a fresh start. So he asked me to connect you to Moose, and . . ."

"You're serious." She took a step back. "You brought me here to *spy* on me?"

"No—I was trying to protect you."

"By lying to me?"

He bit his words back, arched his eyebrow, and then, "I don't think I'm the only one lying here, London."

She gasped. "I don't know what I was thinking . . ."

"London!"

She held up her hand. "Just stay away from me."

Then she walked away.

And he stood there, like the man in the river hanging on to his car, watching the floodwater of his own lies sweep everything away.

"Is your answer always pie?"

Tillie sat in the truck cab overlooking Kincaid Park, the wan light of a nearby streetlight shining against the pavement, the waters of the Cook Inlet dark save for the moonlight tipping the waves.

On the other side of the road, across from the park, Ted Stevens Airport shone like a beacon in the night, and occasionally, airplanes jetted off for the lower forty-eight or Hawaii, or even international destinations like Russia or Seoul.

An empty container sat between them, just the crumbles of an order of hot, spicy midnight chicken remaining, along with a few unclaimed French fries.

But it was the apple pie that seemed to find the right place in her empty stomach. Cinnamon, nutmeg, apples . . .

Or maybe it was the just sense of . . . safety. Of being with Moose, and . . .

She shouldn't be here. But she hadn't been able to stop herself from lowering his bear gun when he'd stepped up to her, his expression gentle and urgent, his soft voice delivering the words she so longed to believe. *"You can trust me. I will help you."*

Starting, apparently, with chicken and pie.

"The answer *is* always pie," he said now, finishing off his own piece of pie. "It's better than a shot of whiskey."

She glanced at him, not expecting that comment. "Oh, really?"

He gave her a wry look. "Yep."

There was so much more there, in his eyes. But they weren't here to unearth *his* demons.

So she took a breath and, "My mom made amazing apple pie." And she didn't know where that had come from, but starting there felt easiest.

He closed his empty pie container and picked up a cup of hot cocoa, sipped it. He'd pushed his front seat back and now leaned back into the door, considering her. "I would have expected key lime pie in Florida."

"Apple is my dad's favorite. He's from Minnesota. He moved to Florida when he was a teenager, and met my mom. She was originally from Puerto Rico, and her family were immigrants."

"Not really, though, because you're a US citizen, too, if you're born in Puerto Rico."

"True. And both of my parents took that pretty seriously. My dad enlisted after 9-11. I was six years old. He became a marine."

"That makes sense."

"We lived in North Carolina for the first four years—he was deployed on a ship, and then he reenlisted and became a Marine Raider."

"MARSOC."

"Yeah. We moved off base and bought a home in Jacksonville,

North Carolina, and then, when I was twelve, my mom died of cancer."

"I'm so sorry."

"It was terrible. Worst part was that they didn't catch it early—she was sick a lot and finally got in to see the doctor, and when she did, it was all over. She died less than three months later. Dad was devastated."

Moose nodded.

"I had sort of stepped up by then. My sister was ten, and I did a lot of the cooking. Made a mean pot of macaroni and cheese. And ramen."

"And milkshakes?"

She didn't know why her eyes wetted. But of course he'd put that together. Because Moose was exactly that thoughtful.

"Yes. My mom loved milkshakes. They tried chemo for a while, but after one round, it didn't work, and she decided not to try any more. So Dad came home from deployment, and we went on a family vacation to Florida and . . . then she died, just a couple months later."

"Wow."

"He didn't know what to do with us. He'd been gone for most of our lives, really, and . . . he could have gotten out of the military, but it was all he knew, so he went back in and put us in foster care. The last thing he ever said to me was that he'd be back. And then we pinky promised, and I never saw him again."

She swallowed, hating how that still made her entire body ache.

"You didn't have family in Minnesota?"

"No. Dad was an only, and his mom had died. His dad remarried, and the stepmom didn't want us."

"I'm sorry."

"Yeah. Mom's family wasn't able to take us either. Her parents were in assisted living, and she had a brother, but Dad didn't know where he was, so . . . yeah, foster care was the only option. Dad worked with a family rep from the military, and we went with a family who understood military deployments. But . . . it didn't make it any easier. Pearl and I felt orphaned."

"I'll bet."

She'd closed up her Styrofoam box and put it on the dash.

"Pearl met Rigger when she was about fourteen. He was my age, two years older than her. That's also when she experimented with drugs for the first time. Oh, I was mad. After our mom died of cancer, I thought, how could she do that to her body, you know? She saw our mom suffer, and all those drugs were destroying her too."

He nodded. "But kids don't think about their health. They're just hurting and need to fix it. "

"Yes. And I panicked. I threatened to turn her in to our foster mom if she didn't stop using."

His mouth made a grim line.

"Yeah, I know. She got mad and ran away, and I went out looking for her, and we both ended up in juvie as runaways. We switched foster homes then, to another military family, but not far enough away from Rigger, and it happened again."

"Did your dad find out?"

"I don't know. By that time, we'd gotten word that he'd gone missing, so . . . I figured I'd have to take care of her."

"So you enlisted."

"I was seventeen, took my GED and got emancipated. Then I joined up. Went to boot camp, deployed to Afghanistan."

"What was your MOS?"

She picked up a plastic bag and put the empty containers in it. "Counterintelligence."

He said nothing.

She looked up.

"You were a spy?"

"No. Hand me your container."

He did and she put it in the bag.

"I was an interrogator."

"Seriously? I mean—don't get me wrong. I know you're smart and tough, but—"

"I scored high on my ASFAB and in the intelligence tests. And I had a gift for languages. I wasn't involved with anything sketchy like you see in the movies. I vetted female interpreters and sometimes questioned Afghani women who came in with information, and rarely—very rarely—I went to get information with some of my team, connecting with Afghani women who worked as informants."

"That sounds *plenty* sketchy. Wow. Do you speak Afghani?"

"You mean Dari? Yes."

He wore what looked like admiration in his eyes.

"What—you thought I just waited tables?" She smiled.

"Clearly, I'm an idiot. You are . . . surprising, Tillie."

"Don't beat yourself up too much. I worked hard to slough off my past, become the Tillie who served you late night chicken." She shrugged. "I liked that Tillie."

"I like that Tillie too," he said quietly.

"I'll bet you're thinking, How did she go from top security clearance to on the run in Alaska with kidnapping charges?"

He held up his hands. "No judgment here. We all have stories, but . . . yes."

"The short of it is that I came home after my first deployment and found that Pearl had run away again. Rigger had moved to Florida, and she'd followed him. I found her living with him. He'd started his MMA career, and she was still using. I asked for a transfer to the base in Tampa and got it, and took her away from Miami and put her in treatment. We were good for a year, and then I got deployed onto a ship for my last year. When I came home, she'd moved back to Miami. He'd married while she was away, and she got jealous. I don't know. . . ." She sighed. "She just couldn't see herself as deserving better, I think. Anyway, she was pregnant, and

I left active duty and went into the reserves. She was so desperate to be near Rigger that she ran away to Miami and refused to return, so I requested a transfer. They have a reserve base there. And Rigger . . . I don't know. I was hoping that after the baby came, she'd see what a jerk he was. Unfortunately, for a while, he wasn't. Maybe he felt guilty, but after the baby came, he started coming around. I'm not sure why—although, seeing how old his kids are now, my guess is that his wife was pregnant with twins then. So yes, a total jerk. But we didn't know that, and then he asked me if I wanted to earn serious cash."

She had folded up the takeout bag. Put it in the back. Now she sighed. "I'd gotten in over my head trying to take care of Hazel and Pearl and so I agreed. And I thought I could learn a few things. I did one event and was done."

"You lost?"

"No, I won, but I . . . I didn't like it. I wasn't filled with rage. I was filled with terror. My only goal was to stay alive."

"Yeah. I've seen those bouts. There are some terrifying people in there."

"Yeah, like Rigger. He was the light heavyweight champion at the time. Billed me as his protégé, so I had to perform. I saw the future, and I tapped out."

"But you still trained with him."

"He was furious with me. That's when I started really seeing the danger. He was getting rough with Pearl, and Hazel too."

Overhead, a passenger jet took off, rumbling the van.

"I agreed to train for the Iron Maiden to sort of cool him off. But I liked it. It was more than just strength. There was strategy and timing and . . ."

"And you were good at it."

"I needed to be. We needed the money."

"Was Pearl using again?"

"No. But Pearl just couldn't say no to him. So I decided that we needed to get out of Miami, but I needed cash. I started putting away my win money."

"And then?"

She frowned.

"You said you could destroy him. How?"

Oh, that. She looked away at the headlights from cars slicing through the night.

"Tillie. Did you see him hurt someone?"

She closed her eyes.

"*Kill* someone?"

She swallowed, then slowly nodded. "It happened while I was training for the Iron Maiden. I went in late one night, after I got off work, and I walked in on him in the practice ring, fighting a kid. I think he was seventeen years old. They were sparring, but it had gotten out of hand. The kid was tough and angry and, I don't know—could be that Rigger just wanted to put him in his place, but . . . I walked in right about the time he got him in a rear naked choke hold and . . . Rigger broke his neck."

Moose groaned, deep inside his chest.

"I saw it. And Rigger knew I'd seen it. And he told me that if I ever told anyone, he'd do the same to me, but . . . I didn't care. I walked away, and I was going to tell the cops, but then he paid a visit to Pearl." She reached up and wiped her cheek. She hadn't realized she'd been crying. "And that's when it all went south."

Suddenly, Moose's warm hand covered hers, held it.

She turned hers over, threaded her fingers through his. Swallowed. "He came over and beat up Pearl and threatened her and . . . that's when we left." There, she'd gotten it out.

His jaw tightened. "Did he hurt you?"

She made a face, then, "Yes. I came in during the attack and I just . . . I lost it. I picked up a tire iron and just . . ."

"I remember the tire iron."

"What?"

"No wonder you attacked me when I came up on you in the parking lot a few months back."

"Moose, I didn't—"

"Hey. Calm down. I get it."

By the texture of his expression, he did. And that might be worse, because now she was broken, damaged, and crazy in his eyes. . . .

"I really hurt him, I think. And maybe that's what this is about. He says he wants the money. And Hazel. But I think he just wants to hurt me. Really hurt me."

"That's not going to happen."

His tone cut through her, stiffened her. A fierceness had entered his expression.

"I don't think you can . . . I mean . . . I *did* kidnap Hazel. Sorta."

"You probably saved her life. And Pearl's."

Aw. Now her eyes really glazed. "Pearl already had cancer by then. She lived for two more years after we got to Alaska."

"Why Alaska?"

"That was Roz's idea. She was a cop I met at the gym. One of Rigger's gyms, ironically. I didn't know where to go, what to do, so I went to her house. Pearl and I were both bleeding, and Hazel was hysterical, and Roz wanted us to press charges, but all I could think was that they'd find out that Pearl had been using, and I was afraid they'd put Hazel in foster care . . . and then somehow, Rigger would get her. . . . I don't know. I just panicked, I guess. Roz always wanted to live in Alaska, so she fixed us up with a guy named Hecktor who made fake passports. I was afraid that Rigger could track us—I don't know why. So I drove to Alaska. We've been hiding ever since. Roz showed up a few months later and became like a grandma to Hazel."

"No wonder she fought so hard for you two to get away."

Tillie nodded, her eyes filling. "Yeah, and I guess she's the one who took the money, too."

"Really?"

"She put it in a safe deposit box, under my name—my fake name—at a nearby bank. The key is at her house, on the lawn-mower chain."

"Smart."

"She told me that Pearl had put a phone in there, too. I have a feeling I know what's on it—and it might be enough to exonerate me. Or at least mitigate the kidnapping charge. But how am I supposed to get into a bank? They have cameras, and by now, I'm sure half of Anchorage is looking for me."

"Not half of Anchorage, but . . . " He gave a tight-lipped nod.

For the first time, a spear shot through her, and she caught her breath. He wouldn't—

"So we need a place to hide out while we figure this out."

Aw. Now she really did want to weep. She wiped her cheeks again. "Are you sure, Moose? I mean—I didn't mean to get you this deep into trouble with me."

"You think I'm just going to let you drive off into the night without helping you?"

She swallowed. "Um, yes."

He met her gaze, his steady, almost painful. "Then you don't know me as well as I thought you did."

Oh. But, "You're such a . . . such a great guy. You're always so calm, and . . . I just never meant to drag you into all this. You don't deserve it."

His gaze didn't waver. "It's not about deserving. None of us deserve grace. But when we get it, we pass it along. You don't know me as well as you think, Tillie, and there's a big part of me that doesn't want you to. But the fact is, I have my own dark past that makes me understand you more than you think." He squeezed her hand again. "And someday I'll tell you about that. But for now . . . let me help you. Because I want to, okay?"

Oh. My. She nodded and wiped her cheeks. "Shoot, I don't mean to make such a mess of your truck."

He laughed then, big and thick, and it cascaded over her, drowning out all her thoughts, her worries, and even her fears.

Because clearly this man wasn't afraid of her past, or her present—

"Okay, first thing tomorrow, we get that key. We get that money. And then we figure out how to clear you and get Hazel back."

—or . . . her future.

And suddenly, sitting in the warm car with him, watching the planes roar out into the darkness, listening to country music, the smells of chicken and apple pie seasoning the air, she couldn't help but taste . . . hope.

She caught her breath.

His gray-green eyes settled on hers, and if there hadn't been a console between them, she might have found herself with her arms around his neck, holding on.

Clearly it was a good thing the car had bucket seats.

"You okay?"

Not even a little. But she might be, if she held on tight. She nodded.

"Do you trust me, Tillie?"

She looked at his hand in hers, gripping it, warm, solid, and she had *nothing* but trust for this man.

Or just desperation. But all the same, she nodded. "Yes. Yes, I do."

"Good. Because I have a plan."

She cocked her head. "What kind of plan?"

He smiled, and she caught a spark of something almost dangerous in his eyes. "It's time for Staff Sergeant Tillie Young to show up for duty."

NINE

AND HERE MOOSE THOUGHT HE'D FOUND the perfect hiding place.

Country music star Oaken Fox's new home sat on a crest that overlooked the waters of Turnagain Arm, in an exclusive neighborhood off Seward Highway some forty-five minutes south of Anchorage.

But it could be hours away, given the seclusion, the tall Sitka spruce, mountain hemlock, and Alaskan yellow-cedar that surrounded the one-acre property.

Moose stood at the railing of the upstairs loft in his jeans and T-shirt, bare feet, listening as footsteps entered the hallway leading to the downstairs garages. Already, morning light gleamed through the two-story windows at the front of the great room, turning the oak floors to gold, casting over the white beams that crossed the expanse in the main room. The place had clearly been remodeled and given an updated shine, from the black leathered-granite countertops to the painted stone fireplace and the updated black-and-gold hanging ceiling fans.

He'd expected something a little more rugged country, with

moose heads and cowhides. It did have bearskin rugs, but the rest was sleek and modern, set against crisp white walls, leather furniture, and white overstuffed chairs, along with a gray granite table that could seat his entire team and then some.

A deep deck jutted out from the great room and overlooked the ocean, now glistening with light.

The footsteps stopped right below the loft, and for a moment, he thought Oaken had returned home. When Moose had texted Oaken last night—he didn't know where the singer had jetted off to for the weekend—Oaken had given him his code with the offer to stay as long as he needed.

Moose hoped he only needed one night. That somehow, getting the money from the bank's safe deposit box this morning might allow him to negotiate with Rigger and even get the guy to head back to Miami.

Except, that wouldn't erase Tillie's attack on Flynn.

Or untangle her from the kidnapping charges.

The footsteps started again, and into the great room walked a dark-haired man dressed in a chamois shirt, a pair of jeans, and wearing a padded vest.

He carried a bag of food and set it on the counter.

Then the man looked up.

Shep.

What?

"Hey, boss," Shep said. "Hungry?"

"Starved."

Shep reached inside the bag. "Oaken gave me the code to this place when he closed. I'm his security alert contact. He texted me last night and said you were going to be here and not to call the cops. So I brought donuts and coffee instead." He also pulled out a Styrofoam container. "And I picked up some egg muffins from the Sunrise Grill."

"Yum."

The voice came from across the room, the doorway to the lower level bedroom. Tillie stood there, dressed in a pair of sweatpants and a flannel shirt—clothes he'd picked up for her at a Walmart on their drive south.

Seemed like a better idea than trying to sneak back to the hospital to retrieve her car, if it was still in the parking lot.

Now she walked into the room, her long dark hair down, and slid onto a high-top stool.

Moose came down the stairs. "You're Oaken's security contact?"

"Yep," Shep said and put water into a kettle to heat on the stove. "I always loved this place—you can see it from the road, just sitting up here on the hill. So I told Oaken about it, and of course, he nabbed it up. Tillie, do you prefer coffee or tea?"

"I'm an anything-that-has-caffeine girl," she said and looked over at Moose as he settled on a stool. She seemed tired but less broken than last night.

Maybe it was just that she wasn't holding a gun on him. That memory still sat in his bones, along with her story of Rigger, and Pearl and Hazel.

And her soft words that had landed like stones on his heart. *"You're such a . . . such a great guy. You're always so calm."*

Right. Clearly she had no idea that he'd tossed the night away in the king-sized bed, staring through the skylight at the stars, reliving a few nights he'd like to forget.

"So, I heard about the fun and games at the hospital," Shep said, grabbing muffins to heat in the microwave. "Flynn's okay, by the way."

How Moose wanted to step between Tillie and Shep's words. But Tillie hadn't exactly filled him in on the details of her escape, so . . .

"Was she hurt?" Moose kept his voice low.

Tillie's mouth tightened and she looked away. "I tried not to hurt her—"

"She wasn't hurt. Just stunned. And bruised—and surprised." Shep pulled out a coffeepot and a drip filter. "Clearly she wasn't expecting you to sweep out her feet and run."

"For the record, I wasn't either. I just . . . reacted. And panicked." Moose nodded.

"Does Flynn know she's here?" Moose asked.

The kettle whistled. "Of course not," Shep said. "I can keep a secret. But it won't be long before Axel figures out you're together."

"I think he already has. I have three missed calls from him from last night."

Tillie looked at Moose, eyes wide. He shook his head. "Don't worry. We're going to figure this out."

"And get my daughter back."

"Yes," he said softly.

Shep took a mug from the cupboard and poured Tillie a cup of coffee.

She took it, and an egg muffin on a napkin. "I'm going to take a shower."

When she'd closed the bedroom door behind her, Shep turned to Moose, voice low. "What's your plan?" Moose took a breath, and Shep added, "Really. I can keep a secret."

"I just don't want to get you into trouble," Moose said.

"Moose. Trouble is always with us. It's how we react in trouble that matters." Shep set a cup of coffee in front of him. "It's never the right thing to let a brother carry a burden alone." He pushed the plate of egg muffins toward Moose. "God tells us to pray that we'll lead a peaceful and quiet life, godly and dignified in every way. We don't do that because our lives are actually calm. But our spirit can be. And we can respond in a godly way to our circumstances. Anyone can see that you're in up to your chin here, and the water is rising."

Moose ran his hands down his face. "Maybe."

"Listen, I know a little about being in over your head." He

picked up his mug of coffee. "I was caught in an avalanche in the Alps many years ago. Took them three days to get me free, and in that time, all I had was faith—and another person, trying to keep me alive. And that was enough."

"How did I not know this about you?"

Shep gave a half smile. "Listen. I know you feel responsible for everyone. But the truth is, you're not the only one wearing the red Air One uniform. And I know this isn't our standard rescue, but it's just as important. Just as lifesaving."

"I don't want anyone ending up in jail."

"Me either. So we bring Flynn into this, tell her the whole story—whatever it is—and get her on our team. The truth is hard, but I think it's the only way."

"I don't know, Shep. That puts Flynn in a bad position."

He set the coffee down. "Or it arms her with truth. And what about your cousin Dawson?"

Dawson did owe him. Or he owed Dawson—Moose had never sorted it all out. *Still.* "Okay. Tillie told me a few things last night that might help. I need you to tell Flynn—and then have her and Daws track down Rigger. If he's still in Anchorage, we need to know."

Shep said nothing.

"Tillie has information on Rigger that could blow up his life."

"Now this makes sense."

Moose nodded. "Sit down. I'm going to fill you in on the big pieces."

Thirty minutes later, after he'd given Shep the rundown, and after Moose had emerged from the bedroom, showered and put together, Shep left. Now Tillie was seated on the black leather sofa, watching the news.

"Where's Shep?" she asked as Moose came downstairs.

"Running an errand," he said and sat down opposite her. "I think the bank is about open. Ready to get your money?"

She sat up, turned off the television. "No more interviews with Julian Richer."

"Maybe he's left town, put this all behind him."

"Maybe tomorrow there will be world peace."

He smiled. "Right."

She leaned forward, clasped her hands together. "Listen, Moose. Let's say I get the money and the phone, and it has what I hope on it. . . . I still can't risk going to Flynn. She'll arrest me and ask questions later, and that means Hazel stays in foster care. I can't do that to her."

Oh, Tillie. "You need to start thinking beyond this moment. You need to start believing that there is a way out that doesn't involve you running."

She blinked at him. "That's what I've done my entire life."

He raised an eyebrow.

"What do you suggest?"

"Trust."

"I'm here, aren't I? Trusting you."

"Not me. I want you to trust *God.*"

She narrowed her eyes.

"What if you started to look for God, his provision, his rescue, his love?"

She swallowed.

"You said you believe in God. Is it so difficult, then, to believe that he might care about you?"

"How?"

"Not to be arrogant, but I believe there's a reason I kept coming into the Skyport during your shift for a year. Maybe we were supposed to meet. Supposed to end up right here. Because God cares very much about our lives."

"If God cared, then my mother wouldn't have died, my father would have come home, and Pearl wouldn't have gotten cancer."

Okay. He got that. Still, "Or that was the natural consequences of a fallen world and man's sinful choices. What if there is a different perspective?"

"What kind of perspective?"

"Faith. Faith that God knows what he's doing. That he loves you, even in the pain. Faith that everything, for someone who trusts God, works together for good."

"Is that like hoping that things will work out? Feels like a platitude."

"Or the only real answer. You can believe, or you can go it alone. I choose to believe."

She swallowed. "It doesn't feel good."

"No, sometimes it doesn't. But that's where the faith comes in. And ultimately, we have to believe that God is for us, in all of it."

She sighed. "Faith. I'm going to need it for your epic plan, aren't I?"

"Might help."

"Fine. For you, I'll try and trust God."

"And not panic."

"And not panic."

"And not run."

She drew in a breath. "And. Not. Run."

"Good. Because you're going to have to do all that if this plan is going to work."

He got up and went over to the counter where he'd taken out the contents of the Walmart bag. "Do you know how to make a hijab?"

She walked over and found the long black scarf. "I can make this work. Why?"

"Because Alicia Torre is now Muslim."

Her mouth opened. And then she smiled. "Okay. Yeah. This could work." She picked up the scarf and headed to the bathroom.

A few moments later, she emerged, her head covered.

Meanwhile, Moose had put on a baseball hat, pulled on his jacket. Hopefully no one at Northern Skies Bank knew him. He grabbed a shoulder bag with a long strap and waited as she walked to the door, carrying her bag of toiletries and extra clothing.

He handed her the shoulder bag.

"What's this for?"

"The contents of the box."

"Right." She pulled the strap over her head.

He held the door open. "First stop, Roz's house. Then to the bank."

But she didn't move, just looked at him.

"What?"

"God will show me he cares by giving me back my daughter. Let's go." She headed out the door.

But he put a hand on her arm. Took a long breath. "Tillie, I need you to hear this. And I hope it find roost. God loves you even if you don't get your daughter back."

A terrible horror entered her eyes.

"No panicking. But I need you to know that." Then he pulled her to himself, held her, and closed his eyes.

"Lord. We don't know what you have planned, but we trust you. We commit this crazy endeavor into your hands, and . . . yes, we ask for favor. For us to trust the outcome you desire. And we humbly ask that you bring Hazel back to Tillie and give us justice. Amen."

When he lifted his head, she was staring at him, her eyes glossy. "Okay." Then she headed through the front door and down the stairs into the garage.

And he stepped outside and looked heavenward. *Please.*

"We're going to get caught," Tillie said.

"No, we're not," Moose said as he opened the door where his truck was parked on the street behind Roz's house near Earthquake Park. He'd told Tillie to stay put, then sneaked into the back door of the garage, bypassing the yellow crime tape in the front. He'd emerged with the key on the ring with the yellow flip-flop five minutes later.

Now he slid into the truck's front seat with a grin.

"Please don't smile."

"We're going to figure out a way out of this. You'll see." Moose put the key in her hand. "Keep holding on to faith."

When he looked at her like that, his gray-green eyes on her, his dark hair curling out of his baseball cap, when he winked and grinned, she might do exactly that. Because Moose just seemed to radiate faith, and it caught her up, made her taste it, long for more of it.

So, yes. "Just drive."

He pulled out. "What's on this phone we're going after?"

"I don't know. But I think it could be a voicemail that she'd saved for a long time of Rigger threatening to take Hazel away if I said anything about Matthew's death. She played it for me a couple days after it happened, and I asked her to save it, just in case." She could still hear his voice, see the expression of terror on Pearl's face.

"Why didn't you take it to the police?"

She looked over at him. "I wanted to. But he had a hold on her that she couldn't break away from."

"Abusers do that."

"Addiction does that. I think she thought she couldn't escape him."

He turned onto Hickel Parkway. "Until someone showed her the way." He glanced at her. "Clearly you're in the rescue business too."

She gave a laugh. "Moose, sometimes the way you see me—"

"Is exactly right."

Oh.

But she smiled. Glanced at him. "You're always so unflappable."

He laughed at that, then, "Not on the inside, honey."

She didn't mind the *honey* so much. Or at all. In fact, the word sank through her, found her bones, turned her warm.

They pulled into the Northern Lights Alaskan Bank. A two-story brick building with windows along the front and two cameras over the front door that had probably already captured them.

Moose parked around the side. "Put on that headscarf."

"Fine." She put on the scarf, tucked it under her chin, around to the back of her neck and even tied it. "I don't think this is going to work."

"It will. Here's the fun part. I want you to speak Dari."

"My passport says I'm American."

"Yeah, but I think you're a foreign bride."

She looked at him. "Your foreign bride?"

He grinned.

"For Pete's sake."

"Say that in Dari."

She looked at him. *Fine.*

He raised his eyebrows at the words that emerged.

"Okay, that was actually the phrase 'the night is long and the dervish awake.'"

"And it means . . ."

"There's a long way between here and success."

"Indeed. So, go in, show your ID, and then I'll translate for you—"

"Listen, even if I speak Dari, they're not going to let you in with me. Not unless I sign paperwork." She stopped on the sidewalk. "Let me take it from here." She looked up at him, patted his chest. "But you can stick around should anything go south."

His mouth closed. "Okay. But . . . I don't want the cameras to pick up your voice, so speak low. Show your ID, get the box, and leave."

"Sir, yes sir."

He rolled his eyes.

They'd started walking in the front door when his words filled her head— *"We commit this crazy endeavor into your hands, and . . . yes, we ask for favor."*

The words lingered now as she walked up to a teller. Not busy, the place held a hush, and she didn't look, but felt a dozen cameras on her.

She pulled out her passport. "Hello. I need to access a safe deposit box."

The teller, a woman in her early sixties, took the passport, then keyed the information into her computer.

Moose had stepped behind Tillie, away a little, head down.

"Yes, Ms. Torre." The teller slid off her chair and walked over to an office, rapped on the window.

A man got up, and they huddled for a moment. Tillie didn't move. The teller returned. "Do you have your key?"

Tillie held it up.

"Very good. You'll meet our branch manager by the security entrance." The woman pointed to a door near the back of the room, and Tillie took her passport and headed over.

Moose followed her.

But when they reached the door, the branch manager held up his hand. "Sorry, sir, just the owner from here."

Admittedly, she felt a little naked walking through the big steel door, opened by a swipe of a card, then a code, and finally a fingerprint.

She didn't glance back at Moose, however, just followed the banker through, into the safe deposit box room. Three walls with white metal boxes, with two key locks in each door.

For a second, she was back at the hospital, Flynn saying she was going to arrest her. She hazarded a look at the banker, who was searching the room for her number, written on a card, and only then did she check behind her.

No one seemed to be rushing to call security, so . . .

"Box 2301." The banker stopped in front of a box and she walked over. Handed him her key.

He unlocked the door and pulled out a long inner box.

It didn't seem heavy enough for a hundred thousand dollars. He set it on the nearby table.

"I'll close the door behind you. Buzz when you are ready to leave." He indicated a doorbell by the massive door.

Then he left her there, closing her in, and she looked up just in time to see Moose's gaze on her. It wasn't unlike a prison, the room austere and cold. She blew out a breath and opened the box.

No money.

She stared at it, not sure why it felt like a punch.

No. Money.

Roz had *lied* to her.

Except—Pearl's old phone sat in the box, on top of an envelope.

She pulled out the phone, then the envelope. Stuck it in the bag, then closed the box and put it back. Shut the door and removed her key.

Then she pushed the bell. A buzz sounded, and the door clicked.

From the outside, the banker opened it.

"All done?"

"Thank you," Tillie said and marched past him. Didn't even look at Moose, although she saw him pocket his phone as she walked out into the brisk morning air.

Only then did she take a breath, the air crisp and smelling of autumn, the scent of loam in the air.

Moose had followed her out, of course, and now touched her elbow. "Keep moving."

Right.

She stood and headed with him to the truck. Slid into the seat, then while she strapped in, he put the truck in reverse and pulled out.

"You look pale."

She pulled off the hijab. "The money is gone."

He glanced over at her. "What?"

"The money. It's gone." She unzipped her bag and pulled out the phone. "Just this and an envelope."

She tried to power on the phone, but it was dead. "We'll need a charger."

"Look in the glove box," he said, and turned onto Minnesota Drive, heading north.

She opened the box and found the neatest, most organized glove box she'd ever seen. And a number of USB charging cables.

"I keep a few in there—never sure what I'll need."

She found an old USB C and plugged it into Pearl's Android phone and then into Moose's console. The phone's face lit up, the battery indicating zero. "It'll take a few minutes."

"Open the envelope." He turned onto Northern Lights Boulevard.

"Where are you going?"

"Trust me."

Her mouth tightened. She pulled out the envelope. Her name was scrawled on the front, and she recognized Roz's handwriting.

The return address was an insurance company—Guardian of Alaska.

She opened it just as Moose pulled onto a side street. Looking up, she recognized Turnagain Parkway. "Are we going to Roz's?"

"Nope. What's that?"

She pulled out a piece of letterhead, the name of the company embossed on the front, the letter addressed to her, and she must have made a little noise because—

"Tillie. You okay?"

"It's a life insurance policy."

He had braked at a stop sign and now looked over at her. "A life insurance policy?"

"It's a cover letter that outlines a whole life insurance policy. It's taken out on Roz, but Hazel's the beneficiary."

He went through the stop sign, continued along Turnagain. "So Pearl took the money and put it in a whole life policy? Why not herself?"

"Probably they wouldn't approve her, since she had cancer."

"That makes sense. And it couldn't accumulate value. What's the cash value?"

"A what?"

He turned on Illiamna Avenue. "A cash value. Most whole life policies have a death benefit and a cash value. Who is the owner of the policy?"

She scanned the letter. "I think I am."

"That Pearl. Smart."

"What do you mean, smart? How am I supposed to pay Rigger back with a life insurance policy?"

He stopped at an intersection. "You use the payout from the cash value. And then, when Roz dies, you'll also get the death benefit minus the cash value. How much is the death benefit?"

"It says it's five hundred thousand, but—"

"When was it taken out?"

"Three years ago, right before my sister died."

He nodded. "It's probably worth that or more by now with compound dividends."

"But why put money in a policy in the first place?"

He pulled up to Lyn Ary Park, found a parking spot facing the baseball diamond. Turned to her. "Let me see it."

She handed over the letter. He scanned it. Then he handed it back to her. "I think so that you would have bargaining power. The hundred grand is yours to access. And if you do, you can give it to him. But I guarantee it's been growing in value over the past three years. My guess is that Pearl knew you'd have legal fees too."

"What do you mean, legal fees?"

He looked up, past her, and she nearly left her skin when a rap sounded on the window.

A man with dark hair, smiling, wearing a jacket and a pair of hiking pants, stood at her door. "Who—"

Moose rolled down his window and leaned over her. "Hey, Ridge."

"Moose."

"This is my friend Tillie."

"Tillie," Ridge said. "Moose says you have a story to tell." He held out his hand. She shook it, then turned her gaze to Moose.

"He's my new lawyer."

What? Her voice fell, whisper taut. "What have you done?"

His smile dimmed. "Tillie. Trust me."

"Moose. What have you *done*?"

"Tillie. He's my *lawyer*. He's not going to turn you in."

"Moose told me a little of your situation on the phone this morning," Ridge said, his hands in his pockets.

How—

"And you're going to need me, if the morning news is right." Ridge pulled out his phone, then opened an app and showed them a video.

Julian Richer stood outside the Federal Building, with its creamy gray exterior, surrounded by reporters, and next to him, Flynn Turnquist.

Tillie held her breath as Julian spoke.

"I'm here as an advocate for all custodial parents who have had their children stolen from them. Seven years ago, I had a child with a woman who, sadly, passed away, and since then, I have been searching for my daughter. She was found last night with her aunt, a noncustodial guardian who fled custody and is at large. On behalf of all parents out there seeking their children, I want to thank the Anchorage Police Department and especially Detective Turnquist for their help in getting my daughter back."

Tillie stared at the phone, shaking.

"Tillie. Calm down—"

"No." She looked at Moose. "I have to find Hazel before he hops on a plane with her—"

"Yes," said Ridge. "Family law is not my specialty, but I called a friend, and they're working on an injunction to prevent Richer from taking Hazel out of Alaska right now. In the meantime, Moose texted and said you might have evidence against Richer that could help your case?"

She glanced at Pearl's charging phone. "I think so."

"Get in," Moose said, and Ridge climbed into the back seat.

She powered up the phone. The home screen showed a picture of baby Hazel.

Tillie's throat thickened as she opened the voicemail app. *Please, please*—

Empty.

What?

"She had a voicemail—it had Rigger recorded saying to stay away from her and Hazel."

"Could it be in the cloud?"

She searched through the files. . . . Nothing but a video file. She clicked on it.

And then she turned hollow as she watched Rigger charge onto her townhome deck and assault her sister while toddler Hazel cried from a nearby high chair.

"That's him?" Ridge said.

"This was on our Ring. I installed cameras when we moved in, afraid of this very thing."

And then . . . silence as they watched Pearl struggle against Rigger . . .

Tillie closed her eyes, remembering feeling it as if it were yesterday. Her, coming into the house, seeing Rigger beating Pearl, then grabbing a tire iron from her car and charging back onto the deck, now on camera . . .

"Wow, that's some swing you have there," Ridge said as the sound of her blow echoed through the video.

She opened her eyes to Rigger, sprawled on the ground, writhing, his head bleeding.

And then she watched as she grabbed up Hazel, then Pearl, and stumbled away from the shot.

The video stopped.

"He was in the hospital for nearly two weeks," she said quietly.

"Did he file assault charges?" Ridge asked.

"I don't know. We left right after that."

"I'll check into that."

"No voicemail about the murder," Moose said quietly.

She looked at him, then Ridge. No cash. No proof. No Hazel.

"If all of Anchorage wasn't on the lookout for you before . . ." Ridge said.

Moose touched his hand to hers, as if hoping that she'd stay instead of bolting from the truck.

"Ridge, I need you to look into the murder of a man named—" He looked questioningly at Tillie.

"Matthew Lopez."

"Yep. A little more than five years ago. He might be listed as missing. And then see what you can do to slow down Hazel's transfer of custody."

Ridge nodded.

"And get out of my truck and pretend you never talked to us. We'll be in touch."

Ridge's mouth made a grim line. "I know that you probably don't want to hear this, but the longer you run from custody, the worse it gets." He slid out of the back seat. "But I'll do what I can."

"Thanks, Ridge." Moose already had the car in reverse, pulling out.

"I want to find my daughter," Tillie said.

"I know." He turned onto Marston drive.

"Where are we going?"

He wore what looked like fury in his eyes. "Someplace where you'll be safe."

"I don't want to be safe."

He stopped at the light. Turned to her. His voice turned low and crisp. "That's very clear. But I need you to be safe if I'm going to get your daughter back."

His words shook through her. And that's when, for the first time, she realized that maybe, underneath it all, Moose Mulligan wasn't quite so safe, so calm after all.

TEN

MOOSE WAS TIRED OF BREAKING PROMISES.
But yes, this might be a bad idea of epic proportions.
As Moose stood beside his Cessna, under the dome
of the Quonset hut near the Tooth, fueling up before doing his
walkaround check, he just couldn't erase Tillie's expression from
his brain.

Hazel going back with Rigger just might be her worst nightmare
unfolding in front of her eyes.

So yeah, he was going to do something crazy. And it started
with getting Tillie someplace safe.

Otherwise called *running*.

Then he'd round up a friend—a.k.a., a former Ranger—who
might know exactly how to grab Hazel from the hands of a man
who was clearly dangerous.

Which meant—perfect—he'd be breaking the law too.

Already was, really.

Moose wanted to bang his head on the fuselage because, really,
this was not how a man lived by faith. This was not how he exhib-
ited a peaceful and calm life.

This . . . this was panic.

He gritted his jaw, hating Tillie's words churning inside him. *"You're always so unflappable."*

Right.

Outside, under the blue sky, the wind stirred the familiar redolence of the airport grounds—the odor of gasoline, the asphalt tarmac, even the scent of the ocean nearby. Tillie had gone into the Tooth to go to the restroom and make a couple sandwiches for their trip.

She'd gone silent when he'd told her his plan. So maybe he should keep an eye on her. . . .

Because certainly, she knew that trying to steal Hazel out of foster care could land her in jail for a decade, or more.

Even now, she was looking at possibly years behind bars.

"So, making a run for it, huh?"

He winced when Axel came walking up. He hadn't even heard his brother's Yukon drive up, so swallowed by his thoughts. Axel wore a jacket, a pair of jeans, and a rare baseball cap. As if he, too, might be on the lam.

"Naw." And right then, Moose made his decision. He couldn't do this. Couldn't fly away, stash Tillie, then return and . . . what? Kidnap Hazel and become a fugitive?

The jig was up.

But he still had promises to keep.

The gas gurgled, and he pulled out the fuel rod and stowed it on the fueling truck.

Axel fitted in the gas cap and closed the door. Turned. "This is a bad idea, and you know it."

"Mm-hmm." Moose pushed the cart away. "It's complicated."

"I know. But if you want to follow God's plan—and I can guarantee you that he has a plan here—you can't panic. And you can't fight without the armor of God. And that starts with the shield of faith guarding your heart."

Moose glanced at Axel as he walked back to the plane. "Since when did you turn all spiritual?"

"Since I had you for a big brother." Axel gave him a grim smile. "You can't know what to do without praying first."

Moose ran a hand across his mouth. "Yeah. You're right. I just . . . I can't seem to hear God with all the clutter in my head."

"The what-ifs."

How— Moose stared at him.

"I've been there." Axel shrugged. "If you want to do the right thing here, you need to stop listening to all the lies and start listening to the truth."

"Trying."

"Right. Okay, I'll help. The truth is that God has a plan. And he loves Tillie more than you do. And if you can show her what faith looks like, then maybe she'll have it too."

Right then, Flynn walked up behind Axel, out of uniform, dressed in a pair of jeans and a jacket, and smiled. "Hey."

Moose's entire body turned stiff. "What—"

"You've got to be kidding me!"

Moose looked past Axel, and his heart nearly stopped.

Tillie stood at the edge of the Quonset hut, holding a cooler and a duffel bag. But she wasn't staring at Moose or Axel—

"Tillie, just calm down," Flynn said.

Tillie put down the cooler.

"Hear me out." Flynn held up her hands in surrender.

Tillie looked past her to Moose, so much betrayal in her eyes. *No, Till*—

"I believe you." The words from Flynn sucked the air out of the hut, and even Moose stood breathless. "I did some digging, and Julian Richer is . . . he's got at least two assault charges in his past, both dismissed. He's also been connected with organized crime and some drug smuggling. Apparently the voters don't seem to care. How he got custody of Hazel, I don't know, but . . . after seeing his record, I believe you."

Tillie's hands fisted at her side. "There's more to the story."

"Shep filled us in."

Moose glanced at Axel.

"He found us this morning, right before the press conference. Flynn had no choice but to go through with the press conference."

"Pearl wanted me to raise Hazel," Tillie said softly.

"I am sure she did," Flynn said. "But Hazel's custody papers list Julian Richer as the father. And he used that to get custody and got the judge to issue a warrant for your arrest in Florida." Her voice lowered. "But Florida did not send your warrant to Alaska. And if you had let me finish in the hospital, you would have known I wasn't arresting you. I was going to help you get a lawyer and sort it out. You weren't under arrest. Then."

"And now?"

Flynn looked at Axel, back to Tillie. "I didn't file a report on the assault."

Tillie's fists unclenched. "So . . . I'm *not* under arrest?"

"Not here, not now. But if the police department in Miami-Dade County sends the warrant here, then . . ."

"And what about Hazel?"

"The court still needs to award her back to her father. I got a call from our CPS worker—apparently a local law firm just filed a motion for temporary child custody on your behalf."

"Where is she?" Tillie took a step into the garage.

"I can't tell you that."

Tillie took a breath, and Flynn held up her hand. "Because I don't know. I do know that she's safe. Richer isn't going to get her."

"That's because he doesn't want her. Not really. He wants *me*."

"And he's not going to get you," Moose said. "But I need to get you somewhere safe while we figure out how to prove everything you said."

"Moose—" Flynn turned to him. "What are you doing?"

He'd taken the wooden chocks from the front of his tires. "Leaving. C'mon, Tillie. Get in."

"Bro," Axel said and put a hand on Moose's arm. "You can't—"

"I can." He shook off Axel's hand, lowered his voice. "This is one thing I can do."

Then Axel drew in a breath and turned. "Get in, Flynn. If she's with you, then she's not running."

Flynn's eyes widened. "Okay."

Moose stood a little nonplussed for a moment as Axel helped Flynn up onto the wing and then into the plane. Axel then held a hand out for Tillie, who settled in beside Flynn in the back seat.

"I'm going to grab my go bag," Axel said and took off for the Tooth.

Okay then. Moose did his preflight external check, then climbed into the cockpit in time to hear Flynn say to Tillie, "Yeah, I'm fine. You need to teach me that move."

He fitted on his headset and did the rest of his preflight check as Axel stowed a duffel in the back, then climbed into the copilot seat.

Moose opened his window. "Prop clear!"

He started up the plane, and it shook to life, the prop whirring. Then he called to the tower and taxied out of the shed, onto the runway.

Axel had put on his own headset. "You sure about this?"

Moose nodded, surer every moment. He needed to think clearly, and there was only one place to do that.

They took off, the lift sweeping through him, scattering his thoughts, his focus on the instruments, the heading, the feel of the air under the wings.

Flying always set him a little free.

He turned northwest, the ridgeback mountains of the Alaska Range to the north, and took them over the shiny blue water of the Knik Arm, then north up the silvery trail of Alexander Creek,

Denali at his nose, rising tall and white. Here, the rivers turned serpentine below him, and he passed Susitna, then took the eastern branch, following the tributaries northwest.

"You sure you're ready to head back here?"

He glanced at Axel, nodded.

If there was one place where Rigger couldn't find them, it would be Pike's cabin.

The forest closed in around roads and trails, the lakes puddling below, deep blue, the terrain a lethal beauty. He finally descended toward a gravel riverbed, packed down, some fifty feet wide, with plenty of runway.

He touched down, the tundra tires finding purchase, and swung the plane around, ready for takeoff.

Axel took off his headset. "I've never been here."

Moose nodded. "The fishing cabin is up the hill." He turned and pointed to a not-so-little log cabin with a shiny red roof over-looking the river. "It's a little hike from here, but not far."

"What's a little hike from here?" Tillie asked.

Moose smiled. "A place that Pike Maguire once called paradise."

Axel had gotten out, now opened the door. Moose shut down the plane, then got out and secured the wheels. He tied the plane down and grabbed his bag—food, his computer, extra clothing. A nearby lodge had absorbed the cabin rental into their fly-in vacation package, but he'd checked his portal on his phone—no vacationers this weekend. And according to the weather forecast, a bit of a cold snap was headed their way.

Tillie wrapped her arms around herself as she turned to stand on the shore. She looked at the water, the blue sky. "I should have gotten Hazel."

He put his arm around her. "You will."

She drew in a breath then and leaned in. "She's a smart girl. Knows how to adapt."

"Yes, she is. I saw that."

"And we talked about this . . . the fact that someday she might have to stay with strangers. That's why she took her stuffed dog everywhere. Pearl gave it to her. It's sort of a security blanket."

"We'll get this sorted," Moose said and glanced at Flynn and Axel, walking up to the cabin.

He wanted to trust Flynn. Especially after she'd found the Midnight Sun Killer this summer. She was a good detective.

Please.

As Moose walked up the grassy bank to the log cabin, he could almost hear Pike's voice in the wind. *"I lift up my eyes to the mountains—where does my help come from? My help comes from the Lord, the maker of heaven and earth."*

He took Tillie's hand, and she didn't pull away.

Adirondack chairs set around a charred fire pit, along with a seasoned grill sitting on a side patio, suggested the rental had been well used this summer. He stepped up to the deck and turned, and of course, mountains enclosed him on all sides, this place nestled in a valley, like a secret.

Solar panels on the southern side of the house generated enough energy to fill the generators—Pike had made sure of that. And he'd installed indoor plumbing and a satellite for internet. Moose had never tried it. But Pike had watched a couple football games back in the year Moose had flown him out here, the place snug after an early snowfall.

Most importantly, Pike had added a cell repeater. In the end, it had saved their lives.

Moose pushed the door open and found Axel and Flynn inside, admiring the vaulted ceiling, the shiny logs, a few hunting trophies on the wall. The place replicated a Montana hunting lodge, complete with leather furniture that Pike had flown in before Moose's time, a long table, and a chandelier made of antlers that hung from the ceiling.

Off the main room was a kitchen, with a handful of bedrooms

on the other side. Stairs led to a lofted bedroom, the master that overlooked the great room, situated over the kitchen.

"This is nice," Flynn said. "It belongs to a friend?"

"Not anymore," Moose said. "Technically, it's mine."

Axel glanced at him, but he raised a shoulder. Truth. Even if he didn't want to face it.

The stone fireplace in the great room lay cold, with logs piled on the raised hearth.

"What are we doing here, Moose?" This from Flynn, who seemed clearly done with playing along.

"Here we're going to go over every detail of Tillie's story about Matthew Lopez. Then we're going to figure out how to prove it."

"Moose—" Flynn started.

"Nope. Flynn, you're smart. I know you can figure this out."

He walked into the kitchen and opened the freezer. Frozen coho salmon dated just a few weeks ago. And trout. And in the cupboard, rice and canned vegetables. "Meanwhile, I will feed you."

He walked back out into the room, looked at his team. "And then we're all going to get a decent night's sleep, for the love of Pete."

Tillie smiled.

And it was as if he heard God speaking very, very clearly.

"Let not your heart be troubled."

Yes. He'd just needed to get away for a moment, clear his head. He smiled back. "I hope you guys like fish."

It couldn't be right to feel this ... safe. This protected.

Even this happy.

Tillie sat on an Adirondack chair, drinking a cup of after-dinner hot cocoa, wrapped in a blanket she'd stolen from a basket in the great room, staring at the streak of remaining sunset that simmered over the mountains, jagged and whitened with the first whisper of snow.

So much beauty in a land filled with peril. And here she sat, tucked away from danger, warm and fed while Hazel...

Oh, Hazelnut. I'm sorry. Her eyes burned, and she blinked hard. She shouldn't have gotten on the plane. But Moose...

But Moose. He'd become a force in her life that she simply couldn't escape.

Even now, as the door to the cabin—ha, that was an understatement—opened and Moose came out onto the deck. He carried a cup and a blanket.

"Thanks for dinner," she said as he sat on the other Adirondack chair, setting his cup on the wide arm.

He wore the blanket like a cape, very Superman, like Hazel said. The man had the devastatingly handsome looks of the man of steel, with his dark hair and gray-green eyes. And under that flannel shirt, probably a frame to match.

He wore jeans and boots and a wry smile as he settled into the chair. "My pleasure. I love a good grilled salmon."

He'd done some magic with the frozen salmon, grilling it on a plank of wetted cedar. She'd half expected a grizzly to show up wondering why he hadn't been invited.

"You're quiet," Moose said softly.

She closed her eyes. "I shouldn't be here."

"Where should you be? Jail? In your car, running and hiding?"

She looked at him. *Right.* "I feel guilty for being..."

"For being." He met her gaze. "Yes, I think you do."

She frowned, looked away. *Huh.*

"I think deep down you're trying to figure out why Pearl died when she had a daughter to take care of, and you stayed."

"It feels cosmically unfair."

"Death always feels unfair, especially when it happens to someone young, like Pearl. Thankfully, God saves us from that unfairness by giving us hope."

"I don't feel saved."

He took a breath. "That's because right now, you're not."

A beat. "What?"

"It doesn't help you for me to lie to you, Tillie. Jesus came to save us from true death—eternal death. It's the greatest rescue mission of all time. But you have to be willing to be rescued. You can't rescue yourself. And that starts with acknowledging that you need rescue."

He met her eyes, said nothing.

"Like me showing up on your doorstep."

"Finally," he said. "The question is, If you know that God wants to rescue you, what is holding you back from reaching out?"

She looked away. "I guess I've never been good at asking for help. I saw it as weakness."

She took a sip of cocoa, ran her thumb down the mug. "Pearl was a princess. She dreamed of happy endings and a prince to save her." She stared at the sky, the streaks of rose gold. "I used to dream that too." She gave a harsh laugh. "I used to dream of my dad coming home, taking us out of foster care, rebuilding our family. He used to take us camping near Bear Island, a little campground with a pool and a slide, and sometimes we'd go out to the beach and bury him in the sand. He'd carry me into the waves, and we'd jump them together."

She leaned her head back. "Sometimes a huge wave would come in, and he'd tell me to duck, and we'd have to go under it. And the wave would crash over us, but as long as I held on to my dad, I was safe, you know?"

"Mm-hmm."

Wow, her chest had tightened, the back of her throat aching with the story. "Pearl sometimes told Hazel about the ocean. Tried to jog her memory. Told her that someday we'd bring her back. I haven't thought about that for a long time. Feels like we're a long, long way from that. A long, long way from giving Hazel the life we dreamed for her."

"What life is that?"

She couldn't look at him then. "A mom, and a dad. A home."

"The life you wanted."

Aw, shoot, now her eyes burned. "The life I had."

She felt his gaze on her.

"God is not a joker. He doesn't give us a dream only to yank it away. He loves you, Tillie, and he's going to help us figure this out. This isn't over."

She didn't want to argue with him. "I don't know how you do it."

He took a sip of cocoa. "Do what?"

"You're always so calm. All the time. I mean . . . you'd come into the Skyport, and I'd know—I'd just *know*—by the look on your face that you'd had a rough rescue. But you didn't ever snap at me or . . . I don't know. Like I said . . . unflappable."

He shook his head. "I'm not calm. But the times I am—it's when I remember that I'm not in charge."

"What do you mean, not in charge? You're the head of the Air One team."

"I guess I mean just . . . not in my hands. Although I forget that, probably too often." He looked at her. "I learned a long time ago that I was in over my head. Still am, I guess." He smiled. "But there's a verse I keep going back to—God keeps in perfect peace the man—or woman—whose mind is fixed on him, because we trust him. I keep trying to remember that."

"And we're back to faith."

"And we're back to faith." He winked.

"It's just . . . it seems so easy for you."

He gave a harsh, almost brutal, laugh.

"What?"

"If—" He shook his head, then looked at her. "The other side of faith is panic. And panic always leads to bad decisions, so . . ."

"I have a hard time believing you've ever made a bad decision."

She'd meant it as a joke, but the look he gave her sent a shard of ice through her.

"Believe me. I've made plenty of bad decisions."

She nearly teased him then, but when he drew in a breath and looked away, lost in thought, his expression dark, she closed her mouth.

"My worst decision is the reason why I have this cabin."

"How can a bad decision—"

"Pike Maguire would have never given me this cabin, my house, or even funded Air One if I hadn't been drinking the night before I had to ground our plane in the bush."

She just blinked at him.

His jaw tightened. "Yep." He sighed, then set down his mug and turned to her. "We nearly crashed because I was under-slept and wasn't fit to fly."

Oh.

"I told you about the crash in Afghanistan, right?"

"You carried a soldier to safety. He reminded you of Axel."

He just blinked at her. "You remember?"

"Moose. I remember everything you tell me."

A warmth shifted through his eyes, and she felt it then, that connection they'd always had at the diner.

And for some reason, that kiss she'd given him raked to the surface too. He hadn't done more than hold her hand, mostly for support, since then.

Suddenly, she very much wanted to kiss him again, feel those arms around her.

"I came home and started charter flying."

"Yeah. Was Pike the hunter who you got stranded with after an ice storm?"

He drew in a breath. "Yes. It was him, and my cousin Dawson and his girlfriend. We put down, and the plane refused to start again, so we had to hike out. Pike fell along the way—broke his ankle—and I had to carry him out."

"You told me."

He looked away. "Thing is, the circulation to Pike's foot was cut off, and he ended up losing it. And then he got a blood infection and never really beat it and . . . he died about a year later from that infection."

Oh, Moose. "I'm sorry."

"I've gone over and over that flight in my mind. Never mind that I shouldn't have been flying that day—the weather forecast had predicted ice, of course. But I could have flown lower, or adjusted to de-ice the wings. . . ."

"Moose—"

"No, Tillie. Really. I'm not being overly hard on myself. I was to blame. And the worst part is that Pike gave me his entire inheritance. Even after I told him my part. He still did it, and . . . I know I don't deserve any of it."

"Because you got him into that mess?"

"Yes, and because his son is the rightful heir, not me. I promised Pike I'd find him, and I tried, but the lawyers hadn't a clue where he was. The truth is, I am ashamed that I haven't found him. It's a promise that burns inside me. And if I'm honest, there's a part of me that fears that if I do find him . . . "

"You'll lose what Pike gave you."

He nodded. "O ye of little faith." He gave a wry shake of his head. "I should start listening to my own preaching."

"God is not a joker?"

"Yes. Although, there's a part of me knows I don't deserve any of this."

She touched his hand. "Moose. From where I sit, I see a man who God can count on."

"Working on that. But sometimes I do feel over my head. Wondering why I'm in charge."

"I don't know. I like it when you're in charge."

He smiled then, something languid and even a little dangerous. And then, as if he could read her mind, he reached for her mug, set it on the deck, and tugged her over to him.

She got up and settled into his lap in the Adirondack chair. "What are you doing?"

"Being in charge." Then he lifted his face to hers, and she couldn't stop herself from leaning down and kissing him.

He tasted of chocolate and smelled of flannel, and with the twilight dropping softly around them, she was there, in the happy place she didn't deserve.

But so craved.

She wrapped her arms around his neck and felt one of his around her waist, the other hand around the back of her neck, holding her there, as if he feared she might pull away. But he kept his kiss gentle, even while nudging her mouth for more.

And sure, she'd kissed him in the cave, but that was different. This was Moose holding her, giving over a piece of himself, but also the sense of being swept up, carried.

Moose's thumb ran down her cheek, striking a flame deep inside her, and even as he kept his kiss light, he made a soft sound in the depths of his chest and deepened his kiss.

And right then she knew.

She loved this man. Had for months, or longer, but here, right here, the truth of it found her soul and settled in.

She loved his patience, his smile, the way he reached out to rescue, and even, yes, his faith. Loved the fierceness in his eyes when she needed him, and the strength of his hands in hers. She loved that he didn't push but always stayed, and never let her forget she wasn't alone.

This man. He was her happy place.

She lifted her head, met his eyes. His gaze roamed her face, then fixed on hers. And then he smiled.

Such a beautiful, explosive smile, it landed in her heart, practically blew it up as it swept through her.

Then, "I—" he started, but Axel opened the door.

"Guys, you need to—oops, sorry."

Moose looked over at him. "Better be good, Lugnut."

Axel gave a wry grin. "I think we found something. But by all means, carry on."

Tillie was already untangling herself from Moose, however, getting up.

Moose followed, but when she rose from picking up her mug, he caught her arm, then turned her to him. Met her eyes, an earnestness in his. "Tillie, I—"

"Don't, Moose."

And she didn't know why she couldn't hear it, whatever declaration might issue from him. Just, "Save it for when this is all over."

He closed his mouth. Nodded.

She turned and walked into the cabin.

ELEVEN

MOOSE WANTED TO FOLLOW ALONG WITH Flynn's sketchy synopsis of Rigger's motive, but really, all he had in his brain was the feel of Tillie in his arms, the taste of her lingering on his lips, and the screaming of *brakes, brakes!* in his head.

So much for calm.

Or control. *Sheesh*, what had he been thinking, pulling her over to him, tucking her into his lap and kissing her?

Really kissing her, like he'd wanted to for months.

And as he'd expected, he'd lost himself.

Shoot. He knew better. Had made rules for himself years back, and again after coming home from war, and most recently when God had given him a second chance.

No drinking. Healthy eating. And he'd closed the door on ro-mance—at least, until he'd met Tillie. And even then, it had taken him more than a year to ask her out. Not that he didn't want a romance, but . . .

But after Pike's story, he never wanted to be a man who walked away from a promise. And one of his promises was to focus on Air One, to be the rescuer God had saved him to be.

And then there was the fact that Tillie wasn't a Christian. And as much as Moose's heart stirred for her and Hazel . . .

He stood behind Flynn's chair, gripping it, trying to focus as she sorted through her information, not looking at Tillie. Not hearing the words that had been about to leave his mouth on the porch. *Tillie, I think we need to slow down.*

"You're right, Tillie," Flynn was saying. "Matthew Lopez went missing over five years ago. He washed up on shore at the Newport Fishing Pier, his body badly decomposed, dead from unknown injuries. I reached out to a contact I have in the Miami Police Department, a friend of a friend. We'll see if he can give us more information."

Tillie nodded, her face hardening.

"As for Richer's gyms, the Fight Factories, they are serviced by one security firm, Sentinel Vision Security, out of Hollywood, Florida. I'm going to call them in the morning, see how far back they keep their security tapes."

That's it? Moose looked at Axel. Probably a good thing he'd interrupted them, but—

"That's not the interesting part, however," Flynn said. She was working on Moose's computer, the glow against her face turning her hair a deep amber. "I kept asking, Why would Richer start a custody proceeding two years after Pearl and Hazel and Tillie disappeared? Why not sue immediately?"

"Maybe he was afraid of what I would do," Tillie said.

"Maybe," Flynn said. "But I watched the video on Pearl's phone, Tillie. There are grounds there for assault with a deadly weapon, and he never filed a complaint against you for that, either."

Tillie stiffened.

Flynn looked up at her. "I think you could reasonably counter with self-defense." She smiled. "I'm just trying to think objectively here."

Tillie nodded. Axel went over and pulled up a chair for her, tapped her shoulder, and she sank into it.

Flynn continued. "According to the current news, Richer is running for mayor against an incumbent whose platform is the fentanyl problem and the import of it through Miami harbors."

"Richer's against the control of fentanyl?" Moose said.

"No, of course not," Flynn said. "He's very outspoken about the drug problem. But his platform is for affordable housing, and he recently spoke at a gathering of people who want to legalize prostitution. Apparently, he says that criminalizing it makes the workers less likely to report crimes."

"Probably wants to keep himself and his cronies out of jail," Tillie said.

"It's hard to believe that he's seriously a candidate for mayor." Moose folded his arms and wore his sentiment on his face.

"He's just one of many," Flynn said. "But let's not forget that every presidential election, there are all kinds of alternative options, not just two parties. And in the lower offices, it gets really muddy. Especially since most people assume that politicians are crooked."

"True, but sad," Axel said.

Flynn nodded. "Consider his list of donors. Like 'Speak for Peace,' a group that advocates for socialism, and 'New Era,' a think tank that nationally supported communist candidates."

"That is crazy," Tillie said. "He's not socialist; I can guarantee that."

"Could be he's just trying to support what will get him elected," Axel said.

Flynn nodded. "So you need to ask why. Why does he want to run for mayor? And I don't believe it's because of what he espouses on his website—to create a fairer and more equitable Miami." She turned back to the computer. "So, again, I had to ask . . . why?

What does it gain him to run for mayor? Or to sue for custody of a child he hasn't seen for five years and seemingly doesn't want?"

Silence.

"The answer might be this." Flynn had opened a new tab to a news article from the *Miami Herald*. "It's an article about the joint operations between the Organized Crime Drug Enforcement Task Force—and a private anti-drug-trafficking organization that apprehended smugglers carrying ten kilos of fentanyl. Apparently, the private organization worked to help the DEA by infiltrating and conducting controlled purchases. The smugglers were arrested with enough illegally manufactured fentanyl to kill five million people."

More silence.

"By the way, the drugs were in powder form, in mini packets of muscle powder."

"Like the kind sold at a gym?" Tillie said.

"Yes. The article doesn't say, but during the arrest, one of the men was killed. Here's a picture of the smugglers." Flynn opened up another screen and now pointed to a man on the screen. "This one look familiar?"

Moose leaned in as Tillie drew in a breath. "That's Rigger's brother."

"Yes. He was the one who died."

"So Rigger's brother was transporting drugs," Moose said. "And was killed by the cops."

"Or the private organization—the article doesn't say. But I did find this."

She opened another tab—Moose noticed about ten more on her bar.

"About four months after the drug bust on Rigger's brother, a Miami DEA agent was kidnapped and later found murdered. This is an article about the execution-style murder of his wife and daughter a few weeks prior to his disappearance."

"When was this?" Moose asked, his voice low.

"The original bust? About three years ago."

"That could be a coincidence," Axel said. "But she also found another article. Show them, babe."

She opened another tab. "This was a drive-by shooting. Occurred outside a school—a girl, seven years old, killed, her mother wounded."

She looked over at the group. "The woman worked as a DEA agent. She was a single mom."

"Any arrests?" Moose asked.

"Yes. He was a member of the Southern Syndicate."

"The what?" Moose asked.

"The same organization that Richer's brother worked for," Flynn said.

"So Rigger is involved in organized crime," Tillie said. "That, I can believe."

"You think Rigger—or at least the Southern Syndicate—is targeting people who killed his brother?" Moose asked.

"I do. It's just a hunch, but tomorrow morning I'll get on the phone with my contacts in Miami."

Moose glanced at Axel. "I still don't understand. . . . What does this have to do with Tillie and Hazel?"

"Yeah. Good question. So . . ." Flynn glanced at Axel, then Tillie. Took a breath. "Okay, so the papers named the DEA agent who was the victim of the drive-by—Amaia Carrero. I looked her up, and that's how I discovered she worked for the DEA. But I also found her page on Facebook. And then I found pictures of her daughter's memorial service."

Flynn opened the Facebook page and started to scroll through the pictures, stopping at one of a group of men dressed in dark suits, standing at what looked like parade rest, dark glasses, behind a seated woman.

"To be clear, these were pictures where she was tagged—she

didn't put these up. So I followed the tagger and discovered she is the wife of a marine, or rather former marine. A Raider."

Tillie glanced at Moose. He gave her a nod.

"So I went back and scrolled through the pictures on Carrero's feed, and I found one—again, not hers, but tagged by this same woman, the wife of the Marine Raider. It was taken six months prior—I think it's at a barbeque. And I think the same men are in it." She opened the picture.

A group of men sat together in lawn chairs. One of them held a little girl on his lap, his arm around Amaia. "I'm not sure who the man with Amaia is, but the tagger is Gloria Belafonte. I think this is her husband, Luca Belafonte." She pointed to an Italian-looking man in the group. "I figured out his name after reading through her post about their Fourth of July party. I did a global search and discovered that Lance Corporal Luca Belafonte was awarded the Silver Star, along with two other Raiders who had been captured by the Taliban in the Helmand Province of Afghanistan in 2007. They were liberated in 2012 during an insurgent capture in the Badghis Province."

"I remember hearing about that," Tillie said. "I was learning Dari at the Defense Language Institute out in California."

"Was that all you heard?" Flynn asked, looking at her.

"I was taking my final exams and then getting ready to leave, so I don't remember much. And my sister had run away from the foster home, so that sort of consumed my thoughts."

Moose frowned at Flynn. "What do you mean, was that all she heard?"

Flynn swallowed, glanced at Moose. "I'm just . . . I don't . . ."

"Flynn," Moose said. "Just tell us."

"Right. Okay. So there is a picture of the Silver Star ceremony at the White House." She clicked on the tab and turned her computer toward the group. "For Lance Corporal Luca Belafonte, Gunnery Sergeant Price Henry, and . . ."

"Master Sergeant Declan Young," Tillie said on a wisp of breath. She leaned forward. "Yeah, that's him."

"He looked like the picture in Hazel's locket," Flynn said softly. "She showed it to me while we were waiting for the social worker. That, and Pearl's picture."

"He still has his dark hair," Tillie said, her voice breaking. "He was—is—Black Irish. Descendant of the Spanish traders."

"He's very handsome. Striking, really," Flynn said. "Memorable."

"Yes," Tillie said, her voice a little small and tight.

Moose couldn't move. "Tillie, is that your . . . your *father*?"

She looked over at him, swallowed, and her face had whitened. She nodded.

"Her father is *alive*?" He stood up.

"It's possible," Flynn said. "That *was* twelve years ago. But he's pictured here too." She returned to the Facebook page, the men with the dark glasses around Amaia. She pointed to one. "This is him, I think."

Same rugged jawline, same build. Even Moose could see it. "What does this have to do with Rigger—"

"You think these are the guys in the private organization, working with the DEA task force," Tillie said.

"I do," Flynn said. "And I think that the Southern Syndicate is slowly punishing them for the death of Karl Richer."

"As in, *Julian* is punishing them," Tillie said. "By killing the people they love."

"Yep."

"And he thinks by finding me . . . Wait. He filed for custody to track me down—but I thought it was because I knew about Matthew Lopez."

"Could be . . . or . . ." Axel said, a brow raised.

"Maybe he was looking for Pearl. But he didn't know Pearl had died, and by getting the judge to issue a warrant on her—and you—for noncustodial kidnapping, and because you'd taken her across state lines, he could make it nationwide. . . ."

"And find me."

"And find you," Moose said, chilled. "And that's why he wants Hazel—because he knows you'll follow her, wherever he takes her."

"All the way back to Florida," said Flynn. "Where your dad is working undercover. And then Julian flushes out the person he's really looking for."

"And takes his revenge." Tillie sat back. She was blinking hard, and Moose kneeled down next to her chair. "But how did my dad end up in Miami?"

"If I was gone for five years and my children were missing, I'd cross the country to find them. And keep looking in the last place they were seen," Moose said, his jaw tight.

"Miami," she said.

Moose lifted a shoulder. Then, as she put her hands over her face, he put his arms around her and pulled her softly, but firmly, to himself.

So much for brakes. Moose didn't have a hope of holding on to his heart.

And she was supposed to sleep?

Tillie studied the wood-paneled ceiling of the lower-level bedroom, Flynn's soft breathing rhythmic in the other twin bed, and tried to ground herself in Flynn's words.

Her dad, Declan Young, *alive*.

Alive and searching for her? Maybe, because Moose's words kept rounding back to her. *"If I was gone for five years and my children were missing, I'd cross the country to find them. And keep looking in the last place they were seen."*

More, why hadn't the military informed her of his return? Maybe they had discharged him and left him to do that.

So. Many. Questions. She rolled over, her gaze at the window, the darkness still deep, still obscuring the mountains, even the stars.

Blackness—outside and in her brain.

She'd rather think about Moose and the way he'd pulled up a chair as they'd searched the Facebook pages of Amaia and Luca and others. The way he'd put his arm over the back of her chair, protective even if he didn't realize it.

Sadly, she'd found no more pictures. Her father was a ghost, so maybe, in fact, it hadn't been him. But even as the others went to bed, as she lay in bed tracing her father's profile in her brain, she knew.

She could almost hear his laughter, the sometimes-Irish brogue he'd brought out from his parents that made her giggle. The way he'd read stories to her and Pearl, sitting on her bed. The smell of him, an aftershave she'd never nailed down.

Alive. The thought simply took everything out of her.

Especially if she let herself imagine what he'd gone through or how he'd survived all those years. But if her dad was the hero she knew he was, he'd still be fighting for the safety of his children. Of his country.

Against men like Rigger, who fought for no one but himself.

Thank God—and yes, that was the answer—she'd left town with Pearl and Hazel.

And that thought sat her up.

She'd never thought of her desperate actions being . . . good.

Or simply *used* for good, like Moose had said.

"Faith that God knows what he's doing. Faith that everything, for someone who trusts God, works together for good."

What if it wasn't a platitude?

Her throat was parched, probably from all the crying. She got up, pulled off the coverlet, wrapped it around herself, and headed out into the main room, shutting the door softly behind herself.

Darkness bathed the room, but she turned on a light, hoping it didn't drain the solar batteries, then headed toward the water container in the kitchen.

Moose had filled it from the river, a filter in the container siphoning out the impurities. She took a glass, filled it, then walked out into the room.

The computer had died and sat dark, and frankly, she was tired of trying to track down clues. Instead, she walked over to the bookcase, to a lineup of novels on one of the shelves. A few Jack Carr novels, a ragtag edition of *The Thorn Birds*, and the Jason Bourne series by Ludlum.

And a Bible. *Huh*.

She pulled it out. Thick, with a cracked leather binding, it seemed like something a person wouldn't leave behind. Unless they did all their big thinking here, in God's country, under the shadow of the Denali and the ribbon of the northern lights.

She brought the Bible over to one of the cigar chairs and sank into it. A frayed red ribbon dangled from between the pages. Setting the book on her lap, she opened it to where the ribbon lay.

The Psalms. She'd heard her mother talk about a psalm. About it being a song of a shepherd. Or maybe they were all songs of a shepherd. But this Bible had markings in it, highlights and notes jotted in the margins, and stars and exclamation points and red underlining the bottom half of the psalm.

She read the words slowly, felt them splash upon her soul. "*If you say, 'The Lord is my refuge,' and you make the Most High your dwelling, no harm will overtake you, no disaster will come near your tent.*"

She could almost hear Moose's low voice from last night. "*God keeps in perfect peace the man—or woman—whose mind is fixed on him, because we trust him.*"

Faith.

She leaned her head back. It always came back to faith.

Moose's words wrapped around her. *The question is, If you know that God wants to rescue you, what is holding you back from reaching out?"*

"Morning."

She looked up, and Axel had come into the room. Barefoot, he wore jeans, a half-buttoned flannel shirt, his hair behind his ear, just as devastatingly handsome as his brother, just as brave, but still they seemed so different. Axel outgoing, impulsive, heroic. Moose quiet, deliberate, protective.

"Morning." She closed the Bible.

"What are you reading there?"

"I found it on the shelf."

He sat on the other chair, reached out his hand. "Can I see?"

She handed it over, and as she did, it flopped and out dropped a letter. "Oops."

He took the Bible. She picked up the letter.

Unopened. *Return to sender* was stamped on the front. She put it on the arm of the chair.

Axel had opened the Bible to the ribboned mark. "Psalm 91. Yeah, that's a good one. A friend of my mother's had a canvas made of this verse with her name in it. She gave it to her when she had cancer."

"She had cancer?"

"Years ago. Breast cancer. She's fine—all clear. But I remember her memorizing this psalm, repeating it to herself. Made me do it too, and put my name in it." He gave a chuckle. "'Because Axel loves me,' says the Lord, 'I will rescue him; I will protect him, for Axel acknowledges my name. Axel will call on me, and I will answer him; I will be with him in trouble, I will deliver him and honor him. With long life I will satisfy him and show Axel my salvation.'"

He looked over at her. "It still sort of blows me away. I need to remind myself of this more often, probably."

She stared at him.

"You try it." He held the Bible out to her.

"No, that's okay." She held up her hand, not sure why. Maybe it just felt too intimate, too real.

Too much hope.

He narrowed his eyes at her, then set the Bible down on the table between them. "You okay? Pretty heavy stuff last night."

"Yeah. I'm just trying to get my head around the idea that my dad isn't missing anymore."

"Yep."

She swallowed. "Do you think God used my running to Alaska to, you know . . ."

"Protect you?"

She lifted a shoulder, because suddenly that sounded so hokey.

"Absolutely. You may not know how God is at work, but I can tell you that he always is. I might not have said that a couple months ago, but then God saved my life through—and this is going to sound equally crazy—through a ham radio. Flynn was on the other end and my ship was going down and I was trapped and in the middle of a storm and . . . it's a long story. But God completely spared my life and then . . . well, he wasn't finished. So yeah, if you ask me, God is at work even if we don't believe it."

"Or deserve it?"

"Especially if we don't deserve it. Fact is, that's his specialty. Rescuing the lost, the broken, the guilty."

"Why?"

"Because he is love. That is the very nature, the character, of God. That's why we can have hope—because it's not about us but him. His faithfulness."

"And we're back at faith." She smiled.

"We're back at love." Axel winked, then stood up. "All I know is that God is sovereign. And even I can't screw that up. I hope Moose brought some coffee in that pack." He headed into the kitchen.

"I did."

She looked behind her, and Moose had come down the stairs. He glanced at Axel, heading into the kitchen, then at her. "You're up early."

"Yeah. I guess it's a thing."

He was barefoot too, his hair tousled, a slight dark layer of whiskers on his chin, and he wore the same attire as his brother, the Mulligan flannel and jeans.

A longing for her sister washed over her. Her dad would be devastated at Pearl's death when she told him.

No. If. If she told him. In fact—"If Rigger is trying to find me so he can do something terrible in revenge, the very last thing I can do is go back to Florida. In fact, it might be better if my dad didn't know where I was, ever."

Moose had sunk down into the chair Axel had just vacated. He put his hands on the arms. Looked over at her. Nodded. "I thought that too. Because if your dad finds you, then—"

"Then Rigger kills me and wins."

He gave her a grim look. "I'll call Ridge today and see if we've gotten any traction on the custody appeal. Could be his team has uncovered some of the same things we have—and if not, Flynn can fill him in." He reached over to the Bible. "Pike's Bible. Where'd this come from?" He picked it up and opened it to the psalms. "Hey, that's my mom's favorite psalm."

"Axel has it memorized."

"I have it memorized too. 'Because Arlo loves me,' says the Lord, 'I will rescue him. . . .'"

"Arlo? From your grandfather?"

He looked over at her. "Good memory."

"I like Arlo. It's a good name."

He closed the Bible, then looked over at the letter on the arm of her chair. "What's that?"

"It fell out of the Bible." She handed it over. "A return-to-sender letter."

He looked at it and his expression slacked. "This was to his son, years ago." He studied the stamp. "Seven years ago. Before I met him."

"You said he couldn't find him. Could be because he moved away, no forwarding address."

"Yeah. But I never had his name. And . . . given Flynn's detective skills . . ." He looked at her. "I'm going to find him."

Something about the smile on his face, the light in his eyes . . .

"You see what God did here?" he said.

Oh. But yes, maybe. Then he grinned at her, and the dawn seemed to cascade into the room, the night gone, the sunshine filling her soul.

Maybe this was what faith felt like. She stared at Moose, hearing his words. *"You have to be willing to be rescued. And that starts with acknowledging that you need rescue."*

The door to the bedroom opened, and Flynn came out, staring at her phone.

She looked up at Tillie, her face so stricken that Moose got up. "What?"

"I just got a text from Dawson. Hazel and her social worker were on their way to meet with her guardian ad litem this morning and were run off the road." She looked up, and her eyes were wet. "Hazel's gone."

TWELVE

H AZEL'S GONE.
The words still punched Moose, even twenty minutes
later as he lined up on the beach for takeoff.

Hazel's gone.

He glanced at Flynn behind him and she appeared wrecked. She should probably figure out how to reframe a declaration like that.

Gone as in *missing*, not dead.

For one excruciatingly long moment, no one had moved, and then Tillie had doubled over and keened, a terrible sound from her soul that ripped him from his shock.

"What—*what?*" He'd put his arms around Tillie, his attention on Flynn as Axel came out of the kitchen. "Gone?"

"Oh—wow—no, not gone. *Taken.* I mean, she's not . . . Tillie—no, she's alive. I mean—the social worker said that she saw a man take her."

"She's not dead," Axel said. "You're sure."

Flynn looked at him. "I'm reading a text! I wasn't there. Okay, hold on. I'll call Dawson."

SUSAN MAY WARREN

She walked out to the deck, and Moose pulled Tillie up, clamped his arms back around her. "It'll be okay, Til. It'll be okay—"

And that's when she hit him.

She probably hadn't meant to hurt him—she hadn't put a fist to his face or a punch to his gut. She just slammed her hands against his chest, pushing him away.

But it felt like a hit, something brutal and dark that filled his soul. Especially when he read the look in her eyes. Heard her low, broken words. "You promised."

"Tillie."

"You promised she'd be okay—"

"I didn't promise." Had he? "And no one saw this coming—"

"I saw this coming!" She hit her own chest now and stepped away from him. "I know Rigger. I know the man he is and the man he's not, and I can tell you right now that the guy we see on the television weeping over his lost child is a *murderer*. And he's going to murder Hazel."

"He's not going to murder Hazel. Everyone is watching him," Axel said.

Tillie gave him a look that threatened his own murder.

"This isn't my fault either, Tillie, or Flynn's or Moose's." Axel kept his voice low. "Although I can understand how you might think that. How you might be feeling betrayed right now. But every one of us is on your side."

"No." She shook her head. "No one is on my side. No one understands what it feels like to be responsible for someone only to . . . to let something terrible happen to them!"

Axel stiffened, and Moose looked at him, then shook his head. Nope, now was not the time to bring up Aven, or their history watching someone they loved disappear only to be murdered.

Especially not that last part.

"Let's get back to Anchorage," Moose said. He reached out again for Tillie, but she jerked away from him.

Held up her hands.

Then she turned and walked into the bedroom, shut the door.

He took a breath.

"This is not your fault, bro." Axel, still unmoving.

"Feels like it could be."

"Now who's blame casting?"

Moose frowned.

"Just a little of your own coming back at you. I'm not to blame for Aven's death any more than you are for Hazel's disappearance. Bad people do bad things."

"And good people stop them."

"Or try to. But only one person can be in all places at all times. And last time I checked, you're not omnipresent."

Moose held up his hand. "Okay, I get it." He headed up the stairs. "We leave in ten."

He made it back down in five, pulling on his boots and a hat, throwing his toiletries in his backpack and shouldering it.

Axel emerged from his room, carrying his go-bag, and Flynn came inside, staring at her phone. She looked up at them. "Okay, so Dawson said the social worker is on her way to the hospital. She's not badly injured, but he's going over there to detain her until I get there." She pocketed her phone. "But we have a problem, of course."

Tillie had come out of her room. Flynn swallowed.

"Tell us," Moose said.

"The warrant from Florida has come in. Tillie can't go to the hospital with us. Not without getting arrested."

"Then arrest me." Tillie was dressed and ready to leave.

Moose rounded on her. "What?"

"If you arrest me, then can I go with you to talk to the social worker?"

Flynn drew in a breath. "I think I can work that out."

"Then arrest me." She held out her hands.

Moose grabbed her wrists, pushed them down. "Let's just go."

He picked up his backpack even as she jerked her wrists from his grip and headed past him outside.

Axel left, then Flynn, grabbing her jacket and shoes; then Moose closed up the cabin and jogged down to the plane.

Axel grabbed his gear while Moose did a preflight walkaround and got in.

Another check, then he started the prop, and in a moment they were airborne.

Twenty minutes later, Moose was glad for the terrible roar of the motor, the focus on landing safely rather than the roaring deep in his heart.

Please, God, rescue Tillie.

Axel was on his phone, texting, Anchorage in sight below.

The sun had risen high now, shining on the Knik Arm, on the seaplanes in the water near Merrill Field. Moose called in to the tower, and by the time he landed, he spotted Shep and London standing near the Tooth, London's arms folded over her chest, looking like she and Shep were in a discussion.

Or a fight.

Boo's Rogue was parked next to London's orange Subaru Crosstrek in front.

He taxied toward their Quonset hut.

Axel glanced at Moose. "Boo called a friend in the ER. The social worker—her name is Donna—just arrived. Dawson is on his way."

As Moose shut down the plane, Axel got out.

Shep came up. "I'll get the plane sorted and tied down."

Moose climbed down from the cockpit. "I'm going to the hospital with Flynn and Tillie."

London had walked up to Tillie, was talking with her. Tillie wouldn't look at him.

"Axel said that Tillie told Flynn to arrest her."

"Yep." He still couldn't get that out of his head.

"Not a bad idea, considering."

Moose stared at him.

"How else is she going to get to Florida? There's a warrant out for her arrest—she's not getting on a plane or across the border. And don't tell me you weren't thinking of doing something crazy like driving—or flying—her down there to get Hazel."

Moose ran a hand behind his neck.

"Yep, that's what I thought." Shep shook his head. "You might want to consider that you're not the only one who has something at stake here with Air One."

Oh.

Shep put a hand on his shoulder. "We're with you. But—and I never thought I'd have to tell you this, Moose—be smart."

Shep walked over to the plane just as Flynn and Tillie got into Axel's Yukon.

Again, Tillie didn't look at him.

Moose went inside and grabbed his truck keys, and by the time he got out, Shep and London were pushing the plane into the hangar to sit beside the chopper.

He called Ridge on the way to the hospital to give him an update.

"I know," Ridge said. "I talked with our family law department, and we're working on a recommendation to the court for suspended custody."

"What are my options regarding Tillie's bail?" Moose pulled into the ER parking lot.

A beat.

"Right. I reviewed the lawsuit documents. The plaintiff asked the court to freeze your assets so you can't sell before the judgment is rendered. If you take out a lien against those to post bail, that might red-flag the courts to allow the injunction. They could shut you down while you wait for the case to be heard."

"Okay, thanks." Moose got out, Shep's words in his ears. *"Be smart."*

And as he walked into the ER, Axel's words followed him in.

"If you want to follow God's plan—and I can guarantee you that he has a plan here—you can't panic. And you can't fight without the armor of God. And that starts with the shield of faith guarding your heart."

He stopped outside the ER, spotting Tillie and Flynn.

Tillie stood, handcuffs binding her hands. So, clearly Flynn had solved the running problem.

They were talking with a middle-aged woman, her head bandaged, pretty banged up, evidenced by the splint on her arm. Tillie nodded, her jaw tight, and the dark, hollowed expression she wore threatened to tear him asunder.

"Here's a coffee." Axel walked up to him. "It's practically tar, so it should hold you up." He carried his own cup. "Sorry about the cuffs, but it was Flynn's only answer to the fact that she was walking in with the suspect. If she didn't cuff her, someone would have, so . . ."

"It's okay. I know she's trying to help."

"About that." He took a sip of coffee, as if fortifying himself. "Tillie is pretty sure that Rigger is taking Hazel to Florida. Flynn has people watching the airport, but at least three flights have already left for the lower forty-eight, and Donna was trapped in her car for a good hour before emergency services found her. It's possible he already left." He shook his head. "Flynn thinks she can talk to the FBI, see if they'll let her accompany Tillie to Florida, hand her off to authorities there. She could do some legwork with the local PD in Miami."

Moose's gut tightened on the words. This couldn't be happening.

As he watched, Donna retrieved a plastic bag and handed it to Tillie. Tillie opened it and pulled out Hazel's floppy, worn dog.

She pressed her face into it, and he had to turn away.

He looked at Axel. "So, you're going to let Flynn go by herself?"

"She's not a puppy. I think she can handle herself," Axel said.

"Really?"

"Okay, I'll bite—what are you thinking?"

Shep came through the front doors of the hospital followed by London and then Boo. To Moose's surprise, Oaken followed Boo in.

They walked up to Moose.

Considered him.

"I'm going to Florida," he said, finally. "Maybe there is nothing I can do. But Tillie is all alone, and I just . . ."

Shep stepped up to him. "This is not on you. You did not fail Tillie. You just did what you felt you were supposed to at the time." He glanced at London.

Then why did everything Moose do backfire?

At the heart of it, no matter what he did, it crashed down over him. Buried him.

He probably wore that on his face, because Shep shook his head. "You've got to stop thinking all this is yours. Air One. Whatever happens with Tillie."

"'Come to me, all you who are weary and burdened, and I will give you rest.'" London said quietly.

Moose looked at her.

London met his gaze, her voice soft. "What we forget about those verses is the first part. *Come to me*. Believe me. Believe in my unfailing love. *Unfailing*. You do not need to rescue the world, Moose, because Jesus already has. You cannot fail him, because you *already have*, and he's *already redeemed* you. So get over yourself."

He stared at her.

"Right?" Shep said.

Moose sighed. "I gave her my word."

"You always give people your word, whether you say it or not, Moose," said Axel. "But it's not your word to give."

Moose drew in a breath. "*Come to me.*"

He looked at Tillie, clutching the stuffed dog. "I can't help but think I'm supposed to follow her."

Silence.

"Okay, then just ask us, man," Shep said.

Moose looked at his team, at Shep and London, Boo and Axel, and even Oaken, and right then, it hit him.

He'd been so concerned about failing his team that he'd forgotten he was part of the team too. He carried their burdens, but . . . they also carried his.

"I know you don't do asking for help, bro," Axel said. "But 'Those who cling to worthless idols turn away from God's love for them.' Something Mom always says, right? It keeps coming back me."

Moose nodded. "Yeah." Idols, like his own pride. His word, his promises had become idols. Moose to the rescue.

He did have a savior complex.

And then his words to Tillie found him. *"You have to be willing to be rescued. You can't rescue yourself. And that starts with acknowledging that you need rescue."*

His team looked at him. "Fine. I . . . I could use some . . . help."

"See, bro, that wasn't so hard," said Axel, his hand on Moose's shoulder. He winked.

"As luck would have it, my mom has a place in Miami," Oaken said.

Moose didn't know why, but suddenly the terrible knot in his chest eased, and for a moment, he simply breathed.

And then Tillie and Flynn came walking out.

"I need to take her to the station for booking. And then . . ."

"And then we'll see you in Florida," Moose said.

Tillie looked up at him. Stopped. "No."

He stilled.

"I'm not your responsibility anymore, Moose. Don't follow me. This is goodbye."

"Tillie—"

She turned and walked away.

It'll be okay. This time, as he watched her go, he didn't say the words.

But he meant them.

There were bigger things at stake than the fact that London had decided not to talk to him. But it felt big as Shep stood in the hangar this morning, waiting for Moose to show up.

He drove to the Tooth, his fight with London last night still in his head, pretty sure that he should have called her or shown up on her doorstep to rewind their conversation. . . .

"Stay. Away. From. Me."

Yep, that was a pretty clear, *don't call me."* He'd gone back to his place and sat in the darkness overlooking the sound, the aloneness of his place thundering through him.

Along, of course, with Colt's words. *"I do know that she can't go missing. And if she does, then we're back at ground zero. So keep her close."*

Hard to do that when she wasn't talking to him.

So he'd expected her folded arms and cold shoulder today when he arrived at the hangar after Moose's call.

But he didn't have to like it. "C'mon, London. Don't be that way." He'd walked up to her, waiting with her as Boo went into the Tooth, probably to check on medical supplies. He didn't know what he expected from Moose's cryptic call about Hazel being missing, and that had him stirred up too. So he and London needed to solve this thing between them and get back to work.

Focus on the work.

"Shep. Just leave it." She wore her blonde hair back in a ponytail, a pair of black leggings, a pullover, and a pair of tennis shoes.

"No. I know you're angry with me, and I get that. I should have told you about Colt and him asking me to keep an eye on you. But I thought . . . well, I didn't think you'd like knowing—"

"That you were spying on me?"

"I wasn't—"

"What would you call it, then? Babysitting? Bodyguarding?"

Okay, mouth closed. He watched Moose's plane circle in the air, coming around for a landing, and she looked at him.

"If I'm the spy you are accusing me of being, certainly I can take care of myself."

It might be a good thing he couldn't see her eyes through those sunglasses.

"Yes. True. And you can keep your secrets, London. I don't need to know them. But . . . I was trying to do right by you. We did have . . ." *A connection. A moment.* But clearly she'd wiped their past from her mind. He swallowed. "You're not just *anybody* to me. So yes, I agreed to keep an eye on you. Like a friend would."

"And report my activities to Colt?"

"Nope. None of that. Just . . . making sure you . . . were all right."

Her chest rose and fell.

Then she nodded. Looked away.

Moose's plane landed and started taxiing toward them.

"Coming here has been the best thing that's happened to me in a long time. I don't want to—" She looked at him. "I don't want to think that it's not real."

Not real.

He didn't have the faintest idea what that meant, but he couldn't help but drop his voice, take a step toward her. "It's real, London. Everything that . . . everything that I feel for you is real."

She pursed her lips as if considering her words.

"Please, London, can't we at least be friends—"

"Yes." She hadn't moved, her arms still folded, but her voice changed, soft, almost regretful.

He stilled as the plane pulled into the Quonset.

"I'm sorry, Shep. I . . . the thing is, I've had people lie to me before—"

"She's been betrayed before." His jaw tightened.

"But I want to trust you. You've been . . ." She sighed. "Yes. We can be friends. But no more secrets."

He had nothing for that.

The plane stopped and Shep walked over. "I'll get the plane sorted and tied down."

And it seemed she meant it because, six hours later, as he boarded the flight to Seattle from Anchorage, he spotted London in a seat near the window. *His* seat, according to his ticket.

"You're in my seat."

She patted the seat next to her. Smiled.

Huh.

He put his suitcase in the overhead compartment, then sat down.

Fine. "Okay, just to clear the air, yes, there are things about my past that . . . I don't want to talk about. And Colt had his reasons for . . . what he asked you to do. But that's in the past. And this is a new start, and—" She turned to him, her eyes searching his. "I trust you, Shep. I have since you saved my life."

"I think you saved my life."

She gave a half laugh. "Okay, so we saved each other. And yes, I think about those three days . . . more than you know." She touched his hand. "Because of you, I found faith again, and hope, and I need to remember that. So yes, we're friends." She smiled then, her gaze warm.

Shoot. Now they were right back in the unrequited romantic tragedy.

"Now, what movie are we going to watch?"

And just like that, it was over. And he saw it afresh, just like he had three years ago, when rescuers had finally lifted the debris from their ice cave and light had pierced the darkness.

Light. Hope.

Tomorrow.

This time, he wasn't letting it get away.

She reached over to his screen and scrolled through the movies. "Let's watch the new *Mission Impossible* movie." They laughed together, and during the layover, bought enough snacks and treats for the entire team—which worked out, since a storm front preceded them across the United States and they had to bed down in the Chicago O'Hare airport.

Even then, lying on a bank of seats, his head on his suitcase, London across from him, this felt like some sort of crazy new beginning.

See, Colt. Not all of his darkest fears came true.

Everything was going to be just fine.

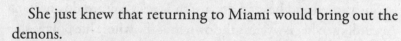

She just knew that returning to Miami would bring out the demons.

Tillie stood outside the women's detention center, her hair wet and pulled back in a hair tie, clutching the bag with Hazel's stuffed puppy, feeling grimy to her soul. The words of her state-appointed defense attorney still hung in her head.

"Don't do anything stupid."

There was more, of course, like her intent to use the defense of *reasonable cause of action against domestic violence* for her actions. Only problem was, the claim on that defense had expired about five years ago.

Which meant she was facing a felony in the third degree.

Alone.

She'd left behind the beauty and autumn redolence of Alaska for the stifling September heat of Florida. The sun was already drying her hair, sending sweat down her back. This was not the prettiest part of town—the skyscrapers of downtown rose in the distance, and across the street, a broken fence cordoned off a weedy track and field, an extension of the nearby high school. Down the street, a vacant lot littered with garbage was guarded by chain link, and an abandoned building covered in graffiti suggested an area forgotten. The persistent grind of construction from a nearby street cluttered the seasoned air.

And God picked a funny time to walk into her head—if it was God at all. *"'Because Tillie loves me,' says the Lord, 'I will rescue her. I will protect her, for she acknowledges my name.'"*

Yeah. Well . . . Still, the thought of it pricked tears into her eyes. If she'd ever needed someone on her side . . .

She pinched her mouth at the memory of her words to Moose— *"Don't follow me. This is goodbye"*—and hated the fact that down deep she hoped, desperately, that he'd be here, waiting for her.

She didn't blame him for finally, *finally*, waking up to the truth.

She turned and headed down 7th Street, toward downtown. According to her lawyer, as the owner of the whole life policy, she could take out a loan against the cash value. She'd nearly maxed it out to pay her bond.

She'd used her one call on Roz, who had sent cash to a Western Union some six blocks from the detention center, and that, along with her old passport, the one under her real name, might score her a burner phone, and then an Uber to Miami Beach.

Maybe.

Her stomach roiled. She'd ignored the breakfast the detention center served this morning before the van took her to court for her arraignment with seven other women. She'd looked at their faces, some of them bearing the effects of drug use or domestic trouble, and seen the life Pearl might have had if they hadn't run.

So no, no regrets. But . . .

She passed a motorcycle rental place, mostly Harleys but also a couple old Suzukis with sale pricing, and an idea formed. *Thank you, Arch Henry, for those lessons.*

Arch. A fellow marine. He'd been a good friend after she'd moved to MacDill Air Force Base in Tampa. Handsome, a Gunnery Sergeant, looking to go spec ops. She'd left him behind when she'd deployed onto the *USS San Antonio*, and when she returned, he too had deployed.

Turning onto a side street, she walked through a couple blocks of hard-living neighborhoods with multifamily housing and a few homes surrounded by broken chain link. A dog ran out and snarled at her, and it dragged up memories of Hazel and Kip.

She picked up her pace, replaying her conversation with Flynn on the plane earlier.

"I never meant for it to get this far. I just wanted to keep Pearl and Hazel safe."

In fact, she'd told Flynn a lot of things, including, *"I know Rigger had a place in Miami Beach. I just don't know where."*

Flynn had typed the information into her phone, and the fact that the woman had believed Tillie had given her the courage to not run. To submit to booking in Miami, to not curl into a ball and weep during her twelve-hour stay at the detention center.

To face the judge today in her orange jumpsuit.

She'd sort of half expected to see Flynn in court. But Flynn had made her no promises.

And frankly, that wasn't fair. It wasn't up to Flynn—or even Moose—to keep her safe.

Tillie spotted the overpass and cut down the street to cross the river. Here the neighborhood turned upscale and clean, sleek, with gated apartment buildings on one side, cobble-roofed, gated townhomes on the other, and after a couple blocks, she picked up her pace, seeing the shopping center ahead.

A Winn-Dixie connected to a dollar store, with Western Union in the back.

She pulled out her passport and used it at the counter to withdraw the money Roz had sent her.

She headed out and bought new clothes—a pair of leggings, a black T-shirt, a pair of running shoes, a windbreaker, a hat, glasses, and a backpack.

Then she walked back to the motorcycle shop, slapped down cash, and haggled for a couple of used helmets. She put one on, strapped the other onto the back.

She'd forgotten the power of a motorcycle, the freedom of weaving in and around traffic as she took the back roads to the MacArthur Causeway over to Miami Beach. Here, the vibe turned to vacation, the tiny apartments bearing art deco styles, the neighborhoods deeply wooded with overhanging palm trees, and cars wedged into tiny spaces along quiet streets. Bicyclers rode alongside convertibles, and music pumped into the air, hip-hop mixing with pop, Adele versus Dr. Dre.

She slowed, stopping at a light, popping open her visor. Sweat layered her skin despite the breeze from the ride, and when the scent of street tacos found her, she angled the bike onto a side street and squeezed into a space between a couple other bikes.

Locking the helmets onto the seat, she piled her jacket into her backpack and headed over to the beachside walk.

The taco stand was set up across from a volleyball net, and after scoring a shrimp taco, she sat watching the players, barefoot, carefree. An old memory stirred up of her and Pearl sitting on the beach watching two-year-old Hazel play in the ocean, running into the waves and back, screaming, falling down sandy onto their blanket.

Wow, she'd made a mess of things. One stupid decision after another.

And now . . . what? She would restart the cycle. She and Hazel always looking over their shoulders. Never in a thousand years had she thought she'd someday end up a criminal.

"God is at work even if we don't believe it."

Axel sat down in her brain, and for a moment, she was back in the cabin.

"Or deserve it?"

"Especially if we don't deserve it. Fact is, that's his specialty. Rescuing the lost, the broken, the guilty."

The criminals?

She finished the taco. Got up. And for some reason, headed out along the path, past the dunes to the long, creamy-white beach.

A few families lounged under umbrellas or played Frisbee in the sand with their children. More bobbed in the water. A few surfers rode boards in the waves. It felt like summer down here, although in Alaska, the kids had already started school.

Hazel should be in second grade, improving her reading, playing with friends, safe and not worried about where she was going to sleep.

Instead . . . what? Tillie didn't even know how to start looking for her.

She walked down to the ocean, pulling up her hair and tying it back after the helmet had dislodged her ponytail. Then she took off her shoes, rolled up her leggings, and put her feet into the warm water.

She wanted to start over. To go back to the girl who'd played on the sand with her father. To trust and believe and . . .

She looked out over the water. *"God completely spared my life and then . . . well, he wasn't finished."*

This couldn't be the way her life was supposed to end.

"What if there is a different perspective?"

"What kind of perspective?"

"Faith."

Faith.

"Is that like hope?"

"Very much."

She stared out over the blue to the sailboat on the horizon, the golden sun upon the water. The smell of freedom and life, the sound of laughter behind her. Yes, she wanted it. Hope. The calm that Moose had.

The faith.

She closed her eyes and lifted her face to the sky. *God, please help me trust you. Because right now, all I can see is disaster. But I want to believe you can save me—save Hazel. Please help me to believe it. Please . . . rescue me.*

The waves washed over her ankles, wetting her leggings, and she stepped back.

"Hey!"

The voice turned her just in time for her to see a Frisbee heading her direction. She ducked, then grabbed it from the air.

A man shouted at her. "Sorry!" He lifted his hand to a boy and started to run over to her.

But the boy reached her first. Preteen, in swim trunks and golden tousled hair. She handed him the Frisbee.

He stopped. "Hey. You look like that lady from Iron Maiden. The Steelrose."

The man ran up, breathing hard. "Sorry. C'mon, bud."

"Dad, this is Steelrose. I recognize her, and she has that tattoo too."

She hadn't thought about the small rose tattoo on the back of her neck for ages.

The man considered her for a moment, then grinned. "It is you. You're one of my daughter's heroes. The Iron Maiden is having semifinals this week, here in Miami, and she's competing."

Tillie stood, stunned. "What?"

"Can I get a picture?" The kid was backing up.

"Um—no . . . I gotta go." She turned to the man. "Tell her to just . . . face the obstacle in front of her. Think out of the box and work to her strengths. And most of all, trust her training."

"Cool." The boy held up his fist.

She bumped it.

Trust her training.

The thought settled into her head as she walked back out onto the street and over to her bike. She'd driven to Miami Beach out of impulse, a tug from her conversation with Flynn. But she'd first trained in Hollywood, north of Miami.

The original Fight Factory.

She pulled on her helmet. If it'd started there, it could end there.

A1A, the highway along the beach, was just as clogged as she remembered, but she followed traffic all the way along the shoreline, past the high-rise resorts and along the cruise ports, past Surfside and North Beach and through Hanover Park. Somehow, being on the road loosened the stiffness inside her, the breeze off the ocean cool.

She passed the Newport Fishing Pier, more resorts on the water, and finally slowed as she reached Hollywood Beach.

Clean and bright, with towering beachside condos and overflowing bougainvillea along tall creamy-white walls. Shaggy palm trees against a crystalline blue sky. Convertibles pumping out a different kind of music—no more hip-hop, more Adele and Celine Dion.

She turned off from the barrier island and headed back over the causeway on the 820, reconnected with Highway 1, past the massive Hollywood Golf Club, and finally slowed as she came into the old neighborhood.

She took a left on Arthur and drove past two-story apartment complexes with tiny yards, a few multiunit single-story buildings, and as she turned onto 19th, tiny flat-roofed homes sitting on mini lots, painted orange or white, awnings over the windows to keep out the sun. She slowed in front of an adobe-looking townhome with a clay tiled roof and a tiny plastic kiddie pool in the yard. They'd had one when she lived here too.

"C'mon, we'll pretend we're at a resort." Pearl, putting her entire lawn chair into the pool. *"All we need is a hot guy with an umbrella drink."*

They had needed a lot more than that, but for a minute there, they'd been happy.

Tillie's gaze went to the back deck area. She didn't see a camera. Just a couple of metal lawn chairs and a snarled, dry hibiscus.

She turned at the end of the block, and there, across the street from the Romanian church, sat the original Fight Factory, with the hanging bags across the front windows and the three central sparring rings, the weight sets, and the wall of champions. Probably, hopefully, Rigger had taken down their picture together.

A few cars sat in the lot, and she drove by, not seeing Rigger's Dodge Charger, but then again, that had been five years ago.

He probably drove something a little slicker now.

Still, she needed a place to hunker down and wait, so she pulled into the church lot, got off the bike, and sat under a palm tree.

She tucked herself in and waited. Tried not to think about Moose and the look on his face when she'd left him at the hospital. *"This is goodbye."*

Wiped her cheeks.

Two hours later, as she debated finding another taco truck, a Lexus pulled up. And under the late afternoon sun, Rigger climbed out, wearing a pair of suit pants and an oxford, pressed and neat. Not a hint of a man who would run someone off the road and steal a little girl out of the back seat. But she'd listened to Donna's account, and in the pit of her soul, she knew it'd been him.

He went into the building.

An hour later, as the sun sent shadows into the late hours, he came out. Got in his Lexus. Drove away.

And so did Tillie.

She stayed a ways back, weaving in and out of traffic, hiding behind trucks and cars, but always an eye on him, and followed him out of Hollywood, north to Fort Lauderdale and then—she just *knew* it—out to Las Olas Isles, with the multimillion-dollar estates, the canals, the tall palms, and gated yards. Driveways paved with cobblestone, where shiny Escalades parked for security alongside Ferraris and Astin Martins.

Rigger pulled into the driveway of a sleek-looking, flat-topped midcentury modern mansion that sat on a corner lot, with a wall of windows and a deck that wrapped around the entire top floor. On the main floor, slatted wooden privacy walls secured a walkway around the house, and beyond that, the entire yard of fake grass was gated with wrought iron. The wide-tiled driveway held at least two Escalades along with a massive garage. She drove around the block and spotted an expansive patio area under a rounded balcony that jutted from the house. Thick pillars held it up on either side.

Beyond that, a forty-foot three-story yacht sat at anchor at the canal dock. Men stood on the yacht, talking amidst armed guards stationed at the bow and stern.

As she watched, Rigger walked out of the house to the yacht. A dog followed him out, barking, and behind him, a little boy ran out, then cannonballed into the pool. The dog—a boxer, from the look of it—barked, worried, as the boy splashed to the edge. Then it turned to warn off the men on the boat as Rigger now glad-handed them.

A woman came out, tall, shapely, and bronzed—Courtney Baker. She wore a bikini and a wrap and sat down on the edge of the pool, splashing the little boy with her feet.

Aboard the boat, Rigger laughed, his hand on the shoulder of one of the men.

And all she could see was Rigger hitting Pearl.

Tillie looked up at the house's windows, scanning them, and then the porch below, and then . . . in the fading darkness, a light went on in one of the massive floor-to-ceiling windows. Her heart nearly stopped at the sight of a little girl standing in the window, staring out into the early evening dusk.

Tillie could make out her daughter's frame anywhere.

I'm here, honey. I'm coming for you.

A black SUV drove by, probably someone's protection detail, and she realized she'd been sitting too long. So she motored around the corner, then down the street, across the canal, studying the house from as many angles as she could see.

"Remember your training."

A half hour until nightfall.

And then she was getting her daughter back.

THIRTEEN

OF COURSE MOOSE WAS TOO LATE.
"Three delays. Are you serious?" He threw his bag into the back of the SUV alongside Axel's, Shep's, and London's and then opened the front door.

"Hey, Moose." The voice came from a tanned and grinning Colt Kingston, who had driven down from his houseboat two hours north in some harbor near Space Force.

Apparently, Colt was part of a top-secret project but could sneak away to help a hometown boy with some reconnaissance and maybe rescue.

Or maybe there'd be no need for recon, because according to a text he'd gotten from Flynn, Tillie had made bail four hours ago and vanished. So there was that.

Apparently, she'd meant her words. . . . *This is goodbye.*

Axel climbed in the back, London and Shep taking the bucket seats in back. London seemed quiet, looking out the window. .

"Have I mentioned how much I miss Alaska?" He pulled a ball cap from the backpack at his feet and shoved it onto his head, donned sunglasses. He was already sweating.

Colt pulled away from traffic and merged into the slow-moving flow of cars leaving the Miami International Airport. Already, the sun hung on the backside of the day, casting long shadows between the shiny high-rises. Palm trees sprouted from concrete, adding a surreal, *Miami Vice* feel to the world.

"So, where to?" Colt asked.

"She's in the wind," Moose said, looking out the window. "But Flynn tracked down Rigger's home address. It's about an hour north of here, in Fort Lauderdale."

"Great. I'll get on 95." Colt wore a pair of jeans, sneakers, and a Hawaiian-print button shirt, a cap over his dark hair, a real surfer vibe radiating off him. "Hungry?"

"Starved," Axel said, leaning forward. "We had to practically run through Sea-Tac, and when we got to Chicago, everything was closed. If it weren't for the snacks Shep and London bought, I'd be eating my flip-flops."

"That's just gross," London said.

"We caught all the thunderstorms heading east," Moose said. "We had to sleep in the terminal in O'Hare."

"Fun," Colt said. "There's a great Cuban place on the Hollywood strip if you want to stop."

Fact was, the last thing Moose wanted was a Cuban sandwich, but by the time they'd travelled north and cut over to the oceanside, his stomach growled, and he could admit that sustenance might make him less grumpy.

Less wanting to hurt someone.

Vengeance wasn't his, but just a little justice? *Please?*

They piled out of the SUV at the Cuban food truck in a parking lot that overlooked white sandy beaches and rolling surf and swilled the smell of salt and spicy pork into the air.

Colt went over to the truck to order, and Moose sat at a nearby picnic table, folded his hands, his gaze toward the ocean.

"You look like a man trying not to combust," Axel said, joining Moose after placing his order.

Moose said nothing.

"Flynn keeps texting, asking where we are."

Moose looked at Axel. "Do not tell her. The last thing I want is for her to find Tillie and haul her back in for another kidnapping attempt."

"Isn't that why we're here? To stop Tillie?"

He hadn't settled on that yet. *Yes, probably.* Because in his heart, he knew he couldn't let her break the law again.

And yet, what was right—to let Hazel sit in peril?

He kept staring at the ocean.

Colt came over, set a sandwich in front of him. "I got you the spicy one." He settled in next to Moose. "Is this about the same girl I met in Copper Mountain? The one who lost her daughter?"

"Yep." Moose unwrapped the sandwich. "Turns out that she's not Hazel's mom—she's her aunt but is raising her. But this guy, Rigger—he's her dad, and he's got custody."

"So what's the problem?"

"He's . . . bad news. This looks good." Pulled pork, ham, and pickles. He picked it up to take a bite. "Tillie has a video of Rigger assaulting her sister. And he's got a slew of other charges against him."

"So this is a rescue op."

Moose chewed his bite, put the sandwich down, and wiped his mouth. "Could be. Right now, I just want to find Tillie and . . . stop her from doing something stupid."

Colt had also dug into his sandwich, the juice dripping onto his paper plate. "What's the stupid part? Breaking the law, or letting something terrible happen to someone she loves?"

"Sounds like you have some history there."

"Some." Colt took a drink of his pop. "What I've discovered is that sometimes God asks us to get involved. Sometimes he asks us to wait. And all the time, he goes with us, even if we do stupid things. The key is to not go alone."

Shep and London had taken their sandwiches and walked out onto the beach. He tried not to read into it, but they seemed to be avoiding them. Or maybe. . .Colt? No, they probably didn't even know him.

Axel sat with his back to them on the bench, eating, and scrolling through his phone.

"Come to me."

The words had been hanging in Moose's head the entire trip to Miami.

He looked back at the sea. *Please. Keep her safe. Bring her help if she needs it.*

He finished his sandwich.

Axel turned and set down his phone. "Flynn is working with her friend Val to track down security footage from the night Matthew Lopez was killed. Val's a former detective with the Miami police. Apparently they were able to track down the security company, but all their files are encrypted. And their current tech can't figure out how to decode them."

Of course.

"And she says that if we need backup, to call her."

"So she can bring the Miami heat and arrest Tillie? Yeah, no."

Axel held up a hand. "Antlers in, bro. I think she meant as a friend. She has no jurisdiction in Florida."

Right. He probably shouldn't have snapped. "Sorry."

"It's okay, Grumpy Moose. We're all on your side here." Axel turned around again, gesturing with his sandwich at Shep and London throwing shells into the ocean. "What's with those two? Are they together?"

"Shep said they have history."

"Looks more like a future to me."

"Maybe. Shep said they shared some trauma together. An avalanche. I do know that she was a missionary pilot in Nigeria before she came here."

Moose looked at Colt. "You were in Nigeria, right? I remember Dodge telling the story—something about you getting kidnapped by the Boko Haram?"

Colt had balled up his sandwich wrapper, was now staring hard at London in the distance. "Yep."

Wait. Maybe London *did* know Colt. So, why the cold front?

"Did you know London?"

He sighed. Again, "Yep."

A weird silence.

Axel looked at Colt, then Moose. "There's something about her. I don't know. Secretive. Like she has a past." He had folded up his sandwich wrapper.

"What, like she's a spy?" This from Colt.

Moose considered him, the strange way he'd said that. "What aren't you telling us?"

Colt gave a laugh. "No. I mean, there were rumors that she wasn't just a pilot."

"What?"

He looked at Moose. "Just some . . . I don't know. Like I said, rumors. But they all sort of circled around the idea that she was really in some branch of the clandestine forces. Even a NOC operative."

"Non official cover?" Axel nodded. "I knew it. A spy."

Colt held up his hand. "Don't go crazy. People invent stuff when they don't know much about a person."

If Moose was honest, he *didn't* know much about London. She'd come recommended by Shep.

Who knew her *how*?

He watched the two of them. Shep calm, his hands in his pockets, London crouched in front of a flock of sanderlings, feeding them bread.

She got up and brushed off her hands, her profile in the sun. Pretty, but no-nonsense and smart. Still, he didn't see her as a spy.

Then again, he hadn't seen Tillie as a criminal.

Still didn't see her as a criminal.

"Let's go," Moose said and stood up. Axel whistled to the pair on the sand and waved them in.

The sun had sunk on the horizon, the shadows long upon the ocean as they drove north along the ocean drive, finally cutting west at A1A, then north again.

"Florida always smells like it's moldy," said Shep from the back seat.

"And the palm trees are constantly shedding," said London.

Moose looked back at them. "Since when did either of you live in Florida? Shep, you're from Montana, and London—"

"Never lived here," she said. "Just visited a few times."

Axel raised an eyebrow from the back seat.

Moose shrugged. He simply preferred to take people as he met them. If London had secrets, let her.

They reached Fort Lauderdale, then turned east to Las Olas. Shadows turned the street dusky. The architecture here turned trendy, the houses white and ornate, most of them bumped up against wide canals, many with speedboats and even small motor yachts moored in their backyards.

Colt turned onto San Marco Drive and slowed as he headed down the street, past the multimillion-dollar mansions now lit up with floodlights.

Everyone went a little quiet.

"This is Rigger's place," said Axel and pointed to a three-story modern home that probably belonged in some fancy magazine.

"There's no way she's breaking in here to grab Hazel," Shep said.

London leaned over him, staring out the window. "Take out that camera on the tree and the two lights on the patio in front and you get in through that upstairs window." She pointed to the massive balcony. "Or you come in off the water, sneak in around the pool, kick out a few of the lawn lights, and go up the terrace. If she has parkour skills, she's on the second-story patio in back, no problem."

Moose just looked at her. "Have you lost your mind?"

She leaned back. "What? You said she was an Iron Maiden. Have you not seen that show?"

He shook his head.

"I downloaded her seasons on my phone, and while you guys were snoozing in Chicago, I watched them. Also managed to find a few interviews. She smashed a world record on the warped wall, and the most tandem pull-ups. She's a rock star."

"Of course she is," Axel said and looked at Moose.

Yes. Of course she was, and the words reached in, took hold. "She is totally breaking in to get Hazel." Silence, and he sat back. "And I guess we're here to make sure she doesn't get killed doing it."

More silence.

"Moose. What are you thinking? I mean, we're not spec ops," said Axel.

"I am," said Colt. He looked at Shep.

Shep's mouth tightened. "Fine. I was a medic, attached to a Ranger unit."

"And you were in the Coast Guard, Axe," Moose said.

"That definitely doesn't count," said Colt.

"Hey!" Axel said. "Five minutes, man. I can hold my breath for five minutes."

"Super not impressive," Colt said. "Let me introduce you to my brother, Ranger."

Axel shook his head.

London stayed strangely quiet. But she was studying the house. "There are two suits in the front, near the door. And one guy in the back. And they all look like thugs Rigger brought home from the gym." She turned to Colt. "You were special ops?"

"Yes."

"And I know you have skills," she said to Shep, and Moose raised an eyebrow.

"One if by land. Shep and Colt, you need to figure out a way to get inside the perimeter and assist her if she decides to exfil over the fence." She looked at Axel. "Two if by sea. You think you can get in by water?"

"I have to get wet for this op?"

"Don't be a baby. If she goes in the canal, you're there to help with Hazel."

She looked at Moose. "And you. What do you think about rescuing that little beauty up there?"

He looked to where she pointed.

On the flat roof of the three-story palatial home sat a small private helicopter.

"Aside from asking how we'd get up there, I'm not stealing a helicopter, London."

"*We're* stealing the helicopter, and I promise we'll put it back. But the last thing we want is a high-speed chase with Hazel in the back."

"London—"

"Okay," she said. "I'll get the chopper. You make sure that Tillie doesn't wind up with that." She pointed to a boxer that ran into the yard, barking at the street.

"I can't believe we're doing this," Moose said. "Do we even know if Tillie's here?"

"She's here." And then London pointed to a motorcyclist at the edge of the property.

He'd seen the person earlier, parked down the street, when they'd passed the house the first time. But they had driven off and—

"That's Tillie?"

"I recognize reconnaissance when I see it."

It was too dark to be sure. "What's she doing?"

And right then, Tillie pulled out, following a pizza delivery car.

"Three if by pizza," London said, looking over at him and smiling. And then he got it. Tillie was going to steal a pizza and deliver it right to the front door.

Oh no, no . . . "This is crazy. We are not going to sit here and plan a . . . a kidnapping assist. This is . . . No." Moose shook his head. "I can't ask you to do that."

"You're not," Shep said.

"This is a felony!"

Nothing.

"Guys. We'd become accessories to a kidnapping, and then what? We'd be on the lam? In a bad *Ocean's Eleven* sequel, all going our separate ways until our next big gig?"

"I get the boat," Axel said.

"This is not funny."

"You went there, with Clooney—"

"And they weren't that bad, Moose," said London.

He glared at London, then Axel, who held up his hands in surrender.

"I'm serious. We do this and Air One is over. I'm already barely keeping us afloat, and with the lawsuit—"

"What lawsuit?" Shep said darkly.

Moose sighed. "The Benton family is suing us for negligence in the death of Grace Benton. The court is considering freezing our assets, which means we'd have to shut down anyway. I suppose it won't matter if I'm sitting in Sing Sing."

"They'll send you to Coleman, here in Florida," Colt said.

"Not if we don't transport her across state lines. Then it's a domestic case," London said, and again Moose just stared at her. "I'm just saying, it wouldn't be Coleman, because that's a federal prison. It would probably be Raiford. At least for you guys. I'd go to Lowell."

And then there was silence.

So maybe it *had* sunk in a little.

"You should have told us about the lawsuit," Axel said, now serious.

"Yes. Yes, I should have. I'm sorry. But now you know and . . . I can't let us do this."

More quiet, the darkness now heavier, their expressions shadowed.

Finally, from Axel, "Okay, then what are we supposed to do?"

And then, as they sat in silence, it didn't matter—

Fire exploded out of a downstairs window.

It rocked the neighborhood, the SUV, the team, and they turned silent as black smoke billowed out of the lower level and sirens blared.

And all Moose could think as he barreled out of the SUV was, *Oh, Tillie, what have you done?*

Yeah, that hadn't gone as planned. In fact, Tillie had planned exactly none of the chaos that now erupted at the back of Rigger's hacienda.

Fire licked from the main floor, windows bursting, and then, from the front door, Courtney ran out screaming, and all Tillie could think as she got off her bike was . . .

Now.

She'd been sorting out how to get inside for the better part of an hour, and it had dawned on her when the pizza guy went by to simply . . .

Make it simple.

He'd parked at the end of the street, and she'd waited for him, planning to grab the red insulated bag when he returned from his delivery—no need to deprive anyone of their pizza—when the absurdity of her idea hit her.

She'd counted at least three former MMA fighters, two she knew personally, surrounding the complex—as if Rigger knew she might be coming.

Of course he knew. Probably counted on it.

Although, it also had to do with what was going down on that yacht.

Even if she got inside the gate, her skills weren't the kind that could neutralize three grown men, no matter what the movies said. She had U-turned the bike and reached the property, her eye on the window where she'd seen Hazel, when the explosion rocked her off her bike.

She hit the ground.

And then she stopped thinking. Because Hazel was *inside* that house somewhere—

Lights burst around the perimeter as if there was a surge of electricity, but she was already on the fence, then over, onto the grass.

This was easy. Columns held up a deck that hung over the pool area, and all she did was run past them to the far side, land on one column, bounce to the other, then spring up to the upper railing, catching it and pulling herself up.

Behind her, the yacht tore away from the dock, heading out of the canal into the passageway, but she was inside, second level, and on the hunt for Hazel.

Smoke billowed up into the night, obscuring her entrance, and she opened the unlocked doors and ran into the master suite.

She braced herself to find Rigger inside, but the doors hung open, so she ran past the massive king bed, under hanging lights that looked like a cascade of tiny pebbles, and then stopped and edged out into the hall.

Shouting rose from below. Whatever had exploded had caught

a sofa on fire, then some kind of fancy wall covering, and smoke blurred everything.

She'd seen Hazel on the second story, east side, and now ran down the hall, slamming open doors.

A kid's room with a television the size of her car and a wall of Legos on display. She ran through a Jack and Jill bathroom to a similar bedroom, then out and down the hall to the next room. Bathroom—Hazel would love that tub—and then to the final room.

An office. But a Murphy bed had been pulled out, and crayons lay on the surface of the bed, and then—

Hazel's locket. It lay broken on the floor. Tillie scooped it up. "Hazel!" She didn't want to shout, but—*aw*, "Hazel. It's Mom!"

Smoke crept up the upper floors. The entire house wasn't burning yet, but certainly, these open-concept homes filled with smoke fast.

Hiding them.

Maybe this was God, on their side, just like Moose had said.

"Hazel—" She opened the closet—nothing. Then looked again in the bathroom.

Please let Hazel have evacuated. Tillie ran to the end of the house and looked down.

Street light brightened the entire yard, and in the distance, red lights evidenced help on the way, sirens pealing down a nearby street.

In the middle of it all, shouting, holding one of his sons, stood Rigger, his white shirt grimy, pointing at the house.

She also spotted Courtney and their other son, which meant— She ran back to the room. "Hazel! I know you're here."

And then she spotted Hazel's pink cowboy boots, poking out from under the curtain.

She pulled it back, and Hazel stood there, her hands over her mouth, her eyes wide.

Then, "Mommy!" She launched into Tillie's arms, her skinny arms encasing Tillie's neck, her legs around her waist, and Tillie scooped her up, pulling her tight, breathing her in. Hazel felt so small and broken and . . . "I'm sorry, Hazelnut. I'm so sorry."

"I was so scared, and then that man—he makes me call him Daddy." Hazel leaned back. "I hate him. He's so mean, and— please, he's not my daddy, right?"

Oh, Hazel. "Let's get out of here." Tillie turned and headed for the door, out into the hallway.

And that's when she heard Rigger shout. How he'd gotten to the second-story master, she couldn't guess—except, he'd taught her some of those parkour skills, so—

He came running down the hallway, swearing at her, and she took off toward the stairs to the third story. She put Hazel down at the steps and grabbed her hand. "Run!"

No railing, just a set of steps, and it led to more bedrooms and another jutting deck. She ran out to the deck, refusing to look behind her, and hit the railing made of glass.

Three stories down, smoke obscuring the landing.

If she were alone, she'd chance it. But even if Hazel held on, the jar of their landing would throw her off.

The pool might cushion them, but again, Hazel. And she couldn't really see the pool anyway.

She looked up. *The roof.*

"C'mere, Hazel. Put your foot here." She held out her folded hands.

"Mom—"

"Do it!"

Hazel put her foot in Tillie's hands. "I'm scared!" She put her hands on Tillie's shoulders.

"I know. But have faith. It's going to be okay. I promise."

She met Hazel's eyes.

"'*Tillie will call on me, and I will answer her, I will be with her in trouble.*'"

"God, help me!" She hoisted Hazel up, nearly catapulting her onto the roof. Hazel clung to the edge, kicking. Tillie grabbed at Hazel's feet, pushing. "Pull yourself up!"

The tackle hit Tillie without defense, middle body, slamming her against the glass wall railing of the deck. She hit so hard she lay there gasping, everything burning, trying to clear her head.

Through the haze, she saw Rigger grab Hazel's foot and yank her to the deck. She fell and cried out, and Tillie rounded to her feet.

Then Tillie threw herself at Rigger. Turned her right hand flat and slid her arm under his jaw. She caught his left bicep, grabbed it, and slid her left hand behind his head, pushing it forward. Then she clamped her legs around his waist, squeezed, and reared back.

He fell—probably on purpose—and she hit the deck so hard she nearly lost her breath again, but she had enough in her to shout, "Run, Hazel!"

Rigger tried to headbutt Tillie. She flexed hard, pulling her shoulders back, fighting for a blood choke, but he slammed his head back again and again and made a pocket under her arm.

Then he grabbed her hand, brought it over his head and rolled.

"You should have locked your hand on your shoulder."

She scrambled back, kicking at him, but he got her foot, pulled her close.

"Always running away from me."

She kicked him in the face, and it loosened his hold.

She jerked free, scrambled up. And that's when she realized Hazel *hadn't* run. She stood, screaming.

"Hazel, *run!*"

Then Tillie rounded to face Rigger.

He charged her. She rolled away, then brought her hand down on his neck, a slice that rattled her to her bones.

He barely flinched. "Really?"

Then he backed up. And maybe he didn't see Hazel behind him, or maybe he knew, but the force of it knocked her against the railing, and she cried out.

"Hazel!"

Rigger turned, and her little girl kicked at him.

"Hazel, no!"

Rigger caught her leg and pushed it over, and just like that, she went over the glass wall.

Tillie froze. *What*—"Hazel!"

Rigger's fist caught her full-on as she ran to the edge. She spun and landed on the deck with the force of a fallen tree, head spinning.

Hazel was still screaming. "Mom!" And when she looked up, Hazel hung from the edge. "Mom!"

Tillie struggled up, lunged for her—"Hazel!"

And then Hazel fell.

Her scream lit up the night, heat flaring through Tillie's body as the horror seared through her. "*Hazel!*"

She ran for the edge, but Rigger grabbed her, pulled her back, his arm around her neck, going for the hold.

But she dropped, rolled, kneed him, and then rolled again, and from her knees, threw everything she had into a palm blow to his jaw.

He reeled back. Fell.

She hit her feet. Ran to the edge of the deck. But the night and the smoke obscured her daughter's body below. Just water now, hazing over the building, and shouts from the deck—

And then from behind her, Rigger, coming back to life.

She turned around. "You killed your daughter."

He laughed. "She's not my daughter. She was *never* my daughter. I don't know who your sister slept with, but she came to me knocked up." Blood gushed from his nose, and he put a hand to it, then shook it away and smiled at her. "Tried to make me think the girl was mine. I'm not that stupid."

Then he swore at her, a litany of vile words that knotted Tillie up and brought her back to a day when her only thought had been murder.

See, this was why she was unredeemable. Because on the inside, she didn't have faith. She just had herself.

Remember your training.

The words shook through her.

Stay calm.

She ducked, rounded away, and his punch missed her.

Stay on your feet.

He dove for her, but she sent up a knee and pulled him down, and pain flared as it connected with his chin.

He pushed her, but she scrambled back.

Watch the body language.

He backed up, jarred, a bull, his neck thickening, his breaths hard. "I knew I'd find you. You can't escape me." He stepped back, and she glanced behind her. He was going to rush her, send her over too. "You belong to me."

And right then she got it. This wasn't *just* about Pearl or Hazel . . . maybe even her father. It was about her. And Rigger wanting control of it all. Her heart. Her thoughts. Her *soul*.

"No, I don't. I don't belong to you."

Know your escape routes.

"You do, Steelrose. You know you'll never escape me." He leaned toward her, his voice low.

She could go over the edge, but without seeing the bottom, she'd hurt herself landing.

She could go up, to the roof—

Weapon. She needed a weapon. A side table sat beside a lounge chair, and she edged toward it, picking it up. "You're the one who won't escape me, Rigger. The police know about Matthew. They know you killed him."

He slammed the lounger away, then grabbed the table legs and jerked.

She let it go. He fell off-balance, stepped back, and she leaped for the edge of the roof.

She pulled herself up, fighting, kicking, nearly there—

Rigger grabbed her leg. "You—" And there went the words again. She kicked at him, he ducked and then jerked.

She slammed onto the deck, the force of it jarring every bone, and this time, taking her breath with it.

Rigger stood over her, blood dripping off his chin, his lip split, and reached for her.

She lay helpless, still gasping like a fish, and could do nothing but close her eyes.

Clearly, this was the end. And she was more hurt than she thought, because all she had was a voice deep inside. *"She will call on me, and I will answer her. I will be with her in trouble...."*

Her escape route.

Please—God! Please, rescue me—!

Scuffling and a smack, and then voices around her, and she opened her eyes to see police—probably police, because they wore tactical vests and gear, boots and helmets—and one of them had Rigger on the ground, his hand in a submission hold.

A man knelt beside her. "You okay?"

She blinked at him, tried to push herself up, her breath finally back, then rolled and ran to the edge of the railing. "Hazel!"

She rounded, and the man stood in front of her. "I gotta—"

"She's okay."

He wore a helmet, a glass visor, and full tactical gear but . . . those eyes.

Those *blue* eyes.

And the dark skim of whiskers, and the way he suddenly, mark-edly swallowed, and . . .

"Tillie."

She stepped back, her hand on the glass wall. Breathed hard. Shook her head. *No . . . What?*

He pushed up his visor, then pulled off his helmet. Short dark hair, wide shoulders—

"Dad?" Her voice emerged broken, a whisper. "*Dad?*"

He barely nodded before she was in his arms, hers tight around his neck, so tight she might be cutting off his breath. His embrace pressed her into his hard-plated vest, but she didn't care.

And then she wept.

He might have wept too, because his body shook as he held her. Someone cuffed Rigger and hauled him away through the smoke and fire and—

Wait. She pushed away, breathing hard, her face a mess. "Hazel."

"The little girl? Someone caught her."

She blinked at him. "What?"

"Someone caught her. I saw it as we came over the wall—he was just there. A guy, a big guy. I don't know how he knew, but . . . he was there and he just grabbed her. She's okay, Tillie."

She's okay.

And with his words, big guy all she could think was. . .Moose?

Somehow, she was nodding, and he put his arm around her. "Let's get a corpsman up here—"

"No more corpsmen, boss. Just the EMTs," said one of the men, and then her dad laughed.

And it was like a promise kept, pouring into her soul, bringing life and light and more than she ever imagined.

And just like that, she was free.

Free of Rigger. Free of running. Free of fear.

Free to believe.

Her father seemed about a thousand times larger than she remembered him. Or maybe that was simply her heart exploding her vision. "I don't get it. What are you doing here?"

"We've been watching Richer and his gym, waiting for a shipment. A couple days ago we got word that he'd brought home a little girl. We thought he'd expanded into human trafficking and were trying to decide when to move. Today he received a shipment of nearly four hundred thousand packets of individually packaged fentanyl disguised as protein powder."

"You came to arrest him?"

"Yes. The smoke was from flash bombs. Courtney knew and was on her way out with the kids, but ops never go quite as planned. One of the flash bombs caught fire."

Right.

"We went after the yacht, secured the dealers aboard, and then came back for Richer. I couldn't believe it when I saw him brawling with a woman. It took a couple more seconds to figure out . . . I mean . . . what are you doing here? Of all places . . ." He shook his head.

"The girl he brought home—that's Hazel. She's your granddaughter."

He blinked at her. Swallowed. "My . . . my granddaughter?"

"Yeah. Actually, she's Pearl's daughter."

He frowned. "Is Pearl okay?"

Oh, Dad. "She's . . . gone. Cancer. Three years ago. I was with her."

He drew in a breath, nodded, but his mouth tightened and he looked away, his jaw pulling. When he turned back to her his eyes were wet. "I tried to find you."

"I know. Or at least, I figured that's why you came to Florida."

"I was discharged, and I found out that you'd become a marine." He shook his head. "Seriously?"

"Semper Fi."

"Your whereabouts were top secret, but your foster mom knew

you'd gone to Florida, so I went looking, first in Tampa, then Miami, but I couldn't find you, so I fell back into what I did."

"Did you know that Rigger was trying to find me?"

He shook his head.

"My friends think he was trying to use me against you. Revenge for killing his brother."

Her father's eyes narrowed.

An EMT had come up the stairs. "Listen, I need to find Hazel." She held up her hand to the EMT. "I've had worse." Then she pushed past them, through the room and down the stairs, still intact, and through the front door.

Outside, smoke still cluttered the air. So many people—firemen spraying water on the house, and two ambulances and cops and . . .

And not a sighting of Moose. Moose *wasn't* here.

Instead, she just wished it with all her heart.

"Mom!"

The voice cut through the clutter. She turned and spotted Hazel, pushing through the crowd, a blanket falling off her shoulders as she ran to Tillie.

Tillie fell to her knees, opened her arms, and Hazel ran in, nearly bowling her over, and again, she wept.

"Hazel—I thought . . . " She buried her face in her daughter's shoulder.

"Mom, you're squeezing too hard."

"Sorry, Nut." She let go. Looked her up and down. "Are you okay? Did you get hurt?"

"He caught me, Mom."

She nodded, looking around. "A fireman?"

"No. Superman."

She looked back at Hazel, the nickname rooting her.

Moose.

"Right place, right time."

She looked up, and there he stood, as if he'd emerged from the smoke and haze exactly like Superman to stand there, magnificent and strong, smiling down at her, so much in his beautiful gray-green eyes that . . .

"I didn't mean it." She pushed to her feet. "I didn't mean it—I mean, I wanted to mean it—my brain said I should mean it, but . . . I *didn't* mean it."

He stepped up to her, cupped her face with his hand. "That's okay. I didn't really believe you anyway." He frowned, then, "You're hurt."

She kissed him—hard, her arms around his neck, pulling him against her, kissing him because he was her hero but also her friend, and the man who kept his promises. *Moose.*

He put his arms around her, held her, kissed her back—not as urgently, but that was good and safe and right in front of all these people and her daughter.

Her daughter. In her heart, for sure, and maybe, after all this was sorted, legally too.

And maybe she'd never know who Hazel's father was, but really, it didn't matter.

Especially when Moose lifted his head and met her eyes. "I love you, Tillie. And I don't care what you say or what you do or how angry you get at me, I'm not leaving you."

"Promise?"

He laughed. "Nope. You'll just have to trust me."

FOURTEEN

TOO MUCH SMOKE.
Moose coughed as he pushed through the front gates, the smoke billowing out of the house. Shouts, and the clutter of people, and flames—his eyes burned.

"She went in the back!" London's voice. It rose through him, galvanized him, and he took off around to the back of the house.

His heart thundered, and in the back of his mind, he knew—he'd get there. It had already happened, but the memory still played out, almost in slow motion, in his dream. Cops coming from the canal, one of them coming for him.

Then Colt somehow in the fray even as Moose kept running.

Smoke clogging the air, turning it hazy, and then a scream and Tillie's voice. He stood on the pool deck, looked up. Barely made out a body hanging over the edge of the balcony.

Then it dropped.

Reflexes, adrenaline, instincts—

He missed. He *missed!*

Hazel lay broken on the sidewalk, her head cracked, bleeding, and he went to his knees. A keening sound emerged from him, high pitched, ripping through him—

No . . . *no* . . .

A siren blared, piercing, cutting through his nightmare, and Moose opened his eyes, shaking, sweaty, and sat up.

Blinked.

The morning rays cast through the gauzy curtains of the main-story windows of the beach home, puddled along the wooden floor, over the creamy white sheets of the queen-sized bed.

Oaken's beach home—or at least, the one he'd given to his mother.

An alarm blared, cutting through the house, and Moose threw off the comforter, pulled on a pair of shorts, and slammed out of his room.

The kitchen connected to the great room, and as he came out of the main-floor bedroom, he spotted Hazel at the stove, trying to put out flames from a pan with a towel. Except the towel had lit on fire, and Hazel started screaming, trying to shake out the flames. Which flew off the towel onto a rack of paper towels—

"Get back!" Moose scooped her up with one arm, grabbed a pan lid, and slammed it over the flames. Then, still holding Hazel, he snatched the hose from the sink faucet and doused the paper-towel torch. He dropped the burning towel onto the tile floor and drenched that too.

About then the screaming from the alarm stopped, and he turned to find Oaken on a chair, pieces of the smoke alarm in his hand.

Boo had also emerged from a guest room, wearing a pair of shorts and a T-shirt.

Tillie stood at the open sliding-glass door, holding a cup of coffee, her eyes wide. "I was out by the pool—I didn't even hear it until—Hazel, are you okay?"

He hadn't realized he still held her. Now he put her down.

She looked up at him, then her mom, and her cute little face crumpled. "I wanted to make you breakfast."

That's when Moose spotted the broken eggshells in the sink, the empty carton on the counter. And bacon—aw, the grease had probably splashed out onto the gas stove.

"I always make my mom eggs at home," she said to Moose as he knelt in front of her.

"It's okay. Are you burned?" He looked at her arms, her hands, and she shook her head.

"She does," Tillie said, coming in. "It's okay, Hazel. These things happen."

"I just want to go home." Hazel turned to her mom, her arms around her, crying.

Moose stood up, wrapped a hand around his neck.

He trembled, the adrenaline still hot inside him. Maybe from the fire.

Maybe from the dream.

Surely from the what-ifs.

Axel had emerged from an upstairs bedroom. "So, that was fun." He had wet hair, a T-shirt plastered to his body, a pair of faded jeans. He leaned over the railing. "If I jump, will you catch me?"

Moose had stood up and now scowled at him.

"Too soon?" Axel winked.

"Never too soon," Tillie said. She released Hazel, then walked over and put her hand on Moose's arm.

And in front of everyone, she rose on her toes and kissed him.

Oh.

She patted his chest. "Listen, Superman. You sit and let me get this cleaned up."

She directed Hazel to a stool. But Boo and Oaken had already started the cleanup. Moose came over to sit next to her.

"You okay, kiddo?"

She nodded. *Such a tough kid.* "I couldn't sleep, and Mom got up, so I did too."

"Yeah, I couldn't sleep either," Tillie said, now sitting beside them. "I just keep—" She sighed, then looked at Moose. "I'm still trying to sort it all out. How on earth did you . . ." She glanced at Hazel.

"I don't know, really. When we saw the house explode—or at least what we thought was explosions—I just lost it. I knew you'd try to save Hazel—"

"You knew?"

"We saw you casing the joint," Axel said as he came down the stairs.

"I wasn't . . . okay, yes, I was. But only to figure out a way to get in." She took a sip of her coffee.

"I don't know why I knew to go to the back—I just did. And then, there she was." He smiled at Hazel. "She just fell right into my arms."

He'd caught her. Nearly gone down with the force of it, but held, pulled her tight. And then she'd wrapped her arms around him and started to wail—something about her mom—but she'd held him so tight he couldn't wrench her away. Then more cops appeared and grabbed him and forced him to the front yard and—

And right then, he rewrote the nightmare lingering in his head. Yes, life was out of his control. And always would be.

But God had sent him there, right time, right place, and that was enough. To trust God to be in charge. Moose just had to listen.

You keep him in perfect peace whose mind is stayed on you, because he trusts in you.

"Right into your arms," Tillie repeated, and gave him a soft smile. He lifted a shoulder.

Axel slid onto a stool. "Flynn and I stayed up late talking last night. Her friend Val contacted a family lawyer here that is filing a fresh custody petition in the Florida courts. They're going to have to do a paternity test to prove that Richer isn't the father. He's on the birth certificate."

"He's not my dad," Hazel said. "I *know* it." She slid off the stool.

"Hazel!"

But she ran down the hall toward the room where she'd stayed with her aunt.

Tillie's expression grew serious. "All her life—at least, after we moved to Alaska—my sister told her that her father was a soldier. A brave soldier who'd died. I think she wanted to put a good memory into Hazel's mind instead of the horror of Rigger, and what went down. I always assumed she was lying."

Hazel had returned, carrying her stuffed dog. "Ask my mom."

Tillie frowned. "What?"

She shoved the dog into Tillie's hands. "I know you're not my real mom. She died. But she told me who my dad was."

Tillie held the worn stuffed animal, frowning.

"Mom. Here." Hazel grabbed the animal back and turned it over, reaching up behind its neck to an opening. Dug her little hand into the space and pulled out a tiny MP3 player. She handed it to Tillie. Then rose on her tiptoes and pressed play.

A voice emerged, soft, bright, clear.

"My dearest Hazel. I don't have a lot longer for this earth, but I wanted you to know some truths, things that I think your mom— your next mom, Tillie—won't be able to tell you. First, I love you more than life. You were what saved me from myself. You made me want to believe that there was a better life for us, but it wasn't until your aunt Tillie made me act on that belief that I was set free. See, honey, sometimes you have to act like you believe even when you're not sure. Don't let your unbelief trap you. Someday, you'll understand that. The second thing is that you *are* the daughter of a hero. His name is Arch Henry. Archie. He served with your aunt Tillie. When she deployed, I was very sad. And Archie made me happy. He loved me, and we would have gotten married, but he left for the war. He was killed before he knew about you. But he would have loved you. When I get to heaven, I can't wait to tell him all about you."

Tillie looked up at Moose, holding his gaze, hers wide, glossy. Yeah, his throat ached too. He took her hand.

"Be good for your next mom. Aunt Tillie—Momma Tillie—also loves you and would do anything for you. I'll always be with you, Hazelnut. Never forget that I love you."

The room went silent as the recording stopped. Tillie didn't move.

Moose had nothing. But *shoot*, he sort of wanted to put his head down in his arms and have a little cry.

"See, Mom, I knew that man wasn't my dad." Hazel slid onto the chair and tucked the recorder back into the stuffed animal. "So, can we go home now?"

Flynn had come into the room and now walked up to the counter. "Hazel, I think a few more people need to listen to that recording. And then we can figure out how to get you home."

Moose squeezed Tillie's hand.

"How do you feel about pancakes?" Oaken said as he dried the pan he'd just washed.

"I love pancakes!" Hazel said.

And that broke the silence. Tillie leaned down and kissed her daughter's head, and Boo took out glasses and poured orange juice, and Flynn grabbed a cup of coffee, and then the front door opened and Shep and London came in, breathing hard, dressed in workout gear—clearly returning from a morning run—and Shep said, "What did I miss?"

Moose wanted to ask him the same, but that's when Axel pulled a folded letter from his back pocket and put it on the counter.

"Is that—" Tillie started.

"Yep. The letter from Pike," Axel said. "Moose left it at the cabin, and I thought . . . Anyway, look at the address."

Moose picked it up and read the address under the *Return to Sender* stamp. "It's in Melbourne, Florida."

"Yeah. About two hours from here." He took a sip of coffee, looked at Flynn. "Tell him."

"My contact, Val Castillo, used to be a detective, and he still has access to resources. He found an expired forwarding address for your contact there—Fisher Maguire, Pike's son. His mother lived in Melbourne, but she got remarried about ten years ago and moved to Tampa. Fisher was seventeen at the time. He then graduated, went to college in Pennsylvania, and eventually came back to Florida, where he now runs a computer security company. Ironically, in Melbourne."

Axel took a sip of coffee, then smiled at Moose and said in a singsong voice, "Road trip."

Oh brother.

But Moose considered the envelope, took a breath.

Tillie's hand came over his arm. "Time to get out of the whale."

He looked at her and she winked, and their conversation from the cave, so long ago, but really just a few days, returned to him.

Out of the whale.

"I'm going to need some pancakes first."

"You didn't have to come with me." Moose sat in the driver's seat of Colt's SUV, shaking his head as he and Tillie pulled into a small neighborhood on the barrier island near the town of Melbourne Beach.

Yes, yes she did. After all he'd done for her—"I'm just here for moral support." She touched his arm. "Moose, breathe. It'll be okay."

He nodded, but she heard their past conversations in her head and had no doubt he was stirring up the same.

"This could be the end of Air One," he said softly. "If I were Fisher, I'd want my father's inheritance. I'd be asking why he gave it to a random guy."

"Then you'll have to tell him about the accident, and how Pike died."

Moose swallowed, and her heart went out to him. She leaned over, caught the back of his neck, met his eyes.

"Have a little faith."

"You're hilarious."

"No, seriously." She leaned back. "If you've taught me anything, it's that God does miracles. That he surprises us with more than we can ask or imagine. I mean, who would have thought that my dad was alive and trying to take down the one man who haunted me—haunted us. That he would show up right when Rigger was—" She swallowed, again, for a moment living those terrible moments when she'd been waiting for Rigger to finish what he'd started. "Anyway—"

Moose turned to her. "You're safe. Hazel's safe."

She nodded. "They were sweet today, weren't they?"

"Yeah. Watching your dad meet his granddaughter was something I'll never forget."

Her throat closed over at the memory of her dad showing up at Oaken's mother's house with another toy puppy, then sitting on the floor with Hazel to play a game.

"I remember when he used to play Sorry! with me. It was like watching my childhood all over again." She drew in a breath. "They'll be fine, right?"

"Yes. Declan is meeting Axel and Flynn at the beach. It'll give your dad a chance to bond with her before we go back to Alaska."

Oh.

And maybe the question played on her face because his mouth opened. Closed. "I guess . . . yeah."

She hadn't thought beyond today. "I'm still out on bond. I have a court date to be at. And we need to settle Hazel's custody. My dad has offered his place for us to land for a while."

"Yes." Moose nodded. "I get that." He gave a wry smile. "I just thought, after—"

"You thought right." And the sense of hope welled up in her—she could almost see it. A future with Moose, wherever that might be.

Have faith.

Yes.

She smiled at him, and he studied her face for a moment before he leaned in and kissed her. Sweetly, softly.

A promise.

Then he met her eyes. "Let's find Fisher."

She nodded. He got out, and she followed him up the path to a modest home with a white painted-brick exterior, a teal-blue door.

Not on the level of the home Moose lived in. She glanced at him. The tightness of his jaw had returned.

He knocked on the door. Took a breath. She slid her hand into his.

The door opened.

Moose jerked. Handsome guy, mid-height, lean, with brown hair, wearing a pair of golf shorts and a white shirt. He looked at Moose and then, "You."

And the word seemed to blow Moose apart, because he drew in a breath, swallowed, and she'd never seen him so completely undone.

So, "Hello. My name is Tillie, and this is—"

"Moose Mulligan."

And now she felt her own bones rattle. "Um, yeah. How do you—"

"Come in." Fisher held the door open, then held out his hand. "Sorry. I'm Fisher Maguire. But my guess is that you know that."

Moose took Fisher's hand, nodded, and Tillie followed him into the house.

Nice place. Not large. Clean, with a sunken living room under a vaulted ceiling, a small galley kitchen, and an inviting blue pool covered by a screen in the back.

"I should have contacted you long ago," Fisher said. "Can I get you anything? Water? Something stiffer?"

"Water."

"Nothing for me," Tillie said.

"What you do you mean, contacted me?" Moose asked as Fisher went into the kitchen and pulled a bottle of water from the refrigerator.

He handed it to Moose. "This is my fault."

And she, along with Moose, had nothing.

Moose, however, opened the bottle and took a drink.

"I knew Dad had gone to Alaska, hunting. He invited me every year, even after the divorce, but I was so angry that I just couldn't go. And after we moved, he stopped writing to me, so I thought he gave up too." He sighed. "My mom sent me the article about how you carried him out of the woods, and even then, I didn't want to talk to him. And then he died. And all I could think was . . . I was a jerk. He left me all this money, and I just couldn't touch it."

"He left you money?"

"Yeah. Dad had numerous investment accounts. He left one to me and another to Mom and . . . a few charities. And of course the endowment to Air One Rescue and all the properties in Alaska to you. He was a good man." He sighed. "After he and Mom got divorced, he changed. He was gone a lot when I was a kid, but suddenly he started hanging around. Going to church, and sometimes he tried to drag me along. I was almost relieved when I moved away with her so that he couldn't bug me." He sighed. "I wish I could get that back. Especially now that . . . well, I met my wife, and she finally talked me into attending church. And then

I realized what had changed my dad. Salvation." He met Moose's eyes, then Tillie's. "I wish I'd figured out how to forgive him and asked him to forgive me before he left this earth."

"He sent you a letter." Moose pulled the folded letter from his back pocket. "It came back, and he carried it in his Bible. Tillie found it." He glanced at her as he held out the letter.

Fisher took it. Took a breath. Then he looked up at Moose. "This was sent around the time of my birthday." He turned it over and opened it with his thumb. Reached in and pulled out a card.

Something fluttered out of it, but Fisher seemed not to notice. Tillie picked it up. A picture of a kid, maybe aged ten or twelve, holding a stringer of fish with his father, who was holding a pole, both of them grinning into the camera.

Fisher opened the card, read it, his hand to his mouth. His eyes glazed, and he nodded. Looked up. "It's, uh . . . he . . ."

Moose held up his hand. "It's okay, Fisher. But you should know that he talked about you over those three days while we tried to make it to safety. He definitely loved you, and more, he forgave you. He made me promise to find you and tell you that."

Fisher nodded. "Yeah." He looked away, blinking, closing the card.

Tillie held out the picture. "Seems like he had some good memories."

He took the photo, and a smile slowly swept over his face. "This was taken near his cabin. We used to fly in to go fishing." He ran his thumb over the picture. "I wish, sometimes, that he knew that I turned out okay. Good job. Wife, kid . . . and I found Jesus."

A car pulled up outside, and Fisher looked up.

Tillie turned, too, and through the door came a boy about ten, a towel around his neck, wearing flip-flops and board shorts, his hair wet.

"Dad! The waves are amazing—" He stopped and looked at Moose and Tillie. "Sorry."

SUSAN MAY WARREN

"That's okay. PJ, this is my friend Moose Mulligan and his friend—"

"Tillie Young."

"Hi." PJ raised a hand.

"Take a jump in the pool and then shower off. You have soccer practice in an hour."

PJ went out through the sliding door, dropped his towel, and jumped into the pool.

A woman had come in behind them too, pretty, long brown hair, wearing a sundress. "Hey there." She set beach gear down in the entryway.

"Lana, this is Moose Mulligan and his friend Tillie."

Her mouth made a rounded O as she came over to stand by Fisher. "Really? It's nice to finally meet you, Moose. And you, Tillie." She shook their hands, then turned to Moose. "What are you doing in Florida?"

"It's a long story," Tillie said. "We're . . . sort of in the middle of a . . ."

"Wait," Moose said. "Do you run an internet security company?"

Fisher raised an eyebrow. Nodded.

"Do you know anything about encryption?"

"Of?"

"Security footage."

Tillie frowned at Moose. The security footage from the Fight Factory? They'd found it?

"I can take a look," Fisher said.

Moose pulled out his phone, and she guessed he was texting Axel.

She turned to Fisher. "You really don't care that your dad gave away half your inheritance to other people?"

He sighed, folded the card on the crease where Moose had, and stuck it in his pocket. "Truth is, I *did* care, for a while. And then

285

I realized that God was in all of this. I get the Anchorage news online, and you're doing good stuff up there. And . . . truth is, I have all I need." Then he looked at his wife and smiled.

She frowned but rose up and kissed him. Turned to Tillie. "Would you like something to eat? I made an amazing key lime pie earlier."

Tillie looked at Moose, and he happened to glance up also and meet her eyes.

And then as he smiled, she said, "Yes, actually. Pie would be perfect."

He laughed, and she laughed too, and deep in her heart she heard the words, *With long life I will satisfy her, and show Tillie my salvation.*

FIFTEEN

MAGIC BEGAN WITH THE FIRST SNOWFALL.
Shep stood in the Tooth, holding a cup of coffee,
watching the white stuff peel from the sky. The last week
of September might be a little early for a real snowfall, but he tasted
the freshness of grace, the hint of the beauty that came even in a
frozen world.

This year, he'd ski with London, put a new memory over the
scar of the past.

The snow lay over the glistening ice along the tarmac, a remnant of last night's brutal storm that had turned the highways into
lethal skating rinks. He'd driven in this morning behind a plow
that salted the roads and skimmed the ice and snow away from
the pavement. With Moose down in Florida for Tillie's custody
hearing, someone had to mind the store.

Looked like that someone was him—and Axel and London,
and Boo, who'd flown in a couple days ago, having visited Oaken
on the road somewhere in mid-America.

Now, with the police scanner playing in the back office, Shep
stood watching the lot, waiting for the team to show up. The state

patrol had called earlier and asked them to be on alert, what with all the patrols and EMS services hauling people out of ditches and attending to the pileup on the Glenn Highway.

His phone rang and he pulled it out of his pocket. Recognized the number.

Colt.

Nope. He was done with this game. Colt had texted him from the beach in Florida. He wasn't going to stop watching over her, showing up in her life—that's what love did.

But no more spying or reporting in to Colt what London might be doing. Not that he'd kept a journal or taken pictures, but yes, definitely he'd call his previous gig spying.

No more secrets.

So he thumbed the call away and repocketed his phone.

The place smelled like the bacon and eggs he'd fried up and left on the island, and now he returned to the coffeepot and poured himself a fresh cup. Behind him, the door opened, and in walked Axel, his hair dusted with snow, wearing a winter jacket and jeans, hiking boots.

"It's an ice rink out there."

"Still? I thought the plows would be out salting."

"I got off at Eagle River, swung by Tillie's place just to make sure none of the trees came down on her house after the storm last night. By the time I got back on the highway, the pileup had traffic backed up for a mile leading to the base. Good thing I was heading west, but yeah, the side streets—we could play hockey."

Axel pulled off his jacket and hung it on a hook by the door. Then he headed over to the counter. "Good, you made coffee." He also picked up a piece of bacon from the plate in the middle of the island.

Shep pulled out his phone. No text from London.

"Everything okay?"

"Yeah. I just . . . I texted London about an hour ago, and she hasn't texted back, so . . ."

"She's probably on her way with Boo." Axel slid onto a high-top stool. Grinned at him.

"What?"

"So, you two a thing now?"

Shep lifted a shoulder but couldn't stop a smile. *Maybe. Almost.* He hadn't tried to kiss her again, but it had been tooling around his mind.

Kiss her, and eventually ask some big questions. But, "We're taking it slow."

"Why?"

He frowned. "Um . . ."

"If she's the one"—Axel waggled his eyebrows—"get on with it, dude. Pop the question."

Oh. "Are you—"

"Yes. Definitely. Not yet, though. Flynn's still getting settled in at the police department. But yeah, she's the one. So . . . I should probably start looking for my own digs."

A car pulled up outside, and Shep looked out the front window. Boo, in her Rogue, snow melting off the hood. She got out, headed inside.

"Okay. I like Alaska and everything, but those roads are crazy!" She pulled off her hat, then her jacket.

"Is London driving separately?"

She hung up her jacket, turned. "She's not here?"

Silence.

"She wasn't home when I got there. I thought . . . I thought she was with you."

Shep set down his coffee mug. "She was—we had dinner at my place. And then she went home before the storm really hit. What time did you get in?"

"After eleven."

More silence.

And right then, dispatch came through their radio.

Axel headed into the office to grab it.

Boo came over, her eyes wide. "I'm sorry, Shep. I didn't even think about it—I got up and came here and just assumed—"

"We have a callout," Axel said. "There's a car in Jewel Lake. They think it slid off the road in the night. Submerged. They need a diver to go in after it. I'll get my gear."

Shep put down his coffee, pulled out his phone. Dialed London's number.

Voicemail. "Hey," he said. "It's me. Please call me."

He hung up and texted her again, too.

SHEP
_____

I'm worried. Please call.

Then he grabbed his jacket and pocketed his phone.

Boo was already in the rescue truck, checking the supplies. Axel came out, geared up in a wetsuit, carrying a duffel bag, his fins.

Shep climbed into the front seat and set the phone on the console.

Axel got in front beside him. "She's okay. We'll figure it out."

Shep looked at him, his jaw tight. But Colt's words had settled inside him in an icy ball. "*Listen, if she gets spooked, she'll vanish again.*"

No, this wasn't that. She hadn't gotten spooked. Last night at dinner, she'd told him about her parents—diplomats—and how she'd grown up travelling the world. Then she'd tucked herself against him, and they'd watched an episode of *Manifest*.

She wasn't going anywhere.

Except his own accusation to Colt was now ranging around his head. "*Are you telling me you want someone to find her?*"

He swallowed. *Just calm down. . . .*

He pulled out of the airport and headed south on Highway 1, down to Diamond Boulevard. His jaw tightened as he glanced at his phone. No call. No text.

He turned onto Diamond, headed east toward the sound, past neighborhoods, Campbell Lake. Jewel Lake sat just ahead to the northwest. Ice from the storm clung to the trees, skeletons against the hazy day.

"This is near our house," Boo said from the back seat. "I can't believe I didn't notice the accident on the way in."

He said nothing as he slowed, seeing the cruisers up ahead parked at the municipal fishing dock. A few cops clustered, chatting. As he pulled in, Axel sat up. "Flynn's here with Dawson."

Shep spotted Flynn with Moose's cousin Dawson, standing with a handful of cops at the dock that jutted out over the water. A haze lay over the water, the air crisp, quiet, as he parked and got out.

No sirens. No panic.

Yet a terrible foreboding gripped his chest.

Sort of like it had so many years ago on the mountain, a moment before the avalanche had roared down over him.

Hello. This was not Switzerland, and he wasn't about to be buried alive.

Axel jogged out to the dock to meet Flynn, about twenty feet ahead of him.

Shep caught a glimpse of the car. Fully submerged in the water, a glaze of ice over the top of the water, unbroken.

So the car had been there for a while.

It sat under the glaze like a pumpkin, orange and squatty, the shape of a hatchback.

Or a . . .

Axel turned and looked at Shep and . . .

It was a Crosstrek.

An orange Subaru Crosstrek.

No—Shep started to run.

Axel caught him. "They ran the plates. It's hers—but let me get in the water—"

Shep didn't wait. He pushed past Axel and ran right off the dock, into the icy water. A thousand blades speared him, but he didn't care. It wasn't that deep, and his entire body had turned to fire anyway.

He swam down to the front and peered into the car.

A body floated in the front seat, hair around her face, her arms floating.

Oh, no—no—

Breathe. He kicked hard, surfaced. Gulped breaths.

"Shep! Wait—" Axel, pulling on his gear, but Shep headed back down.

Grabbed the door handle.

It opened and the body floated out.

So dead.

And then Axel was there, kitted up, grabbing the body, pulling it up.

Shep followed him up, freezing now. Axel headed to the dock, and Shep followed, his limbs turning heavy.

Hands pulled him out, and he lay on the frozen landing, breathing hard.

"Have you lost your mind?" Dawson said, standing over him, hands in his pockets, his breaths captured in the air.

Shep rolled onto his hands and knees as Boo and another EMT pulled the body out of the water. Laid her on the dock.

Axel followed her out, but Shep was already crawling toward the body.

"Shep, buddy, no—" Axel grabbed him, his arms around him, but Shep pushed him away with probably more force than he needed, but—

"Is it her?" He got up, shoved away one of the EMTs.

The body was bloated, gray, frozen, grotesque.

"London—"

Then everything stilled inside him.

"Is it her?" Boo said.

He wanted to look away.

A terrible beating had disfigured her entire face beyond recognition—swollen, cut, the nose twisted, her hair broken off. And the impact of the crash had finished the job, breaking her jaw.

But the body seemed the same lean, strong build, the same size and . . . "This is her jacket." His voice emerged gaunt, broken.

This wasn't London. This body was . . . cold. And clammy. And lifeless. And . . . no, no, it *couldn't* be London.

He reached out to touch her, but Dawson grabbed his hand. "Evidence."

Evidence.

"Her fingertips are gone," said Flynn, now crouching opposite, scanning the corpse.

And that's when Shep turned, scrambled to the edge of the dock, and lost it.

No. This couldn't be right.

Please.

Axel came over, crouched beside him. Boo brought him a blanket. Sat on the other side beside him.

He didn't watch as the coroner came and bagged her up. Or as a dive recovery team came in and hooked up the car, pulling it out with a winch.

Or even as the ambulance pulled away, no siren, on its way to the morgue.

"Shep, let's go. You're freezing."

No, he was numb.

Just like he'd been the last time she'd left him.

And this time, no amount of hope would bring her back.

Sarah Walker was dead.

Get the next book in the series and
continue the adventure!

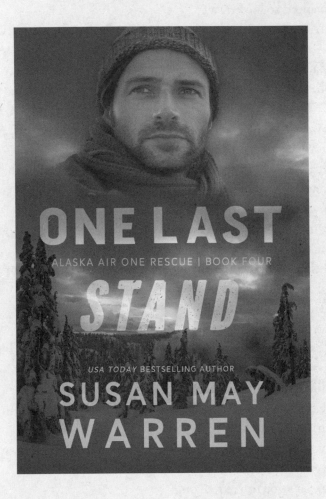

ONE LAST

ALASKA AIR ONE RESCUE | BOOK FOUR

STAND

USA TODAY BESTSELLING AUTHOR

SUSAN MAY
WARREN

She left a life of danger, but when the past
comes back to stalk her, what will it cost
her to save the people, and life, she loves?

Pilot London Brooks never thought her past would find her.

Hiding out in Alaska, as a member of the Air One Rescue team, she's built a new life—one far away from her clandestine past as an operative tasked to take down a branch of Russian terrorists. She has no desire to reenter that world...or endure the grief of losing everyone she loved, including her fiancé. But the past won't stay away, and when she finds herself falsely accused, her reputation tarnished, and her life in danger, she has no choice but to plunge back into the treacherous world she once left behind. Even if she must surrender everything—and everyone—she loves in her new life.

Shep Watson will never forget the day he saved London Brooks from the avalanche that nearly killed her. Sure, he knew there was more to her story—after all, she was one of the few who survived the tragedy. But he is intent on keeping her secrets...and starting over. She's finally ready to let him into her heart—or so it seems—and then someone comes knocking. Someone who happens to be the man she thought was dead. Now, he'll have to choose—does he let her go, or help her make one last stand with her for her freedom?

But when that danger comes home to Alaska, will it cost the Air One Rescue team everything?

Book 4 is the final, thrilling journey through the majestic Alaskan wilderness, where love defies danger, and second chances are won with courage and determination.

Note to Reader

Thank you again for reading One Last Promise. I hope you enjoyed the story! There's more to come...!

If you did enjoy One Last Promise, would you be willing to do me a favor? Head over to the product page and leave a review. It doesn't have to be long—just a few words to help other readers know what they're getting. (But no spoilers! We don't want to wreck the fun!)

I can't help but feel incredibly fortunate to have such a supportive and talented team by my side. A heartfelt thank you to my editors, Anne Horch and Rel Mollet, whose feedback is always spot-on and invaluable. You both have a special way of making my stories shine and I can't thank you enough for that.

A big hug to my writing partner, Rachel Hauck, and to Sarah Erredge for always being there to bounce around ideas, no matter how many questions I throw your way. Your support means the world to me.

A special nod to my husband, Andrew, for all the behind-the-scenes technical support. You keep everything running smoothly, and I couldn't do this without you.

Kudos to Emilie Haney for her beautiful cover designs that give my books the perfect first impression, and to Tari Faris for making the inside just as beautiful as the outside.

And to Katie Donovan, thank you for your eagle-eyed proofing skills when the clock is ticking.

A special shout-out to my friend John for the name Rigger. I told you I'd use it!

I'm grateful to each one of you for your contributions. We're a team, and every story we put out there is a testament to our collective effort and dedication. And let's not forget Andrea Doering and the team at Revell for their partnership and belief in my stories. My heart is full thanks to all of you!

And to you, my readers! Thank you for reading my books. My hope is that the time you spend with these characters and these stories bless you. I'd love to hear from you—not only about this story, but about any characters or stories you'd like to read in the future. Write to me at: susan@susanmaywarren.com. And if you'd like to see what's ahead, stop by www.susanmaywarren.com.

If you would like news on upcoming releases, freebies and sneak peeks, sign up for my weekly email at susanmaywarren.com, or scan the QR code below.

XO!
Susie May

More Books by Susan May Warren

Most recent to the beginning of the epic lineup, in reading order.

ALASKA AIR ONE RESCUE
One Last Shot
One Last Chance
One Last Promise
One Last Stand

THE MINNESOTA MARSHALLS
Fraser
Jonas
Ned
Iris
Creed

THE EPIC STORY OF RJ AND YORK
Out of the Night
I Will Find You
No Matter the Cost

SKY KING RANCH
Sunrise
Sunburst
Sundown

GLOBAL SEARCH AND RESCUE
The Way of the Brave
The Heart of a Hero
The Price of Valor

THE MONTANA MARSHALLS
Knox
Tate
Ford
Wyatt
Ruby Jane

MONTANA RESCUE

If Ever I Would Leave You (novella prequel)
Wild Montana Skies
Rescue Me
A Matter of Trust
Crossfire (novella)
Troubled Waters
Storm Front
Wait for Me

MONTANA FIRE

Where There's Smoke (Summer of Fire)
Playing with Fire (Summer of Fire)
Burnin' For You (Summer of Fire)
Oh, The Weather Outside is Frightful (Christmas novella)
I'll be There (Montana Fire/Deep Haven crossover)
Light My Fire (Summer of the Burning Sky)
The Heat is On (Summer of the Burning Sky)
Some Like it Hot (Summer of the Burning Sky)
You Don't Have to Be a Star (Montana Fire spin-off)

THE TRUE LIES OF REMBRANDT STONE

Cast the First Stone
No Unturned Stone
Sticks and Stone
Set in Stone
Blood from a Stone
Heart of Stone

A complete list of Susan's novels can be found at
susanmaywarren.com/novels/bibliography/.

About the Author

Susan May Warren is the USA Today bestselling author of over 95 novels with nearly 2 million books sold, including the Global Search and Rescue and the Montana Rescue series.Winner of a RITA Award and multiple Christy and Carol Awards, as well as the HOLT Medallion and numerous Readers' Choice Awards, Susan makes her home in Minnesota.

Visit her at www.susanmaywarren.com.